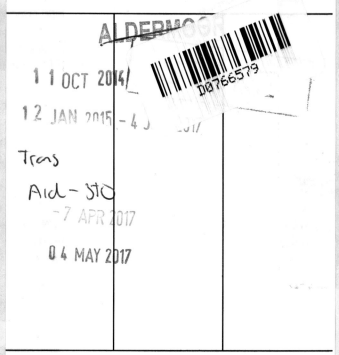

AUTHOR NOTE

As a child, I remember seeing a picture of the Venus de Milo. I didn't understand the archaeological aspect—I only wondered why she didn't have arms. Much later, while thinking about what story to write, I happened to see something on television about her discovery and began to imagine the Venus lying, waiting to be uncovered.

While researching I discovered that part of one badly damaged arm had once been found, and also a hand believed to be holding an apple. But I found nothing definitive about her other hand except the explanation that the fragments around her might have been another arm. It might have been…but it was so easy for me to believe someone took it!

I hope you enjoy my story and uncovering the magic of this wonderful time!

SAFE IN THE
EARL'S ARMS

Liz Tyner

Published in Great Britain 2014
by Mills & Boon, an imprint of Harlequin (UK) Limited,
Eton House, 18-24 Paradise Road, Richmond, Surrey, TW9 1SR

© 2014 Elizabeth Tyner

ISBN: 978 0 263 90969 2

Harlequin (UK) Limited's policy is to use papers that are natural, renewable and recyclable products and made from wood grown in sustainable forests. The logging and manufacturing processes conform to the legal environmental regulations of the country of origin.

Printed by Blac

Liz Tyner began creating her own stories even before she decided on the lofty goal of reading every fiction book in her high school library. When the school gave her a career assessment they came up blank—they double-checked and still came up blank. Liz took it in her stride because she knew that on the questionnaire she'd ticked an interest in everything but scuba diving. She believed the assessment proved she was perfect for becoming a novelist.

Now she and her husband live on a small acreage where she enjoys strolling her walking trails and wishes the animals she shares the trails with wouldn't visit her garden and fruit trees. She imagines the wooded areas as similar to the ones in the children's book *Where the Wild Things Are*. Her lifestyle is a blend of old and new, and in some ways comparable to how people lived long ago.

Liz is a member of various writing groups, and has worn down the edges of a few keys on her keyboard while working on manuscripts—none of which feature scuba divers.

This is Liz Tyner's fabulous debut novel
for Mills & Boon® Historical Romance!

DEDICATION

To Bill, who encourages my dreams
and who buys me chocolate.

Chapter One

Being wrapped in a shroud of sailing cloth—
a shot ball secure at his head and one at his
feet—and tossed into the Aegean Sea could only
increase Warrington's spirits. He linked his fingertips together, braced his elbows against the
railing and ignored the sting of the wind slapping
his hair on to his face.

His brother's sparring remarks didn't help.

Warrington turned his head from the words. 'I
swear you are not related to me,' he grated out, in-
terrupting the flow of Ben's jests. 'You talk more
than any two women I've ever heard.'

Ben chuckled, moving so their shoulders
touched briefly. 'And you've made me proud on
the voyage. Not of you, of course. Of myself. I'm
a fine captain to be able to have an old melancholy miss like you on board and still keep from
throwing you over the side.'

'You've sailed us to an island that doesn't even

have the comforts of hell.' Warrington used both hands, pushing back the hair from his face, and then he rested clenched fists on the railing of the ship.

'You do not give me the respect due me,' his brother said, shaking his head in exaggerated dismay. 'I saved our lives by steering us here when the ship caught fire. You may have the title, but an earl drowns just as quickly as a mere captain when a ship sinks.'

Warrington didn't speak, hoping to let Ben have the last word and himself some silence.

He'd had to leave England—he'd thought his memories would be easier to bear at sea. He'd been wrong. His wife's face wouldn't appear in his mind, but he could see the letters of her name carved on to the crypt.

He leaned into the rocking of the boat, letting it numb his mind from the endless days of sameness broken only by tribulation aboard the *Ascalon*. He wanted dry boots, freshly blacked, and not covering sodden stockings. Sea-misted trousers dried stiff and looked no better than a stable master's discards.

Across the water, he saw the longboat returning from shore, and hoped the *Ascalon* could cast off with the next tide. With the crew back and the repairs almost finished, surely they would leave soon.

In minutes, the longboat thumped against the

side of the ship. Gidley, the first mate, reached his gnarled hands to the top of the ladder. His face came into view. The mate's eyes twinkled and he'd not yet moved on to the ship. 'We have us another one of them problems yer so good at solvin', Capt'n Ben.'

Warrington watched his younger brother take a forceful step forward.

'If anyone has stolen a goat this time, I'll personally throttle them until they are unconscious.' Ben straightened his shoulders and stared at his second-in-command.

'Not goats, Capt'n.' Gidley pulled himself on to the deck, his face showing a barely reined-in pleasure at whatever news he was about to speak.

'What, then?' the captain asked.

'It be a woman.' Gidley spoke slowly and stepped aside to give the other three men from the longboat a chance to board. They rushed in behind him, feet thumping on to the deck, faces anxious to hear the response.

'A woman?' Ben straightened and strode to Gidley. 'The island is practically afloat with whores.' He spat the words out. 'Why can't the men understand how to handle a simple transaction and be done with it?'

'Well…' Gidley gave a demure smile. 'This one claims she be savin' herself for the capt'n.' He stepped back against the railing, one arm resting on the wood, and with the other hand pulled his gangly chin whiskers. 'I tried to give my-self to her in yer stead, but she'd have none of it. *Capt'n,* she said. Kept insistin' she had a treasure for the capt'n.'

Ben smiled, his even teeth too white in the sunlight. 'Is she lovely?'

Gidley shrugged, but his grin flashed back hearty approval. 'She's some kind of mark here.' He touched above his breast. 'The birthmark…' he smiled '…pulled my sight right to her breasts.'

Not a ripple of emotion passed behind Ben's eyes. He turned to Warrington, indicating the shoreline with a quick tilt of his head. 'Go ashore and see what the woman wants.'

Warrington could not believe his brother's words. He examined Ben's face and took a step towards him. 'No.' Warrington shook his head.

Ben's eyes lost all familial ties. 'Captain's orders.' The smug words slashed in the air.

'I'm an earl.' Warrington's voice was tight.

'In case you're unaware, we're not on English soil. Captain ranks higher—*here.*' His brother bit out the commanding words and adopted the cocksure stance he'd perfected by five years old. 'And my crew does obey me. See to the woman, or I will have you left on the island when we haul anchor.'

'Like hell.'

Ben smiled. 'You're going to have to have a go at another woman some time. You might as well get some use out of your little man as to let it wither up and wash overboard.' He raised a hand, summoning three other seamen who'd stilled to listen.

Seven men were ready to toss Warrington on to the longboat should he not go on his own. He stared at his brother's face. He would kill him.

'So go ashore.' Ben crossed his arms. 'Take care of the matter for me—and you might be able to return to England on this vessel.'

'I—' His hands clenched.

'No. No,' Ben interrupted, head dropping but his hand still high. 'Trust me. Once you've been called captain by a woman in that breathless moment—you'll fashion yourself a captain many times over.' He waved his hand in the air. 'Correct?'

Seven male heads quickly gave assent, eyes flashing amusement and watching Warrington.

'Fine,' Warrington snapped out, moving to give his brother a shove from his path, but Ben moved aside—the man was nimble as an eel—and Warrington strode to the port side, stopping to give Ben a bitter glance.

He grabbed the railing and turned, scrambling down the woven ladder. He saw the first mate's boots next on the rope rungs. They would see him to the woman.

When the men reached the bank, the boat's bottom grated into sand underneath. Warrington jumped from the longboat into the water. He stopped for a moment. The immobile land beneath his feet jarred him. He'd been at sea too long.

He sloshed to shore. The others splashed behind him, then pulled the boat free of the waves, showing no more effort than moving a child's toy.

They started on the path. Water sluiced from Warrington's boots. Gidley slogged beside him. 'She's near the town. Said we'd find her 'fore we reached Castro.'

The blowing wind pushed whiffs of the tainted egg smell that lingered at the base of the island. The shoreline reeked as badly as a demon's breath—a scent Warrington supposed left over from volcanic eruptions centuries earlier.

Warrington nodded sharply, but gave no other acknowledgement. He trudged up the path and soon the sand gave way to a coal-hued surface. Glass-like shards of earth now crunched beneath his feet. The unusual land piqued his interest, but the scent didn't. Warrington wished they had risked another island to recover from the ship's fire, which had nearly cost them their lives. This one stank.

Gidley expounded on what a woman such as the one he'd seen could do for a man's pleasure. He described the mark at her breast in fifteen different ways and each one included more details of skin than he could possibly have seen.

The mate spoke so earnestly and with such conviction, he'd convinced at least one of the other seamen the woman was a descendent of some goddess. Warrington wasn't certain Aphrodite herself would be so free with her charms as Gidley recounted. The sailor loved his mythology—but it was all Gidley's tales, not the ancients.

The road disappeared into a growth of olive trees and brush.

Warrington wondered about the woman—this bold woman who shouldn't disturb an earl who'd been a month without a decent mattress, longer without a decent night's sleep and even longer without a deliciously indecent tumble.

Meeting the woman might be interesting, he decided. He would return and tell his brother what it was like to bed a goddess in the flesh. No matter how the events unfolded, Warrington would manage a supreme tale of unsurpassed passion.

Gidley stopped where a path shot out from the road. 'She lives in one of them red-roofed houses up this trail—a home overlookin' the sea.'

Warrington stopped and turned to the seamen. 'I will continue the rest of the way alone.'

Gidley and six other pairs of feet ceased all movement and their faces weighed Warrington's words.

Gidley spoke softly, his downturned lips showing hurt at the exclusion. 'We want to see yer meet her.'

'I can meet her alone and need no help,' Warrington said.

Gidley stepped nearer Warrington, facing him. Gid's worn cap slid into a jauntier position when he raised his head. He clapped Warrington on the arm. 'I wager a earl knows a bit about pleasurin' himself. I mean…' he paused for effect '… with a woman.'

The others snickered. Warrington raised a brow and gave them the glare that hours spent with a fencing master had made him confident to use, and that hinted *Swords or pistols and choose your seconds.*

Gidley took a step back and turned away with a disgusted grunt. 'We be takin' the longboat back to the boat in an hour or so,' Gidley muttered. 'Sun will be settin' not long after. Ought to give you enough time to meet 'er, fall in love and get yer trousers back on.' Gidley's words faded away as he left along the road.

Warrington pushed through a clump of tree branches over the path and saw the roof of a house. The structure had two storeys and the stairs leading to the upper floor had no railing. He knew from his first day's visit to the island that the house was made as the others he'd seen. The first level—a barn—held the livestock. He supposed the tradition of making homes in this manner started because of the houses built near the sea. If a low-lying area flooded, the animals could be released and water would be less likely to harm the house's upper contents. Besides, the structure took fewer materials than if two were built.

He saw a nanny goat grazing near the corner, a kid at her side. And near the cliffs, a woman sat on one of the boulders overlooking the sea. She turned to him. In the chilled air, her red scarf fluttered around her face and she stood. He didn't move. Let her approach him. She'd summoned.

The covering on her head showed scarlet enough to use as a beacon and another garment draped around her shoulders had only a little less colour. She pulled the covering snug as she walked. The wind didn't warrant bundling so.

When she strode closer, he caught his breath. Even with the breezes constantly tossing the head covering against her, she drew his attention. Brown eyes with lashes thick enough he half expected them to flutter in the breeze, as well. She held her shawl closed with one hand and with the other brushed back the hair that kept blowing across her face. A waste of effort.

'I'm Melina. Are you the *Ascalon* captain?'

Her words shocked him. She spoke King's English and with only enough accent to give her words an exotic flair. And her voice—it purred into him, causing a jolt in his midsection that reminded him of how tempting a woman could be.

* * *

Melina appraised the man before her. She'd expected someone silver-haired. Perhaps scarred a bit. This one—she could see how he kept from being mangled. His body showed strength. She doubted he'd be able to scamper across the rigging as she'd seen French seamen do, but he could probably toss another man up to do the job for him.

His clothing fit tight over parts that held muscle, and loosely everywhere else. When the wind blew at him, he stood impervious. His stare trapped the breath in her and caused a pleasing quiver in her stomach.

She'd waited months for an English ship to anchor in the bay because she had to leave the island and discover the truth about the treasure. She had to be right. Her sisters must eat.

'Where did you learn such speech?' He asked his own question, ignoring hers.

'I wish to go to London.' She kept the scarf tight around her.

'I wish for a soft bed at night, but the ship doesn't have one,' he said. 'And it has no room for passengers.'

'I've payment.' She raised her chin. She would not give away this chance. Not willingly. Only certainty of death would back her down.

His shoulders relaxed and he gave her an apologetic smile. 'We've had a fire. Our vessel is near ready for departure and we're finishing the last repairs, but it might not withstand a storm. Another ship will be along shortly. Bargain with them.'

She took a step forward, closer than she would normally stand near someone who'd docked on the island. She looked up at him. 'Before you decide, I must show you something.'

He gave a tilt of his shoulder and raised one eyebrow. 'I told you I'm not interested.' Then she saw his gaze drift to her chest and quickly move back to her face.

She pulled her shawl tight. 'In the stable,' she bit out, taking a step towards the structure.

He reached for her, trapping her arm, but his grip wasn't tight.

She snapped her head in his direction and stood ready to push him back—first with words, then with force if she needed. He had to see her discovery.

'I don't wish—' His voice softened, but he didn't release her arm. His eyes, not true dark but reflecting the same colours as the almost leafless tree he stood near, showed compassion. 'I can't take you to London with us. Wait for another ship.' His voice lowered. 'Or stay here. The world is not kind for women away from their homes.'

Words fled her mind and she couldn't look away from him. He'd trapped her—not with his hand, but with his gaze. His touch warmed her skin and his gentle grasp had taken her will to move.

'Come with me.' She thrust the words out, re-capturing her strength.

He shook his head, still not releasing her arm. The grip held her firm, but she didn't feel impris-oned. She knew a quick tug and she'd be able to slip away.

'I… The ship is no place for a woman—even a…' He tried again. 'I'm sure you could have many times your passage back in your pocket in the time it will take us to reach London—but the men don't need the distraction. They'd be compet-ing for your favours instead of thinking of their duties. You'll not go with us.' He put his free hand in his waistcoat pocket, brought out a coin and held it to her. 'Take it.'

She stared and didn't move.

He kept his hand extended. 'You may keep it. For getting me from the ship for a few moments and for letting me hear a woman's voice. I want nothing more.' His eyes softened. 'I did not bring more funds or I would give them to you.'

She jerked her head in refusal of the coin.

He released her, putting the gold away, and took a step back. She reached out, grasping his sleeve, stopping him.

He turned, his mouth open, and seemed to

struggle for words. 'Miss. Truly. I do not want...
And we cannot take you.'

He could keep his words—she needed a man
who'd free her from the island.

'Let me show you,' she said.

'As long as you understand you're not stepping foot on that ship. The men...' He finished
his words with a soft tone. 'They would not be
able to ignore...'

'I must show you my treasure.' She turned
away and strode inside the barn, knowing he
would not resist following her.

They walked over dirt packed solid from goats'
feet, breathing dust from manure the animals
kicked about. She moved towards a small stack
of firewood branches. She knelt, reaching into the
sticks, and pulled out the cloth-wrapped marble
she'd hidden there.

She turned back to him, pulled away the fabric
and handed the work to him. Even in the dark interior, the richness of the stone glowed.

He took the carved marble in his hands. The
arm was slightly bigger than a human arm would
be and the delicateness of the fingers proved the
hand to be a woman's. 'It's a part of some statue.'

'Yes.' Even as he touched and examined it,
she rested her fingertips against the stone. 'A
learned man came here two years ago. He told
us the island should have artefacts—worth coin
to him—but he found nothing. I uncovered this—

and more, after he left.' She watched this one, noting his study of the arm. He looked at the hand the way a woman might look at a baby.

'Take me to London,' she said, 'and you'll be paid my passage once the British Museum discovers what I have—'

'This is well done. When I get to England, I'll get someone who understands art to look at it and he can send payment back if this marble is worth something.'

She jerked the carving from his hands. 'I have to leave now. Not next week. Not the next ship. I must go.' Already her neighbours had warned her. The man who led the island was planning to marry her soon. She would have no choice.

She turned, picking up the cloth she'd used to protect the arm. When she looked up, she caught his eyes on her. Her shawl had opened and her mark showed. He stopped moving. Her clothing fell open a bit more. With her free hand, she brushed the edge of the birthmark, letting her fingers rest a moment. Desire darkened his eyes.

She took a slow breath. Neither smiled. She stopped the words of caution blowing inside herself, pummelling her with the knowledge she could never turn back if she continued her path. 'Is that what you want for my passage?' she asked.

'Yes.'

'Then we've a bargain.'

He shook his head. 'No. The captain will not let a woman sail with us.'

'You're not the *archigos?*' She pulled the arm into her grasp, cradling it. He didn't answer, but she could read the truth in his face. She'd just offered her body to a man who could not, or would not, say yes. Her mind hammered in rage. Controlling her desire to hit him across the face with the stone took all her strength, except for the amount she used to keep herself from shouting.

'I'm the Earl of Warrington,' he said. 'I own part of the ship, but I don't sail her. I'll take you aboard the *Ascalon* and you may speak to the captain.' His head moved sideways, indicating the direction of the vessel.

'Very well.' She could see his thoughts in his eyes. He believed the captain would refuse her. But if the ship's leader had the same mind as most men, once her foot touched the deck, she would make it difficult for him to say no.

'I will sail with the ship.' She challenged him with her stare.

He turned and walked back into the sunlight.

Melina knew that once she stepped on deck, she'd find a way to stay, no matter what she had to do. Their father had given them enough to live on while their mother lived, but now he'd forgotten his daughters. Without funds, she could no longer escape a forced marriage to a man whose touch made her stomach roil. She could not let her sisters starve, or sell their bodies.

The arm, and a description of the goddess, would let the museum see what she had and they would tell her what the beauty was worth. The statue was valuable. Her heart told her so. She could support her family by selling the stone woman.

She ran to the steps of her house and grabbed the small satchel she'd stuffed together after talking with the other sailor. She'd told her sisters her plans. They now watched from the window. Melina waved and then took a step to the path.

The first footstep was easy. But then she couldn't move. A hollowness in her heart told her she was leaving her home for ever. She squeezed her eyes tight and planted one foot forward, then the other.

Chapter Two

Melina rushed to keep up with Warrington's long strides. As she reached the first bend in the path, her satchel strap slipped from her shoulder to her elbow. The weight pulled at her arm, but she kept the stone cradled. The bag bumped against her leg, slowing her pace.

She paused and he immediately stopped and turned to her. He'd been as aware of her footsteps as his own.

Warrington reached a hand out to her, gesturing for the bag, and she met his eyes. Reassured, she hefted the rock in one hand and let the errant strap slip into her grasp. He took the weight from her, tossing the leather sling over his shoulder.

Muffled tones reached her ears. She focused on the sounds. Two men talked as they moved towards the path. Her heart thudded when she recognised the voice of Stephanos, the man who planned to wed her. He was moving in their di-

rection. A few more steps and he would see them.
She'd be trapped.

'*Skase,*' she whispered, and then remembered
her English. 'Quiet.'

Warrington studied her, but gave a small lift
of his chin in agreement.

She brushed past him, nodding for him to follow her. Snaking through the gnarled trees, she
ran towards a knoll that rose just enough that they
couldn't be seen from the path.

She reached the hiding place and pulled him
beside her, hoping they would not be seen. Listening, she realised the men no longer talked. Stephanos and the other man were silent—unmoving.

Fear crept into her body, clutching at her insides. If Stephanos saw her with Warrington, the
Greek would not ask any questions, but would
find his own answers. Stephanos and his friends
always carried knives and they were skilled with
them.

After a few moments of nothing, she heard the
word, *gida,* and relaxed. Goat.

The men continued on. She heard their voices
fading away and her breathing returned to normal. Warrington put a hand on her shoulder, the
warm grasp somehow reassuring. He tugged her
around to him and put his face so near hers that
the breath of his whisper touched her cheek. He
didn't release her, but his grip was soft.

'Have you stolen the stone?' he asked, words quiet, creating a haven around her.

She would have confessed all if she'd done wrong. 'No. The man who owns the land where I found the treasure knows what I have planned. We are in agreement and he has said he'll keep my secret. I trust him.'

Just the gentlest touch of his hand again, moving over the crest of her shoulder and the merest bit down her back, and the waiting look in his eyes, trapped her in an intriguing web and she could not stop her words. 'When they are sure I am safely gone a long distance, my sisters are to say I've been forced away by a man from a ship.'

His eyes widened and he stepped back as if she'd prodded him away with a burning stick.

He opened his mouth to speak, but she closed the distance between them, stopping almost against him. She could not risk him raising his voice.

'You must understand our reasons,' she said quietly. 'No one will know who you are. My sisters will not describe the true person.'

He pulled the satchel from his shoulder and she could tell he meant to leave her there and go on his way.

'No,' she whispered, closing her fingers over his roughened hand, preventing him from giving her the bag. His knuckles were large in her grasp, startling her, and she knew she didn't keep them closed by her strength any more than she caused the tides. Confusion flashed behind his eyes and something whispered in her that she had trapped his hand—that he could no more move his fingers than if their grasps had been reversed and his strength held her.

She could not lose her advantage. 'I am not a thief. I merely wish to get to the British Museum and find out what my treasure is worth. Then I will be able to sell it.'

'But *kidnapped?*' He remained with his face almost at hers. 'That's a bit much.'

She closed her lips and let her breath out through her nose before she answered, 'I have no choice.'

'I do.' He kept his words tight and lines appeared at the sides of his eyes and mouth. 'I am not at ease with purchasing a woman and I certainly wouldn't steal one.'

The words pleased her, yet they were not what she wanted to hear.

She had to convince him. She held his gaze with her own. 'It is necessary. My sisters can't be hurt by my actions. The man who rules the island would be enraged at them if he thought they had helped me leave and did not search him out to keep me. They would suffer. They could be starved, or beaten, or forced into marriage or worse. I cannot escape and leave them behind to face torture.'

She felt his movement and looked down to her hand. She'd tightened her grip on his fingers. He slowly slid his hand from hers.

'You're leaving behind a man.' His words were thoughtful.

She had to make him understand. 'Our land doesn't support my sisters. The rocks only grow more rocks. I care nothing for the man who wishes to marry me, yet his mother often sees that we have food. If I stay, I will have no choice but to wed him. She wishes for it. So does he. He is powerful.'

Stephanos controlled the island and did so easily. But he had other secrets. He often left the island and returned with goods. One of his shirts was mottled with faded brown stains. Blood.

She could barely keep the kindness in her words when Stephanos called on her and she had to speak to him. Perhaps, as the others whispered, she truly had been tainted by her English heritage.

'I have promised myself to no one,' she said.

Warrington shut his eyes.

She put her palm flat on his chest. When his lids fluttered up, she could feel the change in his gaze. She wouldn't beg, or ask again. She didn't think she needed to.

He spoke harshly under his breath—the words directed at himself.

His hand closed at her elbow and he turned away, again taking the lead, only this time, his steps were careful and he watched the wooded areas around them.

She followed, knowing her sisters depended on her and she risked her life to be able to save them. But it wasn't a choice. It was what she had to do. She was the eldest and that meant sacrifice. If she died at sea, or at the hands of a stranger, then she would know she did it for her family. Her mother's last words to her had been *Take care of your sisters*.

Warrington forced himself not to stare at Melina. They stood hidden among the cragged rocks, watching the longboat and waiting for the sailors to return. The hem of her head covering fluttered in the wind and kept calling his attention to her.

He wished he could see her chest again. Her birthmark did have an interesting curve to it. He remembered the child's game of imagining wisps of a cloud as objects and tried to recall the exact shape the mark formed.

He heard the first mate's voice before he saw him emerging from the road. Once the men reached the longboat, he hurried Melina to them.

'You ready to heave to?' Gidley gaped at the woman even as he directed the words at Warrington.

'Yes,' Warrington snapped. 'Hurry.'

Gidley's voice became butler formal. 'Will his lordship be having a guest?'

'Launch the damn longboat.'

Gidley put his forefinger to his lips in a silencing motion and then lowered his hand. He mouthed the word *lady*.

Warrington mouthed back words for Gidley that neither would repeat in front of the woman. The other seamen beamed as if enjoying a particularly good scene at Drury Lane Theatre.

'Yes, yer lordship.' Gidley helped the others push the boat into the waves, then scrambled into the boat, and took the seat in front of her, facing the woman. Warrington made a forceful circular motion with his hand, commanding Gidley to twist around. Gidley's eyelashes gave an innocent blink as he looked at Warrington, then gazed back at the woman, giving a bow of his head as acknowledgement, and turned in his seat. 'Beautiful day for bein' at sea.' He spoke to no one in particular.

Warrington stepped over the side and took the empty plank beside Melina. His shoulder brushed hers. He thought he detected the scent of rosemary about her, but he wasn't sure he even knew what the herb would smell like.

The other men thumped into the boat, voicing polite comments on the calmness of the sea and the beauty of the island as if speaking in front of their grandmothers. Gidley continued his teatime reminisces as the men rowed, recounting with the other seamen the polite sights they'd seen in their travels.

Warrington shut his eyes briefly. He had no idea where these dainty men came from.

'Correct, yer lordship?' Gidley asked.

'Most certainly, my dear,' Warrington answered. He heard a smothered snort from someone else, followed by a coughing attempt to disguise the sound into politeness.

Melina gathered the bundle closer. He hated that she felt discomfort.

Warrington kept his voice calm. 'The next one of you who makes a sound before we board is going to let the rest of the crew watch him swimming around *Ascalon* and the first seaman who can bounce a biscuit off the swimmer's head can give him orders until we're home.'

Silence followed, except for the rhythmic sound of oars slapping the water.

Her shoulders relaxed and he wished he could retrace his steps. Bringing her on to the longboat had been foolish and she was the one being misled. He'd let himself be blinded by a little spot of skin and now she was on a longboat for no reason. They both should have stayed home.

He didn't feel he'd had the option, though. The Foreign Office knew of his ship and had asked him for help. The trip had been a worthwhile diplomatic mission, in that he could tell them the Greeks still planned to rebel against the Ottoman rule. He didn't know if the Turks suspected or not, but he had the information he'd been sent for.

When the boat tapped against the hull of the *Ascalon,* the men tied the longboat. The men closest to the ladder left first. Then Warrington or Melina would go on deck.

Melina stood and didn't move forward, still holding her bundle and her satchel strap draped over her arm.

He touched the small of her back and she turned to him. He reached forward, taking the sculpture. 'I'll get it on deck. If you dropped it into the sea going up the ladder, we'd never get it back.'

She released the bundle and gave her shawl and scarf each a quick knot. She picked her way to the ladder, lifting her skirts to step over the seat in front of them. A simple, everyday movement. His mouth went dry. The image of her legs sealed itself around him. His imagination began to fill in the rest of her body while his mind generously unclothed her. Long limbs, smooth, and welcoming.

He brought himself back to the moment and saw her at the ladder, staring at the ropes.

'Just go up as if you've done it every day, quick, and don't stop.'

She took a few deep breaths, pulled at the waistband of her skirt, trying to keep the fabric away from her feet, and grabbed both sides of the ladder. She snatched the hemp in a stranglehold and moved upwards. Arms reached out to help her on board.

And now he held her parcel. He couldn't risk dropping the rock.

Warrington looked up and called out to the man who stood at the side. 'Toss me the end of a rope. I need you to haul something up for me.'

In seconds, a rope dropped at his feet and Warrington bound the end around the package. 'Pull it up,' he shouted and the arm went aboard ship. He shook his head at the waste of effort. The rock would be returning to the island soon.

The men were good sailors, but not a one of them was of the clergy and it would take at least that to ignore the woman. He'd send a decent crewman back with her to escort her home safely. No, he'd have to make do with a well-threatened one. All the decent ones were on other ships.

Stepping on deck, he saw the men assembled as if Ben demanded them for a meeting, but he knew the captain did no such thing. The cook sat on an overturned bucket and the cabin boy tangled himself in the rigging like a prisoner in stocks, waiting to hear what was said.

Warrington saw Ben's stare. 'You brought a woman because—' Ben spoke, hands on his hips.

Melina stood, her scarf still knotted tightly and her jaw firm, and stared at Ben. Ben was getting sized up from the tip of his pointy nose to the last thread in his canvas trousers.

Warrington edged just to the side between them so he could see each face. He confronted his younger brother. 'Since I am not the captain and do not have authority as such on this ship, she asked to talk to you.'

Ben didn't speak, but his eyes darted up to the heavens in a disgusted manner.

'Explain your request to the captain.' Warrington spoke to Melina and clasped his hands behind his back. He leaned towards her, challenging them both.

She looked at Ben as if she stared across a battlefield and saw him as a target in front of her, then took a gentle breath—so small to be almost invisible. But the movement signalled a change in her.

Her shoulders dropped no more than a hair. She didn't move her feet forward, but she swayed with the movement of the ship. Warrington was certain she leaned towards Ben as the ship moved and when it rocked back, he did not see her retreat. He locked his jaw and forced himself not to step between them or pull her back.

'I wish *taxidi*—to travel to England.' Her voice became lower—her accent turning into a siren's husky whisper. Her hands reached to grasp the tied ends of her shawl and pull the knot free. 'I have an agreement with this man.' She spared a glance at Warrington.

Warrington commanded himself to remain still. Her voice dripped into him like warm pebbles of desire, bringing back the image of her legs and the spot at her breast. Perhaps he would take her back to her home and work out a true bargain there. The longboat could return him to the ship in the morning. He struggled to attend to the words of the conversation, making his plans for the night.

She reached up and pulled her scarf from her head, sliding the cloth away from her face, and the movements also caused the shawl to drop completely from her shoulders. Warrington watched two seamen collide in their haste to return the garment to her.

Ben's expression glazed over. When Warrington saw that, his eyes followed his brother's gaze.

Warrington stared, his mind not working. The scarf had kept drifting across her face before. He hadn't truly looked beyond the spot on her breast.

Her eyes, he knew they were brown. And her lips red. And her nose, a normal nose. But somehow the arrangement of them and the curve of her chin, and dusts of her hair falling loose from her bun, swirled themselves around her in such a way as to bring them all into a delight for a man's senses.

And that was before even looking lower to a mark that peeked out from the bodice, making one wonder what lay beneath—or making one fill in the imagination of what lay beneath in a stirring way.

'You are in agreement,' Melina said.

'I would prefer not having a woman aboard…' Ben's voice sounded as a kindly father's '…but since we can accommodate you with little effort I'll allow it.' Ben touched a flat palm to his chest. 'I, of course, will be happy to share my quarters with you to make sure you are—'

Warrington knew too much of his brother's life. Snaking an arm around Melina, Warrington pulled her close, sweat forming at his temples. 'She and I have already discussed…the particulars. She will travel with me.'

'Oh?' Ben challenged, lowering his palm from his shirt. 'I—'

'Yes,' Warrington said, feeling her brushing the length of his side. 'We have discussed it. I will handle any expense she might incur. She will share my quarters.' He levelled a glare at his brother. 'I believe you mentioned that it might be best for me to have a woman's company.'

'Should lessen your growls to snarls, I hope.' Ben smiled as he spoke. He looked at Melina. 'If you could do that, miss, the entire ship will be grateful.'

Warrington could feel her hip through her

skirts, pressed at his thigh, and smell the spiced scent again, which hinted at mystical pleasures. He felt nothing like growling.

He pushed the thoughts away and loosened his grip. Any tighter and he feared she would be gasping for breath. As it was, he felt on the edge of it and she seemed to have lost her words.

The captain looked at Melina. 'Are you willing to sail this very night?'

She nodded.

Ben turned to Warrington. 'While you lolled around on the island, the repairs ended. The wind is perfect, and the tide right. We can be at sea as the light fades. Show her your cabin, then get to the foredeck and give a hand.'

Warrington leaned his head towards Ben and spoke in a low voice. 'Helping on deck is not what I had in mind.'

Ben smiled. 'See the tears on my face.' He turned and walked away, his boots clattering on the deck louder than before. With every step he shouted a new order to get ready to sail.

Melina whipped the shawl back around her shoulders. She took the parcel from the man who'd lifted it on board.

'Follow me,' Warrington said to her.

His berth was in the foredeck. The captain and the first mate had quarters in the aft deck, close to the wheel.

Warrington led Melina to his cabin, opening

the door, which barely swung wide enough for his shoulders. He stepped back, letting her inside. He remained in the doorway and saw her survey the surroundings.

'Take the bunk,' he suggested. 'I'll get some other bedding.'

The hesitancy in her movements made him want to reassure her, but he couldn't. He stood immobile, looking into the cabin. Everything appeared differently to him than when he'd first decided he would sail. Then, he'd seen the surroundings as an efficient use of space. Now he was not impressed to stand in the centre and be able to touch both walls.

The berth took no more room than for a man to lie on, with storage above, and below an open cabinet with a railing around it to keep supplies from escaping and a brace midway.

He could not sit upright on the bed and felt he slept in a casket for a man of slight build. He had a chair cinched to the wall and his sea chest sat underneath a table. He had floor space slightly larger than the length and width of his bed.

'Are you certain you wish to sail with us?' He spoke the words to her back. 'This will be the room you and I will share. You can change your mind now and I will see that you are returned to your home. The ship can wait to leave.'

She didn't turn to him. 'I have no choice.'

As he heard her, his mind knew what her

mouth said, but her voice barely touched him.
The curve of her shoulders and the delicateness
of her skin—those things reached him. And he
knew without a doubt in any hidden crevasse of
his mind he'd not overcome his weakness. Not
even facing his own death had changed him.

He could never curse a woman as much as he
cursed himself for his foolishness.

At least on Melos she had a home and family. She'd be soon lost among the dockside light-
skirts at Wapping docks, trying to entice men.
But it wasn't his concern. He had tried to keep
her from the ship.

Thinking of her on the docks, plying her trade,
made him feel angry again. She only thought she
moved into a place to improve her circumstance.
The stews of London took no prisoners and willingly released no one alive.

He forced the concern from his mind.

The seamen could have their abstinence. He
didn't mind so much when solitude was his own
choice. But he did prefer to see noses without
close proximity to whiskers. Before, he'd not noticed how women's presence made the world feel
differently, until he found himself surrounded
by men.

He missed Whitegate, his true home, but he'd
left it well before he boarded the ship.

He'd left a perfectly sound home behind for the
chance to sleep on boards and inhale salt water

through his nose. And instead of a crystal decanter, kegs held stale water. The biscuits sometimes had to be broken into pieces and slowly mushed away in his mouth.

He'd not thought past his wish to keep her from Ben, or his own desires, to realise he was putting himself in such closeness with a woman. He'd never shared a room with a woman. Or awakened with anyone. Not even when he was married.

The act seemed intimate. More than a quick tumble would be. Sleeping near her, very near her, could be… His breathing increased. Pleasant.

Or not.

He examined her carefully, thinking of the rumblings from the ship at night. 'Do you snore?'

She stood and looked at him. 'Do you?'

'No.' He supposed he didn't.

Her eyes opened wide, too wide. 'If I sleep loud, will you go somewhere else?'

He smiled. 'It's an old sailor's legend that if a woman snores it's because she hasn't had enough bed play to tire her into a sound slumber.'

Her nose went up. 'It's a Greek woman's legend that if a man *ronchalizo* it's because of the air moving about where his mind should be.'

'We'll have to find something to do together so neither of us sleeps.'

'I do not snore…' She paused and her gaze narrowed when she realised what she said. Her words were strident. 'And it has nothing to do with bed play.'

'It could.' He returned the innocent look she'd given him earlier.

She huffed, not answering. He preferred the anger over the dread he'd seen on her face earlier. Before he sailed, he'd been concerned about the trip—and he knew his brother was a seaworthy captain and the crew was experienced.

Even so, he'd not liked the voyage and he'd hated the first climb up the ratlines.

'I need to give you a bit of advice for sailing,' he said.

She waited, eyes daring him.

'Stay out from under me when I am climbing above. I am not as experienced as the others. If I fell, I could hurt you.' He paused. 'But if you decide to go up the ropes, please wear trousers. Otherwise, the men…would find it distracting.'

He hoped anger might help her forget the newness. Inside, he smiled at the way she ruffled from his words. Talking with her made the water seem smoother. His clothing less rumpled.

Melina saw the spark of humour in his eyes. He jested. She let her shoulders drop and her lips turn down. 'Then I will merely lose my grip and see how the man below feels about breaking my fall.'

His lips thinned, but not in anger. 'I could catch you.'

'But you would not be able to keep your grip.

The fall would frighten me so, I am sure my elbows might flail about.'

'Would you like to test that?'

'No.' She made herself shudder. 'I need to put my satchel away.'

He turned to the bunk. 'Shove the bag under there. Wedge it tight or you will be fighting to keep it from sliding about.'

She moved, kneeling to be able to see and reach into the space. She lodged the bag inside and a tendril of her hair fell forward, loose from the bun. She finger-combed it back into place as she rose and then took one step to the door. 'I would like to watch the sails as the ship begins to move.'

He moved in front of her, blocking her way out, his expression cold and dark. 'I have to insist you not go about the deck. For the duration of the voyage, your attentions are mine alone.'

She opened her mouth to protest, then realised what he was saying. He thought her planning to sell herself to the men.

'I—' Her denial stopped before she could finish the sentence. She had sold her body and to him. It would be hard to convince him she didn't use her attentions for funds. Every man on the ship thought her a *porni*.

Melina didn't want their eyes on her. She already knew how sailors looked at the women they thought to purchase. She'd known it not safe to get too close. And now she was locked on a vessel with them. Her stomach roiled.

'How many men are on this ship?' she asked.

'Thirty-three.' His lips formed each sound of the word quite distinctly.

She didn't like where his thoughts were going. 'Women?' she asked, her fingers gripping the back of the chair beside her.

'One.' Nothing in his expression changed.

She controlled her words. 'I think I shall stay inside. I would not want one of the men falling from overhead when I am walking below. Nor would I wish to get tangled in the ropes. I have heard how things move about when ships are underway and sometimes mistakes are made.'

'It would be wise of you to keep out of the way.'

She didn't ask what he would have done if she'd not agreed to stay inside. From the look in his eyes, he would have been content with locking her in. And she would be able to do nothing about it. She tensed. She had stepped into a world where she was entirely alone.

'Does the door—' She had to ask. 'Does it latch from the inside?'

He shook his head, one very definite movement. 'No one would dare enter without my permission.' His words held in the air.

Relief surged in her, until the next words he said reminded her where she stood.

'And you cannot lock me out.'

'I did not think to do so. I know what I have promised.'

He indicated the island with a turn of his head. 'You can go back. Now. Last chance. No rock is worth going from your home. Leaving the people who can care for you.'

'But it is worth leaving for the people I *do* care about.'

He stared at her, his eyes disagreeing, and left the room, leaving her alone with the reality of her actions slithering into her body.

Chapter Three

Warrington worked the davit, listening to the creak as it lifted the longboat to be secured on deck. He mustn't keep thinking of her. This would be a bad time to get himself injured.

Taking one last look at the shore, he memorised the sight. If the fates were with him, he'd never see Melos again.

And if he had his way, he'd keep alive until they reached England. He had no sailor's wish to be buried at sea. When he died, he wished to be boxed and put into a properly marked location.

He could understand fascination with sailing. The challenge of it. Men stood on rigging as comfortably as they stood on land.

Now the sailors unfurled the foremast sail, working from the middle, out to the side, and it dropped more softly than a lady's skirt.

When the sun set the magic of the sea came out. In the night, the sails stiffened in the wind and the waters whispered a mesmerising sound. To stand on deck, with the blackness reflecting the heavens and the ship racing across the surface, a sailor could feel as if he were flying in an otherworldly vessel.

The moon rose well overhead and Warrington heard the bell, which signalled midnight and the end of the watch.

'Well, old man…' Warrington heard his brother's voice '…I suppose you should go examine the trinket you've stored in your cabin.'

'I'm in no hurry.' Warrington watched Ben. 'I'm not a man given to speed, but more to quality.'

'It's what we all say,' Ben muttered, looking into the darkness at the rigging, and then patted the mast. 'But I prefer to let the women boast about me.' Ben called out, walking away, 'And if you need instruction, return to me and I'll explain how the deed is *properly* done.'

Warrington stopped, turned back, Ben's form outlined in the moonlight. 'Little brother, I see the error now. You've thought all along it is to be done properly, while the women most enjoy an improper tumble.'

Ben turned, waving Warrington on his way. 'Get along, old man. Talk does not get the job done.'

When Warrington opened the door to the cabin, he noticed the lantern light flickering in the room. He looked to the bed. Empty. She sat in the chair backed against the wall, a bucket hooked at her feet by her heels, and looked up at him, her face ghostlike in the light.

'I have lost…' her voice followed the movement of the ship '…most food…' another gentle sway of the boat forward, and her chin dipped over the pot '…I have eaten in the past year.' The ship moved with the rocking motion of the sea and the breezes pushing them forward. She glared at him, but the look seemed more pitiful than angered. 'No one told me…a ship would float so rough…trying to turn my insides…outside.'

'You get used to it.' He hung his cap on a peg. 'About the time we hit land.'

She groaned.

Turning, he reached into the cabinet to move the brandy bottle aside and take out a cloth bag about the size of his hand. 'Comfits. Don't tell the men I have these. Wouldn't want them to think me weak.'

He reached the bag to her, but she waved it away. He didn't move back, but kept his hand firm.

'I had some made with ginger. A servant I have, a former seaman, swears it helps when a man is at sea and his stomach refuses to settle into the ship. Just let it rest on your tongue.'

She frowned, but took the parcel, opened it and

pulled out one of the orbs. She put it in her mouth and kept the bag clasped in her hand.

'Since you're not using the berth...' he said, reaching to remove his coat and place it on the remaining peg, and over her shawl.

She closed her eyes and leaned her head back, thumping the wall behind her. 'I can't lie down. My feet keep moving higher than my head.'

'Interesting.'

He usually sat in the chair to remove his boots, but no matter. Perching just on the edge of the berth and letting the bottom of the cabinet above him press against his shoulders, he tugged off his boots. Then he lifted them by the tops and pressed them into the railed opening beneath him so they'd not slide while he slept. He took off his waistcoat and stored it. Slipping his shirt from the trousers, his hand stopped when he looked again at her face. Her lashes rested against her cheeks. Her lips pressed together in a thin line and skin showed the same colour as the sails in moonlight.

For a moment he stared, torn between letting her alone and a need to brush tendrils back from her face.

He shook himself from his fascination and reached to the water pitcher, lodged in place and filled by the cabin boy earlier in the day. Warrington took the flannel lying inside the small raised edge, which kept it from sliding to the floor as the boat moved. He dampened the cloth and stepped beside her, putting it to her forehead. She held the compress in place. Their fingers touched, but she didn't seem aware he was even in the room.

'Try to think of something pleasant.' He spoke to her, and in response her lips tightened. 'Sing to yourself—some peaceful tune,' he instructed. 'It might help.'

'Are the seas always rough?' she asked.

He couldn't tell her this was calm. 'You get used to it.'

She nodded. 'I hope.'

Her parcel lay beside her. He took it and her gaze flicked to him.

'The rock can't slide around. Might break or cause one of us to fall.' He knelt at his bunk, trying to keep from brushing against her, and well aware that she pushed herself to the other side of the small room. He tucked the arm away carefully, knowing she watched every movement. Still kneeling, he looked across at her. 'The light needs out.'

'No,' she whispered. 'In the dark, the room moves faster.'

He frowned. 'You cannot fall asleep with the lantern lit.'

'I am not sleeping.'

Warrington stood and undid the top fastening of his shirt, then snapped the garment over his head, putting it on the remaining peg.

He pulled open the covers and slid between them. He turned his head and she looked forward, her gaze locked on the wall.

'Would you speak of something soothing?' she asked.

He stared at her. 'I'm going to sleep.'

'Say anything. Anything to take my mind off my stomach and the treacherous waters. Talk about your home. Your mother. A dog. Anything. Please.'

'I remember a tale of a young child eaten by wolves on a winter's night. What of it?'

'Nothing with food in it—please,' she mumbled.

He studied her face. The pallor only made her lashes seem longer. He decided he didn't need sleep as badly as he thought.

'Ben, the captain, is my brother. This is his first sailing on a ship he is captain of—but he was born with the taste for sea life in his blood.' He stared into the wood above his head. 'I've another brother, Dane, who is looking after things at home while we're away. And a sister, Adelphinia—named after a batty aunt, who even refuses to answer to the full name. We call my sister Adele, which she much prefers over Phinny.' He stopped. 'Perhaps from our telling her the horses called her when they whinnied.' His voice softened. 'She thinks brothers are a curse.'

He looked at Melina. If the sound of his voice

eased her, then the rise and fall of her breasts eased him. The little mark on her might be a scar.

'Keep talking,' she said.

He gave a grunt of complaint, but continued. 'I like Hoby boots, on firm land. I like to be able to look out my window and see oak trees. Solid trees on solid ground. I like my horse, Chesapeake, and I hated leaving him behind. I'm never getting this far from him again. He'll probably wish to bite me or throw me when I get home.'

'You miss...your horse?' She slid the flannel from her cheek.

'Ches—' He shut his eyes. 'I don't know what I was thinking to leave him.'

'There is no person you miss?

'For—' His voice rose, but he stopped himself. He remembered his home. He'd not wanted to speak of family. 'I have a son. And there's his sister. She's younger.'

He thought of Jacob, the morning after Cassandra's funeral. At first light, the boy had darted into War's room and bounded upon the bed with a question or two about death, then a concern about cat's ears.

Silence and darkness around him, he spoke again. 'My wife died a year or more ago. I've not forgiven her. I've not forgiven her for anything.'

She didn't speak.

He didn't want the sombre mood surrounding him so many times to engulf him again.

He turned his head back to her. 'Chesapeake enjoys the same journeys as I do. You can jest and call him any name you wish and he doesn't care. Chesapeake's a good mount. His sire and dam—he inherited the best of both. Father's size. Mother's grace.' The shadows in his world jostled him, taking his mind from the horse. Even though he knew he didn't lie, he left out so much.

She daubed the cloth at her face. 'I already miss my sisters.'

'Women are different.'

'Yes. But you have your brother nearby.'

He grunted his displeasure. 'I intended him to tell you that you could not sail with us.'

'I know.' She patted her cheek with the cloth and stared at him. 'No wonder you don't talk of missing anyone but your children. You've no heart.'

'Chesapeake would disagree.'

'A horse.' She near snorted, and if she only knew—she'd sounded a bit like Chesapeake. He wanted to tell her, but when he saw the paleness of her face he changed his mind.

'A fine chestnut. You'd never get him willingly on a ship.'

'So he's *exypnos*—clever.'

'Very.'

'How did you come to be on the vessel?' she asked, holding the comfits and flannel in one hand.

'My brother convinced me to invest in something he could captain. We both own half.' Warrington let himself settle into a more comfortable place. She needed to snuff the light so he could rest. 'Ben can make having fleas sound like a lark.'

'Should I expect fleas on this journey, as well?'

'Not unless you get too close to the men.'

He saw her lashes sweep up as she checked to see if he jested. Let her guess. 'You'll have to put out the light,' he reminded. 'We've had one fire too many already.'

'In a moment.'

Her head was against the wall. Graciously long neck. A delicious amount of skin creamy beneath it.

'What is that mark at your breast?' he asked.

Without looking, she reached to the colouration, running a fingertip along the skin, tracing the outline.

His gaze locked on her fingers.

'I was born with a smudge and it seems smaller than it used to. My sisters have the mark, too, but none of ours is in the same place or shape. I think of it as an hourglass—to remind me to be useful because there is only so much time.'

'Reminds me of...' he paused and looked again '...two horses' hooves close together.'

Again, she moved her fingers briefly to the mark and then stood, using both hands to brace herself against the table. She edged herself around the furniture and then doused the light, putting them in darkness.

'How did you pry yourself from Chesapeake to get on a ship?' she said, her fumbling movements leading her to the chair.

'I hoped to see different sights and learn about the Turks, but mostly I've seen water not fit to drink, heard jests not worth repeating and eaten food with no appeal at all. I think this ship has no rats because they starved.'

He heard the slop bucket slide as the ship moved and pushed himself from the bed. 'I'll empty the pot for you—otherwise one of us might put a foot in it before morning.' And he didn't intend to sleep with the smell.

Not having illumination didn't concern him. The walls were so close he could feel his way for what he needed. He slipped out through the door, his feet bare, and walked to the side, tossing the contents downwind. When he returned, he opened the small door to slip the pail back inside the cabinet.

'I would like to keep that nearby,' she murmured, stopping him.

He put it on the floor at her feet, and he saw the shadow of her pulling the bucket close so she could hook it again between her shoes.

'Take the bed,' he instructed, standing above

her. He would have to pull together something so he'd have a place to sleep.

'No,' she insisted, moving her head. 'I'm best here.'

'Wake me if you change your mind.' He reached to the bunk, took the pillow and then pushed it her direction. 'At least put this behind your head.'

After she held the pillow, he took his shirt, rolled it and tucked it in the berth.

He slid back into the sleeping space. 'My brother needs to get sailing out of his veins, return home and start a life there.'

'You can't fault him. The boat is his Chesapeake.'

'Well, he'll have to convince me we'll find gold, silver and mountains of apple tarts to get me on board again.'

He could hear her silence. It wasn't only that she was quiet—she was immobile. Not moving. Then she spoke. 'Treasures convince people to risk much.'

Chapter Four

Warrington stepped out of the cabin. He'd not fallen asleep until dawn and the climbing temperatures of midday had awakened him. The sailors cleaned the deck, a daily job. They couldn't risk growth of the green muck that flourished at sea emerging where men might slip.

Ben walked to his brother's side, looking every bit a man without a care—even with clouds bundling above them. Air filling with steam. The sea too calm.

The unconcern in the men around him didn't give Warrington a feeling of ease. He knew the men all too well. They didn't fluster over a storm. They knew they'd either live or die through it and, either way, they'd still be at sea.

The captain leaned close to Warrington and spoke so no one else could hear. 'Did you sleep well?'

Warrington ignored him. The young ferret could sniff for morsels awhile longer.

'I'm thinking the earl is wantin' for Stubby's job.' Gidley walked up. His whiskers quivered when he spoke. 'Men said he emptied the pot three times in the night.'

'Oh.' Ben's brows shot up. 'I may have heard that rumour, too. When we get to London, I'm thinking he might become a lady's maid.' Ben looked to his brother and then jumped aside, dodging the boot swung at his heels.

'For that...' Ben's chin went up '...you're invited to spend the afternoon, *and night,* at the wheel.'

'The woman's in my bed.' Warrington kept his voice light. 'Mine. Slop bucket or no. My cabin. My bed. My woman. She's perfection,' Warrington added. He remembered the night before. Perfection—if you didn't mind the greenish cast to her face. And seeing her fingers rubbing her own heated skin didn't do him any favours. She must have touched that mark a thousand times and each time he'd become aroused.

And now a storm to toss the *Ascalon* about more. He was going to die before they reached port and without getting his own mast climbed. No. No matter what, he'd discover the real treasure before the storm hit.

'You have any more of the medicinal you mentioned when we started out?' Warrington spoke to Gidley.

The older man's chin wobbled. 'Two draughts.'

'See that Melina gets them,' Warrington told the first mate. 'And remove the chair and table from my cabin. Get some bedding for her.'

'Do as he says,' Ben instructed Gidley, his voice light. 'He's not getting any younger and he needs all the help he can get.'

Gidley left to get the medicine and Ben looked at Warrington, saying, 'I'd suggest, brother, that you attempt to manage—if you're able—more than only a single tumble. I speak from experience when I say it *is* possible.'

Warrington's hands tightened.

Ben put his hand at the back of his own neck, shut his eyes and rolled his head, then yawned. 'I've had more than a lifetime of women already in my tender twenty-six—no, twenty-seven years—and probably your share, as well. That's why you're looking so sour at just past thirty. You're fading and I've bedded more women than you could ever hope to count.'

'If we take away the ones you've paid, how big would the number be then?'

'Only ones worth having.' Ben gave another stretch.

'Said by a man who has only the single way of attracting a woman.'

'At least when I pay,' he drawled out the last word, 'I manage to get her bedded.'

'I'm sure they do so quickly so they can see the last of you.'

Ben laughed in response, but Warrington knew his brother had a point. In the night, he'd wanted to touch Melina. And he hadn't. He'd not been able to reach out for a moment.

'Ben...' Warrington looked at the darkening clouds above '...do you ever fear dying at sea?'

Ben shook his head. 'Man has to go some time. Best to be doing what he loves when his toes turn up.'

'Then I will feel no regret for killing you if you don't relieve me from the wheel before the storm hits.'

Ben laughed. 'Give the medicinal time to work. Later, I'll give you time to go "courting". When you get to her, explain you must finish quickly so you may return to your duties.' He tilted his head and stared upwards. 'What's a brother for if not to give the elder an excuse for rushing about?'

'I have not *once,* in my entire life, concerned myself with your bedding habits,' Warrington grumbled, glaring at Ben. 'Not once.'

The captain tilted his head sideways and his tone was mournful. 'Sadly, I know why. You would be distraught at what wonders you have missed in your own experience.' He turned, glancing over the deck, appraising the ship. 'I have some good wine. Come to my cabin and have a swallow while you're resting up for the woman.'

Warrington shook his head and walked towards the aft deck, ducking his head from the ropes jutting out above. He could use some refreshment after the night he'd had, but he didn't relish more of his brother's company.

'The wine is quite good. Worth what I paid.' Ben lowered his head as well when he stepped beside War. 'And I'll not needle you any more.'

Warrington snorted, but followed Ben.

The quiet click of their boots as they moved to the cabin blended with the movement of the boat, and the murmurs of the sailors keeping their voices low so orders could be heard.

Inside the room, Ben reached to pull a bottle from a crate. The cork slid free of the neck with a comforting pop. Ben handed the drink to Warrington, who leaned against the door.

Warrington looked to Ben's berth, which didn't have the storage overhead. The bed wasn't bigger, but the room itself was more than double the size of the others, with two windows instead of one. A miniature was affixed to the front of the cabinet and Warrington knew, if he looked closely, that the painting was of a mermaid—Ben's version of a perfect woman.

The wine's sweetness rested well on Warrington's tongue. He handed the drink back to Ben, who dropped himself in the chair and helped himself to a hearty swallow.

Warrington snatched the bottle before Ben had a chance to put it down. 'Every time the boat touched the smallest ripple, the noises she made woke me. She turned green to her toes, I wager. I'd have had more rest on deck—except the men would have made too much sport of it.'

'You brought her on board.'

'Had to stay awake to make sure the lantern didn't falter. She couldn't stand the dark—made her worse. Every time I convinced her to turn out the light, in a few minutes I was lighting it again. I finally persuaded her to lie down in the berth.'

'So you were able to enjoy her.'

Warrington took a long swallow of the wine, frowned and looked at Ben. 'Think of the width and height of my berth. Two squirrels could hardly mate in it.'

Ben raised his brows and put a hand to his chest. His voice became overly concerned. 'I feel saddened for you and I don't wish you more distress. Send her to my cabin. I'll play nursery maid tonight.'

'Not bloody likely. I did everything but rub her feet to soothe her. I will be enjoying the lady's favours.'

'Maybe you should have rubbed her feet.'

'She wouldn't let me.'

'What can I say, old man, except send her my way.' Ben clasped his hands behind his head. 'I've a special remedy that eases any discomfort a woman might have. One look at it and she forgets all else.'

'You'd best see the ship sails like treacle poured across a plate tonight, or I will be pounding on your door.'

Ben held out his hand, indicating time to return the bottle. He might as well have been looking over the top of spectacles in a schoolroom. 'I think you let her make excuses.'

'I do not,' Warrington repeated, and then smiled. 'Every time I looked at her I could see that little mark, like a drawing of breasts.'

'It looks like a woman's bottom.'

'No.' Warrington spoke with certainty. 'Breasts.'

They were silent for a moment, then Ben held his hand out, palm raised, and didn't lower it.

Warrington gave him the bottle.

Ben took a drink. He put the wine in front of him. 'Just don't forget she'll be plying her trade on the docks when we reach port. Saw an opportunity to get to London and she took it. Doesn't change what she is.'

'I don't care what she is. She's in my bed and she's going to do as she agreed. Then we dock and she goes on her way.'

'Now you're thinking. Not like with—'

'Stubble it, Ben.' He didn't need reminding about his dead wife, the beautiful Cassandra, who always wore chemises that smelled of roses.

He knew he'd been a fool with her, two times over. And both his brothers knew. And the servants. Or at least they all imagined they did. He didn't think anyone but himself realised how truly addled he'd been. At least afterwards he'd been able to let them believe most of his feelings were rage towards her.

But he'd grieved for her and not been able to pretend otherwise enough to fool his brothers. Only the misery of being trapped on a ship at sea, with conditions that might have otherwise driven him mad, had brought back his mind to reality.

He could see Cassandra for what she was, but that also meant he could see himself for what he was.

He'd not been able to stop wanting her. He'd hated himself for his desire.

'Oddest thing came to me when I shaved.' Ben gave a slight shake of his head. 'Think I've seen your berth mate before.'

His thoughts snagged on Ben's words. 'The island?'

'Never been to Melos before. Couldn't be.'

'But how could you forget a woman with a face like hers?'

'Didn't exactly forget her. Just can't remember where I saw her. And I know I saw her.'

'You told me all women look alike to you.'

'In bed.' Ben shrugged. 'But I don't think that's where I saw her.'

Warrington felt the betrayal of his past again and anger with himself for having concern for a woman he didn't trust. 'I suppose I can ask her why she speaks so plain. It would not be unusual if she spoke French, or if she spoke a few words of rough English. But she speaks better than some of the seamen, even with her Greek flavour. I noticed on the island, but once she dropped her shawl, I lost interest in her speech.'

'But she's not said *eros*. Perhaps it's the company she's keeping.'

'So you remembered one word from the tutor you tortured. *Eros*. I am not surprised. But she's been paid—her passage—she'll say it. And you'll leave her be.'

'Of course.' Ben stretched out his arms, before clasping his hands behind his neck and grinning. 'But don't be surprised if she changes affections and decides she can't stay away from me.' He leaned back enough that the front legs of his chair lifted, completely at ease with the ship's motions.

'You touch her, little brother, and there are not enough men on this ship to keep you alive.'

'You talk *here* and the woman is in the cabin regretting she did not get her captain.'

'When we get to London, I'm sinking my half of the ship.'

Ben again leaned towards him. 'Let's just hope you don't sink my half before we get there.'

Warrington kept himself from kicking the legs out from his brother's chair. He truly didn't want him hurt, but unsettled would be nice. Warrington crashed the door shut behind him when he left and hoped his brother's ears rang.

He went to take his turn at the wheel, but knowing, before the night was out, Melina would soothe the memories that plagued him.

Chapter Five

Melina didn't know whether she'd stepped closer to devastation or further away. The boat wobbled so much she thought her knees would buckle as she stood.

The cabin boy fidgeted at the door, holding several biscuits in one hand, and a cup of liquid in the other, which smelled the same as soured goat milk. 'First mate says to drink the broth he had made from his special mix-up and we don't have no choice when he says things. This won't kill you, but it'll give you some ballast in your stern. Keep you from going belly up.'

She took the offering from him.

'Anything else you be needing, I's your man.' He plunked his finger against his chest—or where his chest would be once he grew. She didn't think him aged more than most men's boots. His red hair was streaked with dark strands. The locks fell across his eyes, but didn't conceal the watchfulness behind them. 'Gidley says I'm not to leave your side until you drink the last drop. He says I'm not to let you pour it overboard, either. Gidley says I should watch you with my own vision. Gidley says not to trust you 'cause of you being female.'

'How old are you?' she asked.

His face furrowed. 'I be old enough. I keep working like I do—I'll have my own ship some day. I want to sail on a man-o'-war. I'll be...' he straightened his shoulders and glowered '...tougher than any privateer, pirate or first mate. Gidley says first mates are toughest of them all.'

'Malista,' she answered. 'Yes.' She nodded, about to step back and shut him outside.

He put one scruffy bare foot to block the closing of the door. 'Only toes I have, 'cept on the other side. Would sure hate to lose 'em.'

'If I drink this, you might not wish to see the results.'

He waved a hand, indicating unconcern. 'It's your belly.'

She firmed herself and drank half the cup. 'I'll not take any more and the rest goes into the pot and neither of us will tell Gidley.'

'Won't pickle me none.' He grinned at her, the smudge of dirt on his face wrinkling. 'I'll empty your slop bucket and no one will know.'

She stepped back so he didn't knock her askew when he moved inside. He grabbed the pail, held it for her to pour away the medicine and looked at her.

He whispered, but his words near shouted he spoke so loud. 'Where's the treasure?'

She didn't answer.

He bunched his lips, then moved his jaw from side to side as if the movement helped him think. 'Gidley said you had a treasure for the earl. I figure it has to be in the parcel Warrin'ton hauled up. Jewels?'

She shook her head. 'Some stone. Nothing you'd be interested in.'

'Like rocks?' His eyes lit up. 'Gold ones?'

She shook her head. 'Not gold.'

He frowned. 'I was hoping to see me some gold. No use for rocks on *Ascalon,* 'cept for ballast.' He turned, rushing out, barely letting his dirt-encrusted feet skim the planks.

Melina looked at the boards above her head, remembering the catacombs she and her sisters had explored, but they never stayed long in the darkness. She'd only explored inside to prove her bravery. Now the shadows outside the window increased her fears even as she told herself nothing had changed, but the sea had roughened.

Each lunge of the ship into the unsettled water slapped her stomach with the feeling of being in front of a battering ram. She stood, reaching out to the door, palms against the wood.

The image of Stephanos, the man she had fled, entered her mind.

'I hate you, Stephanos,' she whispered to the empty room while wiping away the moisture at her brow—for a moment, uncaring if the ship dropped under a wave, and kept plunging. Sinking would still the movement and silence the ship. *Ascalon* creaked and groaned, complaining more than any person she'd ever heard. She didn't see how something could stay afloat while protesting so much.

The shadows in the room grew longer. The rocking motion made the walls move as if they reached to squeeze her in an embrace. Her lungs could hardly fill with air. She already felt she was drowning.

Without thinking, she jumped up and pulled open the door. She had to escape—to breathe.

Stepping on to the deck, she could see enough in front of her to realise the vastness of the water. The liquid reached to the end of the world. And she could run no direction to escape.

Melina would kiss Stephanos's feet—each naked toe if he asked—to get back to her home. She pulled the door shut behind her and pressed her back to the wood, her fingers grasping for something to hold herself still. Now she didn't care that she'd planned to leave the island for months and swore she'd do whatever the journey took. The sacrifice was too great.

Taking a breath, Melina took stock of her surroundings. She didn't smile or look directly at any of the men. She did not want more concerns.

Two men sitting on crates immediately dropped their heads and studied the frazzled bits of rope in their hands. They continued twisting the frayed hemp back into shape. Everything on deck, but the boxes the men used, was lashed down.

She let out a breath, putting her hand at her stomach. Walking to the railing, she leaned against the barrier keeping her from the water, facing forward, feeling the comfort of the breeze.

Only a day before, Melina could not have imagined herself drinking a vile concoction, after spending the night inside a bobbing box at sea, with a silent man watching her cast up her accounts and him trying to calm her so he could bed her.

She'd bargained with Warrington and taken a risk, and she didn't regret it, but she wasn't certain her promise wasn't troubling her stomach as much as the ship.

Shutting her eyes didn't help. When she opened them nothing had changed.

Something—a hand—grabbed her elbow and she jumped, darting back from the railing.

'You needin' help, miss?' The reedy voice of Gidley jarred her, and even in the dusk, she could see enough to recognise him leaning towards her in concern.

'I'm well,' she muttered. 'I just needed air.

My—' She pulled her elbow from his grasp and touched over her stomach, taking care not to pat it. 'I am not good over water…and…' Things kept moving in front of her when she knew they were really immobile. 'I keep being ill.'

He stepped back, a bundle tucked under one arm. 'If yer need the earl, he's at the helm.' He lowered his voice, whispering, 'He can prob'ly hear us yappin' now. ''Less the wind is howling, yer can hear a sniffle from anywhere on deck. But yer need to take care. This be the bit of quiet before the storm slaps our masts up our…nose.'

She shook her head. Her bun slid back on her head and she hoped the darkness covered her dishevelment.

'Yer want me to show you how well sound can carry, I'll start singin' and in a whisker shake, his lordship will start swearin' at me to shut my mouth.'

'No. I thank you,' she answered.

He tipped his chin to her. 'Well, I'm puttin' this bedding inside yer cabin.' He let his words ring loud. 'Yer get tired of that peer and want to see what a real man can do, just say the word. Might not be the sea makin' you ill. But the comp'ny yer keepin'.'

He gave her a fatherly pat on the arm before scooting her aside to open the cabin door and toss the bundle inside. He left, humming.

'Melina.' She heard the muffled shout of Warrington's voice and turned towards the sound. She crept slowly until she saw his outline at the stern, holding the wheel. The night made him darker, and maybe taller, she wasn't sure. Even the wheel seemed smaller with him holding it.

'You should be in the cabin. You could fall against something, or stumble overboard.' He raised his voice. 'Or have to speak to someone like Gidley, who can't sing and wouldn't know what to do with a woman.'

She heard a chuckle wafting back through the air—and then another.

One more voice—a strong baritone she didn't recognise—called out and she wasn't even sure of the direction. 'When I'm finished with a woman, she's the one singing—my praises. Send her my way if she can't sleep.'

Warrington snapped out, 'You're going to find yourself upside down and hanging from a mast if you don't take care.'

'Best leave his lordship be,' an unrecognisable voice shouted.

Melina guessed the words came from Gidley, but she wasn't sure.

'His mama didn't teach him to share,' the man continued to taunt.

Warrington put his words low, snapped them together and spoke to her. 'Are you pleased with the discussion you have caused?'

'The only grumbler is his lordship,' Melina said.

'You tell 'im, sweet,' a voice rang out.

'Anyone touches her, they go overboard,' Warrington said, his voice not overly loud, but with enough force to take the sound to the tips of the sails.

'Including the captain?' someone asked from the shadows.

'*Especially* the captain.'

Melina crossed her arms and put challenge in her voice. She turned to face him. 'It is a good thing I am fond of his lordship, then, so no one will have to go into the sea.' Her lips turned up and she put her chin closer to his. 'Besides, he's the only man who's ever emptied my pails.'

Whistles sounded, mixed with a few muffled hoots.

He stepped sideways enough to hold the wheel with one hand and snake the other around her waist, pulling her so close she could feel the heat of his breath and hear his rough whisper. 'I should never have brought you.'

She turned, her hair catching in the bristles on his chin. 'I know,' she replied in kind. 'But I'm here and the ship can't turn back.'

His fingers loosened on her waist and as she moved away, he took a step, scooping her closer. Before her feet settled, she found herself tucked between the wheel and a firm male. Both his hands steered *Ascalon*. She had room to breathe and little else.

'You might as well learn to guide the ship.'

Warrington leaned to whisper to her ear. 'You're not going anywhere for a while.'

She tried to push away, but he trapped her and she couldn't leave.

'Let's not let the seamen think we're having a lovers' quarrel,' he whispered.

'I don't feel well.' She spoke between gritted teeth.

'Then try to miss the boots.'

Chapter Six

Melina's warmth overpowered Warrington. He gripped the wheel hard, trying to ignore her body—but he could not ignore anything about her. He could only tell his heart to quit beating so loudly she might hear.

Her skirts tangled in his legs and when she moved the slightest, her backside brushed against him, causing his fingers to lock on to the wheel's spindles with such force he expected the wood to shatter. And when she put her foot down on his boot, and then sidestepped to avoid his feet, even more of her pressed against him. He was stoked into heated readiness.

The sea's moisture penetrated her clothing, bringing the scent of a stringent soap to his nose along with the spiced fragrance he'd noticed. But he inhaled again—because mixed with her skin, the soap reminded him of a woman's purity—something he'd never felt before in his arms.

He savoured the moments with her and, for the first time since the newness had worn thin, relished a moment at sea.

'I think you've impressed the men enough with your mastery over me now,' she whispered. 'You may release me.'

He didn't answer immediately. Instead he lowered his head. 'I do not think they are convinced—yet,' and as he said the last word, his lips tasted the skin at her neck. He wasn't disappointed.

A shrill, vulgar whistle interrupted and he pulled back.

'I cannot believe you men are ignoring your duties,' he called out after he'd turned his head so he could raise his voice without hurting her ear, 'simply because Melina cannot stay from my side.'

He heard her intake of breath, but before she could speak, he put his fingers lightly over her arm. 'Don't say more,' he whispered, 'and they'll go back to their work.'

She gave a quick nod and he dropped his fingers.

'Melina.' He made sure no one could hear. 'If I release you...' inwardly he cursed himself '... will you go straight back to the cabin?'

She opened her mouth to speak and then took a breath before answering. 'Yes, but...'

'You may stay if you wish.'

Her voice was hushed. 'The room—the walls—it reminds me of a cave... I hate caves...'

He held her waist and his hand instantly warmed from her skin. 'I understand. I was daft to step foot on this ship. I never plan to let my feet leave dry land again—but I'm pleased I sailed. I saw what I left behind.'

'Your wife is gone, but you have a woman there you care for?'

He shook his head. 'I do not.' He heard the coarseness of his tone and softened his words, speaking low, near her ear. 'I've spent little time with a woman this past year.' A breeze blew over his face and whipped at his clothing.

'My wife, Cass, died nearly a year ago, or beyond,' he said. 'I'm not sure. I refuse to remember the dates. The days. She left behind two children. But I have to get home to my son. I've left him too much. I had him brought to my town house to visit me, but I've not returned to Whitegate since my wife died.' He paused. 'No. I have no woman. I have not had one for a long time.'

'I would have still bargained with you had you been wed. I had to leave.'

'I understand.' His lips were only a shudder from her ear, and he let his face rest against her head. 'But my brother would be holding you now, not I, if I still had a wife at home.' She shivered, but he didn't know if it was from his actions or his words or his nearness.

'Truly?' she asked.

'Yes, I suppose. Perhaps not. But Ben would

have known had I been untrue to Cass and that would have bothered me, though he wouldn't have cared. As I am the eldest, I should lead the family.'

'Not all the oldest of the family lead.' Her voice, soft, brushed against him like a caress. 'My mother cared for us on Melos. Father would leave for a long time and then he would return, laughing at how much we'd grown. Sometimes he would stay a short while. Sometimes a year or more. Mother still took care of our home just as she did when alone.'

'My wife left all in the hands of the servants, but they took great care not to anger her.' He'd never spoken such to anyone. Nights with poor sleep and wondering if he might die when the ship caught ablaze, and then having such warmth in his arms melted into him had loosened his tongue. And made his memories not so harsh.

'In her youth,' he continued, 'my wife nearly died and her family feared for her life.' He brushed at the hair fallen from Melina's pins. She had as much of her locks on her shoulders as she had in place. 'Her parents adored Cassandra. Plus, she was a beauty and they treated her as porcelain. Her older sister, Daphne, missed Cass when we married, so I welcomed Daphne to visit. Daph loved her sister so much. In no time, Daphne was family to me and Cassandra was a doll we both adored.'

He stepped back, moving aside. The talk of Cass had stirred unpleasant memories. And he had a woman in his arms who could take his mind from Cassandra. Now was not the moment to think of the past. Any longer with Melina and he would not be able to keep his hands from roaming her body. 'Your hair is falling to your shoulders. Go to the cabin and try to sleep if you can,' he directed her, feeling a distant coolness replacing the warmth of having her close. 'I will follow soon.'

She gave a quick nod and walked away, staying away from the outer rails.

He sniffed the air. He was not a seasoned sailor and he knew a storm was on the way. The seas had roughened. He called out for someone to take his place at the helm.

And while he waited, he told himself to remember that Melina was little more to him than an imagination. When they docked, she would disappear—just like the dream he created of her.

Melina sat on the floor, head back against the wood, eyes closed, propped against a bundle of bedding. He clicked the door shut behind him just as lightning flashed at the window. She jumped, blinked twice and struggled to find words. 'The sea is rough,' she said, voice unsteady.

'We'll take your mind from it.' He leaned towards her, took her hand and pulled her to her feet. Just the touch of her made every bucket worth it. He slipped his arms around her and buried his face against the soft skin of her neck. He smiled when a hint of sweet spice reached his nose. She smelled like something of a holiday. Of gaiety. Mulled wine. Exotic treats.

Her clothing bunched under his hands and he covered her back with his touch. He needed nothing more than her in his arms. She soothed him— something he'd not expected. Feeling the softness of her earlobe with his face, he savoured her. But she remained still, letting him caress and giving no response.

Warrington stood back from her and took off his coat, putting it on the peg. After wishing the ship's movement hadn't hit her so hard, he remembered the rough days when he'd first set out. No one should feel so unsettled.

Warrington took her chin, lifted it and brushed a kiss across her lips. His body flamed from just the merest touch of her. He whispered against her skin, 'You'll have to imagine all the fine things that should surround someone as lovely as you.'

He understood her reluctance. She didn't know how they'd find the room, probably expecting nothing more than the sort of encounter a rushed man gave a woman who had to be on to her next business. The two of them simply could not fit on the bed. Not only could they not lie side by side, but the cabinets overhead prevented other arrangements. He'd spent some time thinking of the best way to accomplish a blissful encounter. Even as he released her, the ship kept rocking in such a way they could hardly keep from stumbling into each other.

Warrington reached for the bedding bundle, which rolled about, knocking into his legs, and with a few tugs and a quick flick spread the bedding on the floor. The chair and table were gone. She stepped back, flattening herself against the wall.

Pulling the mattress and coverings from his berth, he put it against the ones on the floor, adding softness. He fell to his knees to finish making the pallet. He'd never, ever knelt in front of a woman—but no matter. Running a hand over the bedding, he smoothed edges together.

He stood, examining her in the lantern light.

Brown eyes—lovely, enticing—stared back at him. She didn't look pleased to see the covers on the floor, but he couldn't fault her.

'I assure you, if we were in London, I'd find a bed for us so soft you'd think of clouds.' He wanted her to understand—he took this seriously.

The pallor in her face slowed his movements. She had to know the bed wasn't his choice.

'There's no bigger cabin, except Ben's,' he told her, 'and he is captain, so it's rather hard to shove him out through the door.'

'I'm… This is fine.' She dropped to her knees, pulling the top covers in place and brushing her hand across them. She lowered her chin. 'You know I'm not… The ship is moving more and…' She touched her stomach.

He knelt, reaching out for her shoulder, feeling the roughness of the sleeve. 'Melina—if you've any compassion at all, try to keep from being ill for a bit longer. I can… But with the storm coming and…'

She pulled back. 'This is not the storm?'

He'd said the wrong thing. 'A few raindrops. Ben thinks we'll sail through without a bobble.'

The ship heaved and she moved backwards, sliding with the makeshift bed. He shifted with the momentum, putting his arm around her and arranging so his back was to the wall and he held her at his side. He felt stronger than any wave—but she didn't.

A blast of anger hit him. The fates—he knew them well, they were his bedfellows—they were conspiring again. They thrust another wave against the ship and he held her tight, seeing the press of her lips.

He was not some rutting beast—and she would still be here tomorrow—assuming they didn't die in the storm.

Warrington stood, extinguished the wick and looked to the window. He had no time to get a hammer and nail a covering over the opening so the flashes of lightning wouldn't illuminate and accentuate the discordance outside.

He'd been graced with this woman whose ancestors could have been from Thessaly, where mythology began, and he would not be allowed to touch her. Lightning wove gold threads into her hair, but illuminated the pallor of her skin and reminded him she didn't feel well.

At least on deck he would be forced into thinking of staying alive. He reached to the door, but her voice stopped him.

'Please,' she said, and touched the bed beside her. 'The ship shakes so. I don't want to be alone. I feel better with you near. Here.'

Lightning kept flashing through the glass—giving her a mythical glow, freezing the unmoving image of her into his mind, painting her like a statue, a work of art.

The intensity of her gaze caused him to stare—her eyes clear as a harvest moon, surrounded by lashes dipped in the flashing light. He dropped to his knees, landing beside her, entranced by the flickers of lightning on her skin. He swept his finger over her bottom lip. Now he knew what magic felt like. His skin tingled with anticipation.

More thunder crashed. He heard a crack of lightning. With the sounds, and the sight of her, sensual energy surged in him, heating him until an internal maelstrom engulfed him. The memories he made tonight would some day take on larger-than-life images in his mind. Melina, different from all he'd seen before, and all he'd see again, would remain in his thoughts—like a precious gem hidden away in a safe. A secret only for himself to have.

A wave tilted the ship and she wrenched her body around, clasping the front of his shirt. She buried her head against him and he held her.

'Have you ever been in seas this rough?' she asked.

Lightning crackled much too close. The very air could not be still, as if it had an awareness of their moments, and told them to hurry, hurry, hurry, and grasp every second of sensation.

He ran his fingertips across her back, and the lightest touch of his hand against her took his breath. The fierce waters faded from his mind.

When he could speak, he said, 'Once is too many times. I didn't tell you before. Suspected you'd worry if you realised how brutal the waves can be when the sun heats the water in the day and the storms take us at night.'

He pulled his coat front aside, sliding into a sitting position, and then tucked the garment around her back, hugging her inside with him. 'This ship was built to handle such weather and the men are the best sailors in the world. Nothing will happen.' Assuming the repairs held and the storm did not get too violent.

'Shut your eyes, and think of… Think of this,' he said.

His mouth closed over hers and the kiss was

nothing more than a simple touch, almost the same as he might give a tavern maid who'd plopped down on his lap, before he scooted her away to get to his ale or talk with his companions. But the pulses stirring in him ignited.

When he pulled back, she reached out, running her hand along the side of his jaw, seeing him with her fingertips.

'I have wanted to touch your face since I first saw you,' she said. 'You're so foreign from the men I have known all my life. And the other sailors. I think you even look at me differently.'

He rested his forehead against the side of hers. 'I wanted…since I saw you…so much more.' His lips explored her skin and he cupped her breast, letting the fullness feed the sensations in his fingertips. The fabric didn't prevent the yielding flesh from rolling beneath his caress with her softness and he discovered the hard nipple, and stretched his hand over her, so he could take in as much of the feeling as his mind would allow. No corset. He'd never felt through a woman's clothing to find so much of her underneath.

Just as she had explored his face, he traced her, keeping the fabric of her garments as a barrier between skin and mapping out the feminine twists and turns of her.

The storm would frame them and their bodies would gain sensations from the hint of danger in the air. And she would be the essence of every sensual mythological being ever imagined.

He couldn't read her expression and didn't know if it was a flaw in him, or if she hid herself well. But when she parted her lips and moved towards him, he didn't have to. She slipped her arms around his waist, mumbling his name, muffled words against his chest, and she clung to him. Her breasts pressed against his shirt, causing his clothing to feel tight over his body. She moved with the lunging waves, too, but not in the same way as he. She kept herself upright by pushing herself into him at the same time as she pulled. He braced against the wall, one hand clutching the edge of the bunk, leg jammed against the opposing side. His body was forced still within the movements. And she burrowed and snuggled and wove herself against him, holding on like a handkerchief might be wrapped around a blowing limb. When the ship created even the smallest distance between them, she moved to fill the space, keeping him as her anchor.

Using all his strength in one arm, he kept them steady while he held her with the other hand.

He found her lips with his and at first she paused, but when she moved again her hands wouldn't be still, roaming his body with a hunger in her fingertips, searching him out as if she were afraid she might miss touching some exquisite part and wouldn't be able to bear it.

Somehow she'd settled herself into the movement of the ship and now used it to keep herself thrust against him. He savoured the desires her body created. If she was a goddess to lure men to their doom, he was prepared to die.

'This helps. And the waves are not so strong now,' she whispered, and he could feel the movements of her lips against him as she spoke.

'Just ripples.' But they weren't. Everything had intensified. He reached to pull free the last bits of his shirttails, which remained tucked in his trousers, and her fingers tangled with his, helping him.

The water outside crashed against the hull, but he no longer cared.

She leaned into the side of him that he used to hold them steady, leaving him one hand free to rub the small of her back. But her fingers remained under his shirt, clasping him, leaving heated handprints, which encased his whole body.

'You feel so…pleasant,' she whispered into him, her face moving up so that her lips were at his neck.

And for the first time since he saw her, she was in exactly the right place, saying exactly the right thing.

Letting her sway into him, her rocking against him when the ship moved caused the fire inside him to smoulder so intensely he wondered if he should just let their clothes disintegrate into ash instead of removing them. He had no time to wait for such an event. He didn't fear her not holding up well in the storm—he felt concern for himself not surviving the intensity within him.

His lips lingered against her hair, and skin, taking in all of her he could. This truly was the woman of his imagination—the night cravings that woke him with seconds of pleasure lingering in his mind and hours of hollowness facing him. But this time, he would sleep after the dream, un-tortured—soothed.

He buried his face into the curve of her neck. She did feel like Aphrodite—and he had the imagination of her vanishing from his arms, fad-ing, mocking him for desiring her so intensely. But he couldn't be imagining this because he'd never tasted a dream and he tasted the nectar of her lips, and this time, he relished the hint of salti-ness at his tongue.

His fingers brushed over the strands of her hair loosening from the pins and he slid his palm down, closing his eyes and closing all his senses except the ones at his fingertips.

He knew they had to separate so he could get past the clothing. But one moment apart was a moment for ever lost. He savoured her cheek, her ear and the hollow of her neck. A banquet for his starved senses.

She might as well have already undressed.

She kissed him, he thought. He wasn't totally

sure. He pulled back, only enough to look into her face to make certain she was real. Dark eyes stared back at him.

She'd not tugged at his clothes again, or spoken much, but she didn't need to. Her expression now told him all he wanted to know.

For the second time in his life—and he'd never tell her—he felt like a virgin. Yet a different sort of innocent. One who knew all the pleasures he could unleash with his hands, his mouth and his body.

He forced himself away—aware of his own breathing echoing in the cabin—knowing if he did not move back, he couldn't get closer. Melina's hands, hesitant but bold, didn't lose their purchase easily and that knowledge alone washed him with a satisfaction he'd not experienced before.

He pulled off his coat and lifted his shirt over his head.

The luscious heat of her—against his chest—hit him harder than any wave could have tossed him. When he touched her breasts, running a finger over the mark just at the top of her bodice, he could barely breathe. This was his Aphrodite. She would vanish soon, but not until she left him truly sated for the first time in his life.

'You are to be savoured.' He wanted to feel all of her and adjusted her on to her back, moving her so she was tucked between his body and the wall. He released the buttons of his trousers. The sight of her, in this thrown-together bed where another woman would never rest, clutched at him, filling him with a reverence that arrested him. He stopped for another moment, just a moment, to look at her. He wanted to see her face even when he shut his eyes. He needed her locked into his mind so that all other memories of women on the earth were erased—Melina alone remaining in his thoughts.

For this, he would have sailed around the world—twice—to capture her so she could bring him to his knees and let him rise back up, unburdened.

He kicked his trousers free at their feet.

Hooking his arm under her leg, he pulled her knee to his mouth for a chaste kiss on the coarse cloth of her skirt. Now the fabric felt leaden, thick and suffocating for skin soft as hers. Much too rough.

He wasn't quite sure how her clothing worked. This wasn't the same dress of an English woman, which slipped off easily, only to reveal rigging underneath as well structured as the ropes holding the sails.

She sat up and reached behind, tugging her garments. She slipped the blouse over her head and removed her chemise after pulling it from her skirt. His jaw fell. Nothing tied underneath. Not a thing. Lightning flashed again, somehow only illuminating her breasts. Even though the burst lasted less time than a blink, the image of the white softness with pebbled peaks lodged in his mind. His body reacted with the same intensity of the storm.

Then she reached to the side of the skirt and undid a knot, and slid herself out. The thunder increased. The bursts of light showering the room must have meant he'd done something right in his life.

'You are perfection,' he whispered.

Leaning forward, he cradled her and swept her back to rest on the covers. Her eyes widened. She reached up and clutched his shoulders. The wind almost drowned out her whisper. 'I am not a whore.'

'It doesn't matter,' he reassured her. This time, he didn't care who'd been before him. He was with her. 'We are the only two people in the world. We must savour this.' His fingertips traced the mark at her breast and he trailed downwards, over her nipple, and to her stomach and the curve of her hip.

When he bent to kiss her and let his hand rest at her thigh, she slid sideways with the ship's movement and he followed the momentum, but didn't let his full weight go against her. His bent knee rested over her, his foot pressed against the ledge that had once cradled his mattress. He reached up, holding the edge of the bunk to keep them from rolling back.

'Are you hurt?' he asked, his face resting against her hair.

'No. Please don't let me go.'

He had no intention of it. Nor could he have. She rested inside the crook of his arm. Her hand nearest the deck captured his shoulder, the other held his back.

When the ship lunged and she grasped, fingernails clenched at his skin. Instead of feeling pain at her fingertips, he ached for her. His cock nudged her thigh, pressed against her smooth skin.

The weather slammed the ship down and he held firm so they would not slide backwards. He hooked his heel inside the opening at the bunk, lodging his leg over the ledge that framed the base next to the deck planks. His hand was momentarily freed to trace the outline of her hip and, with her head still on his arm, he reached out to grip the base at the other end of the bunk. He was as comfortable as in a cradle. The waves rocked them.

He felt where her waist curved in and then let his fingertips trail downwards into the soft curls and the wetness beneath. She was ready.

But he wanted her more than ready. He wanted her gasps and cries and release. If they died in the storm, he wanted her to be pleasured first, more than she'd ever felt before.

He began a rhythmic caress while his mouth rested against her face, her neck and her hair.

Her teeth grazed his shoulder and her hands pinched into his back. She writhed and he felt his own pleasure bursting inside. He watched, mesmerised with the moment, until he knew she peaked, her gasps plunging desire into him so that his whole body burned an aching need for her.

Forcing himself to wait, he pulled his hand from her and gave her a chance to recover while he brushed his face against her, lips caressing her.

He tugged, sliding her so she could move above him. Both her hands went out, resisting movement.

Releasing her, he pulled back from the kisses. 'Sweet. It might be better if you got on top. The waves. The hard bed.'

She breathed her answer. 'No…' Her disagreement registered in his mind, momentarily giving him pause. But only for less time than it took for lightning to flash.

Brushing his face against hers, he rose over her and gently lowered himself, entering her, and her fingernails plunged into his back, and she gasped.

Something forbidding flashed through his mind. An unease hit him. But the moment couldn't be stopped or interrupted. He held the woman of his dreams, bodies bound together with intensity.

Carefully, he rocked into her, whispering tenderness against her ear.

Her legs, he felt one wrap around him and he forced himself to go slow, to savour. To let the riches of her body wash over him.

Now the ship seemed to smooth, to ease across the waters, and the storm raged inside—inside him. The waves rolled through his body, taking him on their skyward roll, their deepening depths.

'Are you…' He meant to ask her something, but his mind got lost in the feel of her and he could not form another full thought. She was everything at this moment—a world for him.

He tried to move a hand up to brush back her hair from her eyes, but he couldn't. He could not let the ship control his movements. He had to be careful, gentle and not let himself plunder her, but show her the tenderness he felt for her.

'Melina,' he whispered. The sound of her name, even that increased the sensations. He could feel so much more of her. Not just where their bodies touched, but the way she breathed, the richness of her voice, all the things of her that made her who she was.

The room brightened briefly again and he saw her face clearly. The sight of her was too much. He could not last any longer for her, didn't want to last any longer for her, because he wanted those seconds, the endless flashes of time where they were completely together, taking them into another realm of the world.

He released, but it was something different. A connection and blending of their bodies, holding close, melding together in just those heartbeats.

Moisture covered his body, as if he'd felt the rains and they'd cleansed him,

He pulled her against him, falling back with the ship.

When the room became silent—silent even with the storm mocking the tempest that had raged inside the cabin—Warrington's mind hurdled ahead. Instead of a wash of satisfaction overtaking him—dread nudged the warmth into oblivion. His stomach churned.

He looked into the shadows of her face and slowly pushed himself to the side. Lightning still splashed through the window, but the storm no longer concerned him. She made a sound, no more than a sigh, but the illegible sound of settling in for a jaunt through her own thoughts.

The ship lunged and he reached out, not wanting her to be overwhelmed by the movement of the waves, and pulled her firm against his side.

'Had you...before?' he asked, hating the words. Dreading the answer.

She murmured, 'No.'

She could not have understood what he asked. She could not have said what he heard. He spoke to the walls, letting his mind untangle the puzzle around him. '*No one's a virgin.*'

He tried to examine her face in the flashes of light. He saw the truth. 'How could—'

She scooted forward, pulling a bedcover over her. 'I decided—for passage. I knew what I was doing. And tonight, I wanted to know…how you felt…'

'I didn't know, though. I didn't know. You didn't…tell me.'

'Yes.' Her brows bunched. 'I said…something.'

He sat up, looking over his shoulder at her. He felt betrayed. How could he feel betrayed again—this time? 'I thought you were a lightskirt.'

'I told you I wasn't.'

'I thought you meant you weren't a common whore. That you expected more… That you chose who you…' He'd been misled again. He didn't know what to think or do. She was *not* supposed to be an innocent.

'I had to bed you or Stephanos, the man who controls Melos. We have leaders, but he is the one who has coin and the leaders do not cross him.' She sat, pulled her knees up and put her chin on them. 'I would choose anyone over Stephanos.'

He stared at her. Strength left him. He could barely keep himself from sliding with the ship.

'But… You offered— I did not misunderstand you in the barn. I did not. You said…' He heard the volume of his voice rise, embarrassing, and he regained control and pushed to his feet, un-concerned by his nakedness. He noted her quick intake of breath and jerk of her head when the lightning illuminated him. He reached to the washstand, bracing, and poured some water on to the flannel, then lodged the pitcher securely back to its base.

She could avert her eyes, close them or watch. He did not care.

He pressed the cloth to his forehead. 'How could you be an innocent?'

'Stephanos. Years ago, he put it about that if any man touched me, his family would be punished.' She raised her voice. 'I have no care for Stephanos. But unless I gave myself to him, I couldn't marry. I didn't mind not having the choice of another—but Stephanos decided he was tired of waiting. I was not.'

He knelt beside her, followed the length of her shoulder to her hand and placed the flannel in her palm.

Then he stood. The oilcloth coat left behind by the previous seaman didn't fit his shoulders and the arms of it stopped just below his elbows, but he dressed quickly, donning the coat last.

He hadn't been Cassandra's first and had been too green to realise it until she taunted him with it.

Now, when he least wanted one, he'd bedded a virgin.

Chapter Seven

The sky sparked and the rain pounded with an unthreatening insistence. Nothing inside Warrington flowed as serene as the sea.

Lowering his head from the drops hitting his face, he kept close to the ship's upper cabin walls, moving slowly towards the bow. He stood with the wind behind him, facing the bowsprit, and his back pressed into the outside of the cabin. Shadows concealed him. Only men who must stayed out in the weather and they would be too busy staying alive to notice him.

He'd had to be away from Melina and think.

A virgin. She'd been recompensed, but he'd actually paid nothing for taking her innocence. Having her on board the ship had taken no funds from his pocket.

The London docks at Wapping couldn't come quickly enough. He should not have agreed to the journey. He'd never step willingly on a ship

again, unless the whole of the world began to fall
into the ocean, and then he would consider sailing
briefly before drowning at peace with his decision to avoid the vessel.

A movement at his side, not in harmony with
the rhythm of the sea, caught his attention and he
stepped sideways, avoiding being stumbled into.
The slight build could only belong to one person.

'Stubby.' He spoke to the small form of the
cabin boy, who'd huddled into the space beside
him. 'You are not to be on deck. Go below. Now.'

He heard no sigh, but saw a heave of thin shoulders.

'Gid says this storm's still just a baby. Shouldn't
scare anybody but a lady. Supposed to get worse
by morning, though.'

'Stubble it. You're to be asleep.'

'Can't sleep. The thunder pitched me from the
hammock.'

'Stub. The bed wraps around you. It's hard to
fall out of the hammock once you're in it.'

'But once you're out, it be hard for me to crawl
back in without help. I'd sleep under it, but I'd be
rolling around all night.'

'I'll get you a place to sleep.' He moved to the
stern of the ship, borrowing one of the quartermaster's lanterns, and Stubby trudged along behind him.

'You be out here because the woman's in your

berth?' Stubby said, his voice still imbued with youth.

'Yes.' Warrington truly didn't want to speak.

'I want to stay here with you.'

'You're going below.'

The lad who could scamper through the rigging faster than a breeze immediately changed his speed to that of a sore-footed turtle, grasping at the sides of the ship's cabins, as if he could hardly stand upright. Warrington locked his jaw and grabbed Stubby's shoulder, turning the lad around the edge of the cabins and towards the opening to the lower decks.

Stubby stopped. 'Gidley says the woman's showin' you her treasure. You seen her treasure?' His voice bounced with excitement.

'Just a bit of marble stone.' He gave another push, moving Stubby faster. The lad would not take a step without a nudge. Warrington kept a hand on Stubby's shoulder, propelling him forward.

'Can you show me?' Stubby moved to the steps to go below deck.

'No.' Warrington ducked his head and followed Stubby down the rungs, into the bowels of darkness, the lantern giving just enough light to guide their way. They followed the men's snores, which made *Ascalon* sound like a beast with a rumbling stomach.

'Why?'

'Stubby.' He spoke sternly, hoping to quiet him.

'I know. I know,' the cabin boy grumbled in the darkness. 'Stubble it. Stubble it. That's not my real name. But I been called Stubby so much I forget the other one.'

'You'll remember some day.' Warrington hoped he told the truth. 'Or you can pick out something you like.'

Stubby paused, a delaying tactic. 'I'm trying to think of one.'

Warrington reached the crowded hold and, clutching the shoulder of Stubby's shirt, walked by hammocks with sleeping men until he found an empty one. He hung the lantern, the scent of burning oil mixing with rain and musty men.

'But that woman I give the medicines to—is she hidin' gold?' Stubby's voice was a whisper, but the kind that bounced from walls.

War stepped back to the empty hammock and knelt to make a step with his interlaced fingers for Stubby's foot.

'I wager it be gold,' the waif continued, moving close to Warrington.

Stubby's small fists held the edge of the hammock. He secured his foot in Warrington's hand and tumbled into the ropes. 'Gidley says having gold is better'n having teeth 'cause if you have gold, then someone will chew your food for you.'

'Go to sleep,' Warrington said, turning to retrieve the lantern.

'I'd like to have me a big hunk of gold. I'd like to have me a gold ring to wear in my ear and a gold sword to fight pirates, and gold buttons and gold—'

'Do not go back on deck tonight.'

'If Capt'n says all hands ahoy, I will. Capt'n says all hands ahoy, even cook goes.'

'Not in this storm. If Captain Ben and Gidley both think the storm will be angry, then you should stay below. I'll take your place.'

'I be man enough. Been in more storms than you could even think of. I be a sailor.' His head wobbled with pride, then his voice dipped to smugness. 'You be just an earl.'

'One big enough to thump your backside. You will not go on deck.'

Stubby didn't answer, but turned his head. 'I be real sleepy now and you be keepin' me awake.'

'You had better not go on deck before sunrise.'

'I might need to piss.'

'Then you best hold it.'

Warrington turned away, leaving with the cabin boy scooting around in the bedding and swinging the hammock even more than the waves did.

Warrington returned to the spot where Stubby had interrupted him. Stubby's chatter had reminded him of Jacob and caused a longing for his child. But he could not expose Jacob to the risks of the sea and he had not been able to stay on land where the memories were disastrous. Now he wanted to get home and see his son, and throw him up in the air, and pick him up around the waist and carry him like a sack with flailing legs.

And Jacob—how could anyone ignore a blast of life like him? If Jacob were on the ship and saw the men climb the rigging, he would be serenely waiting until a head was turned and he'd be scampering to the top, five years old, thinking himself a man.

Warrington was only days from seeing his son again and this time, he'd not leave him. Jacob needed a father. Well, he decided, perhaps Jacob did well without a father. The child had a nursemaid, servants around who doted on him and an uncle for guidance. Jacob would do well—father or not. But Warrington knew he needed his son's laughter. Now, when Warrington was too far to see his son's face and too far for the sound of delight to carry, he knew where his heart belonged. Warrington wanted to be the one Jacob followed.

Being away had helped him find his compass. He'd put the starkness of the *Ascalon* into his past, along with this woman he'd happened upon, and begin anew with his life.

And if Jacob ever saw the scar across his father's back, and asked about it, the version he heard would be a tale of a cutpurse attempting a crime.

He'd send his past into the depths and not even

let Melina linger in his thoughts. But he could still feel the brown-eyed siren. She had skin softer than any touch of silk. Lips that caused his body to boil with desire—not to mention the mark that drew his eyes more than any breasts or arse.

But she wasn't a goddess. She was human. Like everyone else. Their coupling had been a transaction for her passage. She'd been straightforward. And no foolish words of love. *Anyone would be better than Stephanos,* she'd said. No false praise there.

She was, in a way, the perfect woman, drawing his eyes, setting a price for her affections and taking herself away when they docked. But he'd not touch her again. Not risk giving her a child.

If he could only forget she'd been a virgin.

'All hands ahoy.' The voice rang out, carrying through the cabin walls.

Warrington opened his eyes, coming awake instantly. A true storm was upon them.

Melina sat with her back against the wall and her feet stretched against the base of the berth. She'd wedged herself, holding firm when the ship moved. Her hands held the slop bucket. Lightning illuminated the room and her head was relaxed back, and her lips were softly parted in sleep.

He'd not undressed earlier, knowing the call would sound in the night. He left the cabin, giving a quick glance over his shoulder before pulling the door shut.

The wind popped the sails like a whip. The *Ascalon* rolled and he braced himself. The storm bucked the vessel and raindrops pelted like thrown pebbles against his cheeks.

'Get the helm.' Ben appeared from starboard side. Flashes of light illuminated the rain-soaked strands of hair spiking from under a cap he wore.

Warrington gave a quick nod and moved past the quarterdeck. He had no more time to think when the ship jerked, tossing him forward.

The bow of the ship plunged downwards, well into the waves, then bobbed up again, like a drowning person gasping for breath, only to be slapped back against water. He forced his eyes open in the onslaught of wind and rain attacking them. Water saturated his hair, but none ran in rivulets down his face, instead the wind dispersed the drops like shattered glass.

When he stood at the wheel, Warrington braced his feet and locked his body so he could find enough force to control the rudder's movements while the momentum of the ship pulled him forward, then pushed him back.

The main sail was furled. Warrington thought of nothing but keeping the bow of the ship sailing into the waves. He stood, each muscle in his body used to keep tight control and every sense focused on his job.

He couldn't tell how long he'd been fighting the sea, but he had lost the strength to protest the movements and only survived them, when he heard shouts, and saw men scrambling. They were taking risks moving swiftly on deck in a storm and only one reason would cause such a pace. A chill scraped into his stomach and he forced himself to remain on task. Whatever had happened—the sea moved with such quickness and finality that even if he could have dashed to help—the outcome had already been determined.

Pushing aside the knowledge of possible tragedy, he couldn't risk letting his mind wander or make conjectures. If he didn't know, then everything remained the same. He had no choice but to stare forward, ignoring the water blasts in his face and the thunder around him. The ship needed him now more than anyone else.

'Yer had yer two hours.' The shout at his side surprised Warrington. He'd been so focused in his concentration he'd not realised Gidley stood near. 'Yer need to see Capt'n.'

'Why?' Warrington did not release the wheel. Now, instead of bracing himself against the storm, he steadied himself for the first mate's next words.

'He tossed agin' a spar. No blood coming out his ears or mouth, so it looks to be a bump.'

Warrington stepped back as Gidley clamped a meaty hand on to the wheel spoke. 'That boy bounces better 'n any frog I ever seen.'

Warrington left, keeping close to the cabins,

grasping rigging to keep balanced and praying
Ben was not deeply injured. Warrington had always spent more time with his middle brother,
Dane, than Ben, until this venture. Dane shared
a more serious view of life. But Ben—

Both the older ones had watched over him and
tormented him. His sister, Adele, would never forgive him if he let anything happen to Ben, just
as she'd never forgive Ben if Warrington went
overboard. Well, she would forgive Ben. He was
the youngest.

When he reached Ben's cabin, he opened the
door. A scent of camphor, or some similarly pun-
gent medicinal, hit his nose. The light cast everything into garish shadows. Stubby sat in a chair,
feet hardly touching the floor, and looking as if
a jib had caught him between the eyes. His thin
face had grown in just hours and his nose would
likely bear a reminder of the night for the rest of
the lad's life. A streak of dried blood caked between his nose and lip. Stubby's wet shirt plas-
tered against him.

'We'll both be a bit colourful in the morning.'
Ben's words sounded tugged from his lungs.

Warrington looked to his brother, resting on
the berth. His arm lay over his stomach and the
fingers of his right hand gripped, but held nothing. He wore no shirt, only dry trousers. His sodden clothing hung from a peg.

'Gid says you thought to dance in a storm.'

Warrington moved inside and pulled the door shut against the rain. The water pooling at his feet added wetness to the planks.

'The wind led the waltz and gave me a turn I'll never forget,' Ben said. His cheek looked to have been dragged along one of the stones they used to clean the deck. Pain pinched his face.

'He saved me. That he did.' Stubby's words ran together and he looked at Ben, adoration bursting from the young eyes. 'The capt'n just caught me and snatched me back from that wave like it was nothing. Capt'n didn't say a word. Just scared that water into letting me go.' His voice dropped, memories floating behind his eyes. 'Was a big fight.'

Stubby rose to his feet. The words were too important for him to speak while sitting. 'A big ol' wave.' He raised his hand high over his head, and tiptoed. 'A wave. Jumped 'cross the boat and reached for me, just reached out and— Then I was—' His words became faster. 'I grabbed with my toes to the deck because my hands was full of water. Capt'n pulled my shirt, but couldn't hold me. He seized me and a spar and fought that wave—bigger'n two ships and a house. The monster came back.' He made clawing motions. 'Capt'n, he squeezed on to me.' Stubby made a choking face, with his tongue out. He collapsed back into the chair. 'The wave—it were really angry 'cause it couldn't pull us overboard or drown us while we was standin' and just slapped Capt'n hard into the spar.' Stubby's adoration for Ben shone from his eyes. 'Capt'n is stronger 'n sea devils.'

'You able to get out of your clothes by yourself?' Warrington asked Ben.

Ben nodded at the same time Stubby answered for him. 'Capt'n had to have Gidley pull his shirt and Gidley even had to put dry trousers on him. I'm supposed to be watching him now—Gid says—see if Capt'n goes belly up before the storm finishes, but I don't think he's going belly up. Capt'n still holdin' to all his fingers—even if some of them's more crooked than they're supposed to be. He's not missing any halves like Gidley or quartermaster. Gidley said he bit his own fingers off because they was on his nervous side—and he says I get on his nervous side, but I don't think he's going to bite my fingers off because he says I'm wormy and he don't like worms.'

'Stubby—put your hand over your mouth and hold your lips shut.' Ben's voice rasped in the air. He closed his eyes.

'You do look like you've been mopped around the deck.' Warrington moved closer, studying his brother.

'I've moved across the ship on my backside before and I dare say I'll do it again. Best way to check for splinters I know.'

'You find any?'

Ben's lips twitched, but he took a moment to find the strength for words and open his eyes. 'Gidley gave me a scant spoon of laudanum. He said he's saving the rest in case someone gets hurt.'

Stubby looked at Warrington and the child's voice became a loud whisper. 'Gidley told me about the demons of the deep afore. I know it was them. Capt'n said no. Said a mermaid sent the wave because she wanted to meet him 'cause he's so manly.' He cocked his head. 'You think a mermaid can make waves do that—or you think it was a spirit tryin' to swallow me whole?'

'*Captain* Ben Forrester,' Warrington said. 'You're filling his head with nonsense.' Then he turned to Stubby. 'It was just a wave and no spirit or mermaid.'

Ben's eyes were shut. 'It's not nonsense,' he muttered. 'It may not be truth, but it's not nonsense. It's a *yarn* and we seamen spend much time on yarns.'

'Stubby…' Warrington turned to him. 'Don't believe anything anyone on this ship says but me, unless it is something you see with your own eyes.' He stared at Stubby. 'And even if you see it yourself, on this ship, you will check with me to see it is true.'

'I saw the wave reach for me.' Stubby's chin quivered and the purpling on his face seemed darker. Warrington's throat closed. Stubby was scarcely bigger than Jacob. Warrington put his hand on Stubby's shoulder, resisting the urge to pull him into his grasp as he would have his son.

'It was a big hand.' Stubby pushed free and showed the actions with his own arm and fingers. 'Reaching out to pull me to the bottom of the sea.'

Warrington watched the boy. 'You'll have to learn not to believe sailors' tales.'

'Why not?' Ben's eyes were shut. 'Mermaids are truly handsome. Sometimes they leave seaweed behind, though, and they don't always smell pleasant.'

Warrington met Stubby's eyes and then shut his own while frowning and shaking his head.

But Stubby spoke to Ben. 'Do they make mermaids in my size?' he asked. 'I hope to see one 'fore long.'

Melina slept sitting, with her back against the wall, and one hand clasped over her fisted other one. She woke when the pressure of a foot sinking into the pallet jostled her.

She didn't move, even when he slid beside her, scenting the air with a salty-tinged masculinity. He tugged at the covers and pulled them around himself.

'Pretend to be asleep,' he muttered. 'Just don't step on me when you get up. I've been awake two nights straight, part of a third—and I must rest. Drowning is starting to sound pleasant.'

She could tell he rolled so his back was to her. She couldn't move. Her stomach was hanging on to her insides and as long as she kept her back straight she could believe she had stayed alive. The waves had lessened in their violence. Even the thunder had moved on.

'Once we get to London, I'll see you have passage back to Melos.' His voice broke the silence.

'I can take care of myself.' She spoke before she intended, jerking her face in his direction. She bit the inside of her lip, reminding herself to be motionless.

She couldn't see his eyes, but she watched him turn in her direction. He examined her, his face a mask.

His words sounded unwilling. 'Your stone won't be enough in England to protect you.'

She spoke again, controlling the intensity of her words. She'd risked everything on this ship and this stranger. But once she reached London, she could find her father there. He could help her raise funds and search for more artefacts. She was certain she'd seen more carvings at the place she'd found the woman. But the woman was the prize. 'We're too far at sea. You can't turn the ship around and return me.'

He touched the bare skin of her arm, soothing her. 'Once we get to England,' he repeated, 'I'll stay a few days in London. I have to meet people to discuss the details of the voyage. And if you wish to return home, I'll make sure my brother finds a way to get you back to the island.'

She gave a quick toss of her head. 'I will find my way. The arm will help me.'

'This Stephanos. Surely you can find someone you prefer better than him?'

She shrugged.

'The men you see at the docks will have one thing on their mind when they approach you— and they won't pay generously. They'll haggle over a pence and be angry with you for any coin they give you. And then they'll take your body and they won't be kind. They'll feel they've paid you so they don't have to be gentle and they'll want every ounce of your skin for their coin.' He paused. 'You can't find a more troublesome lot of humanity. I'm sure they're even worse than this Stephanos you think so highly of.'

'It's not your concern. I won't sell myself because I have the arm. The museum will want the rest of her.' She turned her face from him and bundled herself up, raising her knees and resting her arms around them. She dipped her chin. 'Go to sleep.'

He sat up and clasped her shoulder. She was amazed at the warmth a single touch could send and pleased deep within herself that he wanted to protect her from selling her body, but angry he would send her back to the island. She could not go back without funds.

His words were soft—sleepy. 'If I'd known you were an innocent, I'd never have let you set foot on the *Ascalon.*'

'If I'd know you were such a tender heart, I'd have thrown myself into your brother's arms.' She considered the words she'd just spoken, and realised the untruth of them. When she looked at Warrington, she could see behind his eyes. The anger she saw wasn't directed at her, but at himself. And sometimes she saw pain, moving quicker than the flashes of light in the night, showing through the struggle she saw within him.

'You've no sense at all if you prefer my brother.' He rested back into the covers.

'I'll find my own way in England.'

He tugged her down beside him and she kept her body stiff. Being held by him teased her of a life she'd never have, unless she made enough from the sale of artefacts to have a dowry not just for her sisters, but also one for herself. A husband of any value could cost a considerable amount.

The warmth of his breath touched her when he spoke, his words little more than a haze of sleepy murmuring. 'I won't waste a worry on you, then. Just be still and quiet for a moment so I can drift off.'

She didn't move, knowing he should fall asleep soon. But even if he slept, she couldn't move from him. His arm around her trapped her with the strength of iron.

'I can't let you be like her.' His voice confirmed tiredness when she heard his slurred words. 'Cassandra. My lovely wife. Not a man on *Ascalon* who wouldn't have given all they owned for her. Even our captain. And I was the lucky one.'

'She's gone.'

'Not to me.' His words barely rose above his breathing. 'The bitch still burns in my heart.'

Chapter Eight

Melina opened the door and stepped into the morning air, pleased to have her shawl keeping out the chill. The *Ascalon* briskly skimmed the water, bow up, proud.

The men showed the effects of the night. They worked, trance-like, eyes focused on the task in front of them, whether it be the ropes in their hands, the buckets or the stones they used to scrub the slippery mould from the deck. She looked to the stern and saw Gidley at the wheel. His eyes had the red-rimmed look of too much wind and too little sleep.

'We near lost 'em both.' Gidley's head trembled in a negative shake and he turned his face to the sea.

'Who?' Melina asked, stopping a few inches from his side.

'Capt'n and Stubby.' He turned back, searching her face. 'Warrin'ton didn't tell yer? Guess a man's thinking of other things when he's close to a woman.' His voice faded. 'Stubby wouldn't ever grow old enough to make a single whisker if not for Capt'n.'

Melina waited, feeling a coldness splash into her. 'Both are well?'

Gidley shrugged. 'Stub's shook or he'd a been dancing 'round my feet this mornin'. Capt'n Ben—' He paused. 'Take more'n a bump to do him in. Prob'ly be walkin' again before we get to shore. One leg's lamed up and he's prob'ly listenin' to a few ribs shouting at him. Though none stick out. Always a good thing when the bones stay skinned over.' Gidley squinted at Melina. 'Yer ever took care of a sick body?'

'My mother.' She hated to say the words. Her mother had died slowly, death taking her by squeezing health away a heartbeat at a time and replacing everything inside her with pain.

'Well…' He took his time saying the word. 'Capt'n is sayin' for you to care for him. I've some laudanum in him and when he wakes he'll not be fine, but I'm needin' to keep my eye on the sails.' Gidley tilted his head, indicating the cabin closest to the helm. 'Go see to him.'

She gripped her skirt, raising it just enough so she could walk quickly, and moved to the captain's quarters. Melina rapped on the door and when no one answered, she peered in. He was asleep.

Melina took stock of her surroundings. The cabin, spacious by comparison to Warrington's, gleamed with polished wood and accentuated the paleness of the captain's face.

He slept because of the tonic and she knew not to give him any more until he complained of pain. She touched his forehead and didn't feel burning. His eyelashes fluttered. Compassion stirred in her. He'd survived the night, but death from an injury could wait days. And she owed him. Without the captain agreeing to let her sail, Stephanos would still be a threat.

She moved back the covers to look at the bruising on his chest, then sat in the only chair and settled herself for whatever care he'd need.

Hours later, when the door opened, she jumped awake and Warrington strode in—his eyes appraising everything. The light emboldened his ragged features. Whiskers darkened his chin and blended with the shadows under his eyes. His hair—neatly combed—contrasted with the rest of him.

'How is he?' Warrington moved to the bedside, staring at his brother.

'He rests *eirinikos,* well enough, but I believe it is because of the draught he was given. He did wake long enough for a thimbleful of water. But he has the right speech and doesn't appear worse than he was earlier. His side is bruised. Leg is straight, scraped some, and his knee is swollen nearly as big as his head.'

Warrington studied her for a moment longer than necessary, then he turned to his brother. He stepped to the edge of the berth and put a hand lightly on the captain's shoulder.

Ben's eyes flickered, but remained closed. 'The boy still alive?'

Warrington's head jerked up in answer. 'Stubby is doing better than you. You look like a man who danced with the wrong fellow's wife.' Warrington's voice remained gruff.

Ben opened one eye. 'You, on the other hand, look like hell.'

Warrington's smile changed his face, bringing a life to his eyes she'd never believed possible.

'You infant,' Warrington continued, his words light. 'You'll try anything to convince me to sail the next voyage with you—but it won't work.'

Ben kept his eyes closed and talked, barely moving his lips. 'I guess expecting a soft old earl to be able to sail is daft.'

'I'd better get to the helm.' Warrington took his hand from Ben's shoulder, still smiling. 'Since Captain Lackbeard looks to lie about all day.'

'Remember,' Ben said, 'keep the masts to the sky. The hull side to the water.'

'I'll do what I can.'

'So will I.' Ben's brows rose. 'I will rest here and look at Melina all day to ease my suffering.'

His head didn't turn, but he glanced sideways. 'Would you give me a drop of brandy, sweetness?'

She rose, which caused her to brush Warrington. He gave a haughty smile to his brother. Then Warrington reached around Melina. His hand was firm at her side and the quick motion surprised her. She stumbled against him.

His lips closed over hers before she expected it. Her heart pounded warm blasts throughout her body. The taste of him was not something she could name, but the flavour of strength and warm male.

He pulled back and kept his hand at her waist while he spoke to his brother. His voice had challenge in it. 'Take care, little brother. Don't test me on this. Or you will get *truly* hurt.'

For days, Melina knew she had less sleep than the seamen while she cared for the captain. She'd not known a person could complain so. He had her searching his cabin for a silver toothpick once, as if his very life depended on it, and then he remembered he'd lost the shining bit on a different voyage.

The captain would send her in search of a sailor he wanted to speak to and she'd find the man at the very spot Captain Ben mentioned, doing exactly what he had expected. Even Warrington did as commanded.

Gidley would sometimes stop to check on Captain Ben, and invariably, the captain would send her on a task. He'd need a biscuit, or for her to take a question to a crew member—she suspected the duties unnecessary ones so he could talk privately with the first mate.

The captain was keeping Warrington from the cabin when she was in it, or else Warrington had no wish to be inside if she was there. She was too tired to sort her thoughts.

They only passed each other briefly, an impossible occurrence—unless planned. From the humour in Ben's face, and the glare in Warrington's, she didn't think it the earl's suggestion.

She'd seen Warrington on the ropes once or twice, with his lean legs scurrying up the rigging. She'd been wrong about him—he could climb the ratlines as well as the others. Perhaps better as he'd kept himself balanced using his legs while he worked.

Almost as soon as Melina reached her cabin and fell upon the pallet, she heard a tap on her door and forced herself upright. A voice through the wood told her the captain requested her.

She stood, pushing at the knot of her hair, pulling at her skirt to straighten it, and left the room. The cabin boy waited. If she'd dallied longer, he would have knocked more insistently. 'I think I have stolen your job,' she told him when she walked through the doorway.

His bruised face burst into a smile. 'I be fine

with it. Won't be long till I be an able-bodied seaman. Gid says I have some growin' left, but I'll
get that done quick enough and be taller 'n him.'

She found a shirtless Ben sitting in his bed, a
map sprawled around him. He looked up at her
when she entered.

He hadn't worn a shirt since he'd been injured
and his side had darkened more, leaving a yel-
lowish cast around the bruising. She heard the
ship's bell. Warrington would be leaving his post.
The captain grinned. He rolled up the papers, his
hands moving slowly and with excessive care. Finally he tipped the cylinder in her direction. She
put it in the cabinet. 'I'll try sitting in the chair for
a while. Lend a hand,' he said. He put his palm
to the bruise.

'It would be better if Warrington or the men
helped you. Your weight is too heavy for me,'
she answered.

'They move me about like a potato sack.' He
stretched out his naked arm, rubbing the muscle.
'I'm sure you'll do just fine.'

She scooted the chair several inches closer,
leaving enough room for him to stand beside the
bed before sitting.

She let the captain's weight shift on to her, and
helped him to the chair. Just as he was pulling his
arm from around her neck, Warrington walked
in. She supposed an earl never knocked when entering his brother's quarters—at least one didn't.

The captain slid his arm back to Melina's shoulders and took a bit more time righting himself.

Warrington's hair gleamed with the mist of seawater still on it. His coat hung open, but his shirt looked crisp underneath.

The three of them were nestled in the cabin so tight they could reach out an arm and touch the others.

'I believe I've wrenched my shoulder,' Warrington said. 'I need Melina's care.'

The captain kept his injured leg motionless in front of him. His mouth opened, but he didn't speak. He shook his head at Warrington in an arrogant wobble. She moved to leave and Warrington turned to follow her.

'Stay a moment, War, I need to talk to you,' Ben said.

'I've better things to do than listen to a man who lies about drinking brandy all day.' His eyes were chips of coal. 'Much better things.' He looked at Melina.

'I know. But it won't kill you to spare a few minutes with your brother.'

'Might not be so good for you, however.'

Warrington opened the door, standing aside. Melina moved to step out, but when she passed Warrington, his hand caught her waist and he stopped her movement.

When she looked into his eyes, nothing light

looked back at her. But he brushed at a lock of her hair, leaving a trail of warmth she could feel to her toes. 'If my brother is tiring you too much, Melina, you don't have to assist him. Stubby can.'

She saw the intensity in his eyes, and more behind it, and gave the barest of nods. 'I'm well with it.'

He snorted in response, but handed her gently out through the door. 'Rest, sweet.' His voice caressed. 'I don't want you overtired.'

As the door closed, she heard the captain's muttered comment to his brother. 'Arse Hat.' She didn't understand Warrington's reply exactly. She didn't think she'd ever heard the word before.

Inside the captain's quarters Warrington glared impatiently at his brother. 'I'm not letting you keep her from me any longer. I only have scant time left with her.'

'I would never get between a man and his sweetheart.' Ben's eyes half closed. 'I am merely a weak younger brother, not as strong as you, and I need help getting back on my feet.'

'Having a bed that smells of a woman's warmth, and no woman in it, is not doing me any good.'

'You'll survive.' Ben stretched, gingerly, keeping his movements slow. 'But I know where I saw her. I remembered.' Then he let the room fall into silence.

Warrington remained on his feet. 'Tell me or not, I'm leaving.' He wasn't letting Ben trap him into a long discussion. He had better ways to spend his time. One way in particular.

'Somerset House. A painting.' Ben touched his chest. 'The spot. I remember the spot on the girl. The painting captured the mark. Odd to leave a blemish and I noticed it more than her face. At the time I decided the artist added it to make his painting different.'

Warrington waved away the words. 'Any artist would want to capture her.'

'War.' Ben shook his head. 'She has ties to England. Ties we don't know about. She speaks too well. And she has some piece of marble you say she believes she has to get to London.' He waved a hand. 'Probably has a man she's going to. Using the stone as an excuse.'

'If she has a man in England, all the better.' Warrington spoke with authority. He only needed Melina long enough to get the past behind him. To get over his foolishness of letting his lust control his mind. No, that wasn't what he needed to stop. He needed to stop letting his foolish heart control his actions. Lust was much safer than love.

When he returned to Whitegate, he'd have no time for a woman while he took back his duties. He wanted to teach Jacob about the country estate. And Warrington would be travelling back and forth to London after taking his seat in Parliament.

Someone knocked. A double thump, pause and double thump on the door let Warrington know Stubby stood outside. He opened the door without taking his eyes off Ben while Stubby bounded in.

'Melina will be on her own soon after we dock. She thinks the cracked rock is a treasure of some sort and will earn funds,' Warrington said. 'She's wrapped the thing in cloth and it stays under the berth. She put my second pair of trousers around it and has the stone secured tight. Has a bit of rope tying the parcel snug to the edge.'

Ben shook his head. 'You've seen it. Does it look like it could sell?'

Warrington didn't take his hand from the door. 'No. It's cracked badly. I've no idea why she decided it valuable.' He held his arm out, moving his fingers into a grasping position. 'It's an arm shaped like this. One of the fingers is broken off, as well. Just an arm. Should be tossed in a dust bin. Like your collections you've stored around the town house.'

'Then she must have a man in London who wants the stone. A sweetheart she hopes to see again.' He grinned at Stubby. 'But she does keep good company. Believed me when I had her searching for a toothpick.'

The boy, only a hint of bruising left on his face, glared at Ben.

Ben winked at Stubby. 'Every cabin boy has to search for a silver toothpick. Proves their mettle by how long and deep they dig before giving up.'

Warrington looked at Stub's mutinous jaw. 'He *did* save your skin and I *did* tell you not to come on deck.'

The little face didn't soften. 'Well, my looks is ruined for ever. Now I don't know how I'll get me a woman when we get to London.'

'Stubby.' The shocked word shot from both Warrington and Ben at the same time.

'The men say they can't wait to get home and get a woman,' Stubby said. 'They be wantin' her apple dumplin' or a tart. I like confectioneries and if I have to smile pretty at a lady to get me some sweets…' he showed a toothy smile and touched his stomach '…then I be plannin' to have a belly full of smiles.'

War looked at Ben. 'You need to have a talk with him. If you can figure it out yourself.'

'I'll tell Gid to explain—' He stopped. 'No. Cook would be better.' Ben sat, rubbing his knee, and grimaced in pain. 'Not so sure our lovely Melina doesn't have some bad luck with her. A lifetime of sailing and I've never been hurt this bad.' He probed against the trouser leg. 'I suppose I should have expected it. We do have a woman on board. Never know whether they'll be bad or good fortune until afterwards.'

'You've spent too long bobbing about. You're

starting to sound like Gidley.' Warrington kept his fingers on the open door, ready to go to his cabin. Stubby stood listening, nodding as if he'd sailed a score of years and seen everything to see.

Ben's voice lowered, and he fell back on the bed. 'I shouldn't have sent you in my place to meet Melina. I would have just...' he raised a brow at Warrington '...put a smile on her face and we would have sailed smoothly home.'

'You may be right. You see me unhurt. I put a smile on her face.'

Ben interlaced his fingers on his chest and turned his head towards Stubby. 'Go get Gid. Tell him I need him. The earl's imaginations are giving me pains.'

When the door closed behind the lad, Ben's eyes darted to Warrington's face. 'I don't trust her. You won't keep her near once you get to land?'

Warrington didn't immediately speak and he frowned. 'When it is your concern, I'll tell you. But, no. She'll be on her way soon after we dock. I'll remain in London a few extra days because I have to meet with the Foreign Office. Then I'll see Jacob and deal with...Whitegate. I can't leave it all in Dane's hands for ever. He'll be wanting to get back to his confectioneries.'

Ben turned his head to the wall, but his words carried directly to Warrington. 'Don't make the same mistake twice.'

War stepped out of the door. *The same mistake twice.*

When the sea air hit his face, he slowed, thinking. Dane had been wobbly-legged foxed one night after Cass died and damn near cried when he told Warrington how they'd hated Cass. They'd seen the truth before he had. With Melina, he didn't need to be warned. Just like Cass, she made her plans and only said enough to further them. A woman in a household wasn't necessary or needed. He'd had enough of broken crockery, tears and lies to last a lifetime. The whirling dream of love he'd had had turned into a whirling nightmare of the wrong kind of passion.

Instead of going directly to his cabin—or whatever part of it he might share—Warrington paced the deck, trying not to long for Melina's touch. Every time his heart beat, desire pumped through his veins. He shook his head gently, trying to force her from his mind, but he couldn't. And his feet didn't co-operate and wouldn't take him a second turn around the ship, or let him stay out in the air. He had to get back to her.

When he walked into the room, he looked to the floor. Melina lay fully dressed on the pallet. Her hair still remained in a twist and she had the shawl pulled over her for a cover. Her half-parted lips and regular breathing reassured him. She hardly looked old enough to be the woman she was.

He knelt, his fingers barely grazing the skin of her cheek. 'Wake.'

She half opened her eyes. 'My legs are near run off. The captain keeps me at his side while he sleeps, and when he stops dozing, he sends me to sleep. When I begin to dream, he calls for me again. He's unkind.'

Warrington shook his head. 'No. He's not. Gid's keeping Ben's mind in a fog so the pain will not get to him. The medicine has addled him a bit, and the injury, and he's used to a life with men around him.'

'And bad women.'

'He's not called Saint Benjamin, but Captain Benjamin.' Warrington braced himself again against the empty bunk, still devoid of any mattress. 'He's keeping you from me.'

Warrington rocked back with the movement of the ship, and sat, tugging his boots from his feet, taking stockings with the footwear. He slipped his scuffed boots under the bottom railing. He wished for a bed. A real bed. With bed coverings and pillows that didn't smell as if a horse had used them first.

'I know.' Melina shut her eyes as she spoke. 'Neither of you wish me to sleep.'

Warrington knelt, taking her face in his hands, and her eyes quickly opened. 'I hope for you to savour being awake with me.' He saw the tightness of her lips. 'This time will be better. I'll show you what it can truly be like between a man and a woman who—'

He stopped. How would he know what it was like to be with someone who loved him? After Jacob was born, Cass had once taunted him by calling him by someone else's name when he bedded her.

But he hadn't given up on Cassandra—at least not then. She glowed at soirées, entertained society with the charm of royalty. Everyone wanted to be within the beam of Cassandra's smile. When she desired, she would sit and converse with him in such a way he could feel the love in his heart and believe so easily she loved him.

Then one day, during the flash of her smile, he caught the smugness behind in her face and he knew that the sweeter she talked, the deeper her machinations were. And he looked pleasantly back at her and continued laughing with her while his world crashed.

She was Jacob's mother. The woman he truly loved. And she was flawed. No matter that she had no true love in her, she went through the motions on occasion. She did want the appearance of perfection. And without a doubt, she wanted to be a countess and enjoy the luxuries he could provide. He'd purchased a wife, just as he'd acquired the carriage she rode in. Only he'd not realised it at first.

He looked at Melina. 'It's all for pleasure.' He

took her hand, but the memory of holding Cass's fingers when he asked her to marry him flashed in his mind and his vision blackened. He couldn't keep thinking of Cass.

He pulled his hand back and undid his shirt and slipped it over his head. Then he gazed at Melina. She looked so different than Cassandra. The darkness fled his thoughts and he cradled Melina in his arms. He could not sense artifice in her. She didn't use her body to turn his desire against him and to her own advantage. She felt pure.

'Melina.' He bent, pulling her so her head tilted back and he could let his lips and face take in the soft skin of her neck and nuzzle the warmth of her. He kissed her pulse. 'You remind me that there's a harbour, dry land and real floors. And I want to see you lying in the middle of my bed, waiting for me.'

'You should not think of such things. I have to be on my way once we reach land,' she said. 'I will see to the stone's sale and return to my sisters.'

He reminded himself to take care. In all of his life he'd never bought a woman's body, until Melina. And she'd not been willing to settle for one of the men from the island. *Captain,* she'd said. *You're not the captain?* Now she knew he was an earl. As always, he was the highest bidder. Only because of the small size of the island had she kept her innocence. If she'd lived in London, she would have realised the real treasure she had was in her face and her body.

'It won't be easy to remove a stone from the island if this man you dislike controls the land,' he said. 'He will be angry at you because you left.'

'Stephanos does not own the land of the stone. Yorgos does. Yorgos said the stone was only rocks to him and that I have sand in my head if I think it is worth coin. He will help me slip it by Stephanos, or convince Stephanos to let it go. I am near the same age as his children and he calls me *kori,* daughter. The museum will have to pay the Turks because they will hear of her leaving and have to be given money. It is better to be done while she is still seen as rocks.'

Currents of relief slid into his body. If she meant to leave him, she could not be planning to ensnare him. But, he couldn't forget himself. He didn't need a child on some island, not knowing whether the babe was being fed or the funds he sent given for some man's ale.

Yet he could not look at Melina without wanting to push her back on to the bedding, and if he thought of her longer than it took to say her name, his body readied itself to join her.

He frowned, rocking back on his heels and leaning against the wall of the cabin, pulling her close. He could control himself for a few moments if it meant the peace of having her in his arms.

He traced the outline of her jaw and then

moved to grasp her shoulder, dismayed by the coarseness of her clothes. A body such as hers should only have silks against the skin. Or his touch.

He rested his chin on her head and took her hair down. Having no place to put the hairpins, he saw his coat hanging on a peg and dropped them in the pocket. He finger-combed her hair around her shoulders, pleased deep within himself at the dark hue. 'Not much time left before we reach London. We must make the most of it.'

'I cannot even imagine the towns.' Her eyes were wistful.

'Where did you learn to speak English so plainly?'

'At Melos. I understand French, too. I speak it some.'

'Who taught you?' He didn't really care. All he cared about was the perfect shape of her breasts and to let his lips trail to the mark. But then he remembered Ben's mention of the painting. 'You could have chosen a French ship to take you to France. What ties do you have to England?' Warrington watched her face.

She gave a shrug. 'I see the French seamen often and they talk badly of the English, but I have also heard pleasant tales of London and the English life. And it is the biggest city I know of and the best museum. They will have a larger purse.'

Because of the French vessels harbouring at Melos, he would have expected her to approach one of those ships, but they would have less freedom to take a passenger.

'Your ties to England?' he asked again, just as he repeated pressing his lips to her neck. He shut his eyes, tasting her skin, letting the sweetness of her flow into his body and melt the tightness of his shoulders, and ease his memories.

She pushed him back. 'I do not ask you of your life'.

'How did you learn the language so well?' he asked, stilling.

'We are a natural harbour with many travellers on the island. I speak to them.'

'Melina—I don't believe you are telling me all.'

Brown eyes met his. 'No. I am not. And I won't.'

A knock interrupted her and a voice commanded. 'Captain needs the woman.'

'She's busy,' Warrington shouted through the door. His hand clasped her wrist and he saw reluctance in her face.

'Go ahead. But if you do, I expect a few nights once we hit land to make up for the ones you don't give me on ship.' He let his hand slide to hold hers and knew he made a mistake. 'Melina... Soft beds. Clean clothing. Food made by someone who knows what it is supposed to taste like. Water—

real water—fresh, not stale or salty, to bathe in. Compared to this, we'll be royalty.'

He saw her chest rise in a deep breath. 'Very well,' she murmured, her hand at the door. 'With the ship rocking, and the food, my stomach feels one step from death. Hearing the men shout outside the walls and the captain calling me, I feel surrounded by watching eyes. On land, surely the world will not rock so and will have some quiet about it.' She sighed. 'I would like to be free from all the men shouting and scratching. It feels as if we all smashed inside a large bottle and someone has put the cork on it, and shakes us about.'

'We will get out of this bottle, and we'll have a bed of clouds.' He stood with her. 'And now I will go to the captain's cabin with you. I can trust Ben with my life, but I don't want him too near you.'

She touched the mark at her breast. 'He thinks it looks like a fish.'

Warrington snorted. 'He lies.'

He put a hand to her back and guided her to the other cabin, aware of how much the men watched her. He didn't blame them. If they looked the other direction, all they could see would be an expanse of nothing. And to look at any part of Melina was a treat.

When Melina reached to knock on the captain's door, Warrington leaned in, touched the knob and pushed the door open for her.

Inside the cabin, the air was bitter from some

stringent herbal. Ben sat on the bed, head back against the wall, eyes closed, chest still bare. His bruising had faded. He half opened his eyes, then frowned when he saw Warrington. In one hand, he held a poultice pressed to his ribs, and in the other, a brandy bottle Gidley must have collected for him.

'Melina will care for me.' Ben spoke with command. 'I like the touch of a lovely woman—even if she is not a mermaid.'

'You tell Gid to quit giving you so much of the poison,' Warrington said.

'I missed you also, old man.' Ben laughed, then winced and moved his shoulders. 'If I wish to see you, all I have to do is call the goddess.'

'Her *name* is Melina.'

'A beautiful name for a goddess. Did she not rise from the sea inside the shell of a giant oyster?'

Warrington walked closer and looked at his brother's eyes. 'Melina.' His voice was low. 'Let me know each time Gid gets near him with a medicinal and how much is taken. And the brandy.' He glared at Ben, challenging. 'I am telling Gid to ease up on the laudanum. If the sea couldn't have you, then I'm not letting you slink into some addled state. You're daft enough without help.'

Warrington looked at his brother and opened the small cupboard, pulling out another brandy bottle. Then he reached and jerked the one from his brother's hand. 'I'm finding Gid now and giving him strict instructions on Ben's care. And if the captain annoys you, Melina, let me know and I will twist his good leg to match the other.' Bottles in hand, he marched from the room. He slammed the door so hard she wondered the boat didn't roll to its side.

The captain opened his eyes and had no smile behind them.

'I've told Warrington, Melina.' The captain's vision didn't rest on any one thing in the room. 'I've warned him. If he wishes for happiness, he must throw you back to the sea. An appealing woman is no better than a serpent, wishing to put her fangs in you and suck the life from your body. That is why I like mermaids. They are not true women.'

Captain Ben gave her a smile. 'Warrington is right. Probably should keep the medicinals from me. I'm beginning to see fins on you.' He frowned. 'It is the laudanum making me dream of women. The evil ones.' He shook his head, shuddering.

'One,' he continued, 'looked like Cassandra and she had a grappling hook in War's throat.' He nodded. 'I keep thinking of the beautiful Cassandra, and then—then I wonder what memories my brother has of her. No woman I've seen deserved her fate more. War finally had to keep a *companion* for her. A big beast of a woman, who

stayed near, and would let him know if his wife
strayed, or acted out of hand. A gaoler, at Cass's
side every minute, and she deserved it. Early on,
at War's house, I woke up with Cass in my room,
on my bed and her hand stroking my cheek. Not
a pleasant moment—waking up with a demon in
front of you.'

He looked at Melina. 'It is not that I don't find
you pleasant, Melina. I do. But you sold your body
so easily. Cassandra held out for a higher price—
and she received it. I'm sure she's making deals
with the devil now.' He laughed.

Melina kept her voice sweet. 'Did she ever
wish to put a pillow over your face?'

'I would imagine.' He spoke the words lightly.
'When I told her War would believe me over her
and to never come near me again.' He looked
around the room. 'I wish War would not have left
with the brandy. It's not as if he's still married and
needs it.' He raked his eyes over Melina. 'Cassandra wouldn't like knowing you're in War's bed.'
He grinned, and then took a breath. 'Thank you
for that. I never expected I'd pity Lucifer, but if he
is with Cassandra, he should be wary.' His eyes
were unfocused and he nodded, the slow movements of a man unaware of his surroundings. 'She
might take over Hades.'

Chapter Nine

When Melina returned to Warrington's cabin, she shut the door behind her in a rush. She had to be thankful Warrington had met her first instead of the easygoing captain—who was not so pleasant when foxed. Cassandra had been called whore in Greek, French, English and some languages Melina didn't know.

She saw the empty berth, and underneath, empty. Her pulse stuttered and she fell to her knees beside the bed. She stared at the space. Her body couldn't move, locked in place. The stone was gone.

Warrington. He could not do this to her. The thudding of her heartbeats brought her movements alive again. Warrington could not hide the rock from her. True, she had not kept her bargain well, but the marble was hers. She must have it.

She knelt lower, looking all the way under the berth. She stood, tore at the bedcovers and then opened each cabinet. Nothing. Turning, she ran from the room and rushed to the helm. Warrington stood by Gidley, who steered the ship.

'My treasure,' she gasped.

She ignored the startled look in Warrington's face and grabbed his arm. 'My treasure. Where have you put it?' Her hair blew across her lips, but she didn't brush it aside. 'Tell me. Now.' The words came out too slow. She wanted to speak faster. She wanted to have the answer now and he only looked at her, his mouth half-opened and silent.

'Tell me,' she insisted, her grip tightening on his arm.

'Melina. What are you speaking of?' He took her hands from his arms, stepping back, and pulling her so they faced each other. 'I've not touched the blasted thing. It's a rock.'

'It's gone.'

'It's under the berth—resting better than either of us.'

'No.' She moved backwards. 'It's not. It's not in the room.'

'I'm sure it is.' He nodded to Gidley. 'I'll be back as soon as we get this sorted.'

She rushed ahead, not waiting to see if he followed. Maybe she *had* imagined the loss. Maybe she had become addled from listening to the captain and perhaps the arm still lay wrapped safely.

But when she ran inside the room, leaving the

door open behind her—she hadn't dreamed anything. Her treasure was gone.

Warrington trudged in behind her. She stood silent as he touched the bunk, then repeated her earlier movements, looking through the small space.

After he finished searching, he grasped her shoulder. 'You are sure you didn't move it?'

She grabbed on to his waistcoat with both hands. 'My treasure…'

His mouth pinched. 'It's a rock, Melina. Rock. Not treasure.'

She put both palms flat on his chest. 'It's a treasure. The French museum curator visited Melos two years ago. He told everyone on the island we might have artefacts buried in the ground. Most of the others ignored him. But I remembered the rocks and seeing the white shards mixed with the dirt, left from a structure long before my grandmother's time. Every time I could, I went to dig. And then I found the arm, and more. I knew I had discovered what the Frenchman wanted for his collection. Now someone has taken the arm.'

'Melina. No one on this ship believes the marble is anything but a carved stone. And we've all seen carved stones before. And it's broken. Cracked and chipped both. Any sailor here would prefer a drop of ale to your treasure.'

'Open your eyes.' She clenched her fists and

wanted to thump at his chest. She would have if it would have done any good.

He touched her chin. 'Don't get overly worked up. How is a man going to take the arm from the ship? It's too big to hide in his shirt or his trousers—and he knows we can search everything he has before he leaves.'

'You truly believe the marble is worthless?'

He nodded. 'Why would you think it valuable?'

'I know more of art than you'd expect.' She spoke the words softly. 'My father told me of art constantly. He spoke of nothing else. He's not dead—at least I don't think he is.' Pulling back, she watched his eyes. 'He's a painter. Robert Cherroll. Have you heard of him?

Warrington shook his head. 'I haven't. But Ben has. At least, he mentioned seeing a painting of you. In London. It showed the birthmark.'

She nodded. 'I had to sit, for hours and hours, and couldn't move while he painted. At first, my sister Thessa stood behind him and made faces, but then she grew tired of it and left. I ached from not moving, but I did it. I wanted to see my face on the canvas. My mother wanted to keep it, but he refused. He said some day he'd paint another one, but I knew he wouldn't. He took it, along with all the artwork he completed on the island. Taking them to England, always, to sell. He had to have funds to support us, he said. The work had to be sold, he would tell us, and leave.'

She backed away but held her shoulders firm. 'My father once told me of the British Museum.'

She tilted her head. 'If the stone is seen as a treasure, then both the English and French may want it. Think of it—how much more valuable something is the more it is wanted. I already know the Frenchman will make an offer if he can see part of it. I think the English will, too.'

'I'll get it back for you,' he promised. 'I'll spread the word through Gidley and the rest. Your rock is gone. We're hours from sighting land—but the ship will not dock until the stone is found. You'll have all the men hunting and one person who will be discovered. But, Melina, it's only a broken arm.'

She reached a hand out, steadying herself against the wall. 'But I have the rest of her hidden. I found her under the earth and then I covered her back up. I had lived always with shards of rock around me. The Frenchman made me want to look closer. I found the statue, which has a look of my mother's face, and behind the eyes I see the thoughts she is trying to tell me. She is *polytimos,* priceless. When I return for it… If I could get her before Stephanos realised I didn't intend to stay… And I could take my sisters…' She shook her head. 'But now it's stolen.'

'The men on *Ascalon* are good men. Not perfect, but they are loyal. Most have sailed with my brother for years. *Ascalon* was in those waters to meet with leaders and discuss the possibility of an uprising against the Turks. So, though these men are rough, they've been entrusted to an important voyage. They wouldn't steal a rock that means nothing to them.'

She took the lantern from its hook. 'I'll search everywhere myself. I have to find it. I have no choice.'

Warrington followed her while she hunted, moving to each corner of the ship and looking in any space large enough to conceal even half the stone.

She examined the hold where the food stores were kept. Barrels pressed against her back.

'Melina,' Warrington said, 'you'll set the ship afire again if you aren't more careful with the lantern. You must stop rummaging about.'

'I'll find it. It must be reunited with the statue.'

'Think, Melina. The stone did not walk out alone. You've been throughout the whole ship. Nothing was kept from you. The only place you've not examined is Ben's quarters.'

'I was there when it disappeared, and besides, he can't walk. He couldn't have taken it.' She put her hand to her head, pushing at a dampened tendril. 'But that is where it must be. It must have been stored there when I left to look for the piece.'

Warrington took the lantern she held. 'Not unless Ben was asleep. He would never let someone do that to you, Melina. He might send you about for an imagined stick, but he wouldn't take your property.' He guided her along the narrow opening and towards the stairway, to the light and fresher air. She took in a deep breath when she stepped on deck.

The men worked the sails, tugging ropes to tighten them. No one looked her way. No one paused. But their backs turned just a hair more from her. Their faces tensed. They knew quite well where she stood. The ship had little privacy, yet her stone had disappeared.

Warrington moved her into the cabin, hanging the lantern back in place and snuffing it. 'Forget about the rock and think about how you will proceed without it.'

She stood on the sleeping pallet. Sliding the covers aside with her heels, she put her shoulder to the wall so she'd not stumble with the ship's movements. Something had addled her. Because she wanted him to hold her like a child and tell her everything would be well. And he was speaking the words, but they would have meant so much more if he held her close.

'I have no place to go forward without the stone,' she said. 'Only backwards.' She touched over her heart. 'I feel something for the stone woman. She is still hidden, buried. But I saw her eyes and knew she wanted to be in a place of honour again. And without the arm… I do not know. She was going to save us…'

'I'll discover what happened to your treasure, Melina.' He brushed his knuckles against her cheek, leaving streaks of fire where his fingers trailed, and then he did take her into his arms. 'Someone on this ship knows and I'll get the men together and scare it out of them if I have to.' His steps thumped as he left.

She touched her cheek. He would find it, for her. She knew.

When Gidley stood at the cabin door, summoning her, he looked at the wall over her shoulders. 'Warrin'ton be wantin' to speak with yer.'

Her stomach churned, even though the ship sailed smooth. 'My stone?' she asked, searching his face.

'He's thinkin' he's found out who took it.' He raised a hand to silence her. 'But he be wantin' to tell yer hisself.'

Gidley turned and walked away, head down. Executioners had more joy in their steps. She followed, a feeling of death grating in the hollows of her heart.

On deck, Warrington stood by Stubby, who'd perched himself at the edge of the ship, his hands sliding along the polished railing and his eyes inspecting the dark flecks inside the wood. He appeared entranced in some imaginary task. Warrington stared at the boy.

'Where is it?' she asked, standing an arm's length from Warrington.

He turned his head to the cabin boy. 'Come here.'

Stubby moved, taking two dragging steps to stop in front of Melina. He took a deep breath, but didn't raise his eyes from staring at the deck. 'I heard it were a treasure, so I went to see it. Like pirate's gold and silver. But it were evil. I saw it and I knew. Just like the wave.' He lifted his right hand, making a claw of his fingers, and his mouth moved into a snarl as if he had fangs about to pounce.

'Evil?' Melina asked. 'The arm?'

'Yes.' He lowered his hand and raised his eyes. 'White like a drowned body. The spirit who lost its arm is sendin' storms and waves to pull us to the deep and drown us dead so it can have its hand back. Nearly took me and Capt'n Ben.' His gaze, along with his upturned eyes and quaking chest, reminded her of the way her youngest sister had looked when their mother died. 'You wouldn't want us drowned, or sunk. I know you wouldn't want to see me all guts loose and swolled up in my face...' He puffed his cheeks and held out his arms to show how he would look. 'I had to throw the rock back to the spirits.'

Melina turned and rushed to the cabin. She imagined the arm sinking, landing with a silent thud into the mud. The filth from below sweep-

ing around it, locking it into a silted grave. Gone
for ever. A new death. And it didn't matter if the
arm was exactly as it had been—a world of water
prevented her from ever seeing it again. It existed,
but was as lost as if it had been crushed into sand.

The arm could never be reunited with the marble woman who stood larger than a true female,
with a covering draped low on her hips. The English museum would not want a statue of an arm-
less goddess, even this majestic one.

She still wanted the statue and she'd return to
it, if only to see her mother's face. But her hopes
of wresting it from the island were now at the
bottom of the sea.

She could have stayed with Stephanos—given
him marriage in exchange for the carving. But her
mother would not have wanted that. She wouldn't
have wanted Melina to have been trapped by the
rock.

Now Melina wished she could run her fingers
over the statue's countenance again. To feel her
mother's presence and the life behind the stone
eyes.

The statue appeared so serene. Her hair pulled
up into a bun. One shoulder raised slightly more
than the other. Breasts free. The covering around
her hips sliding low, about to fall. Unconcerned
she no longer had arms to hold the draped cloth
for modesty.

Melina concentrated on the statue's face, trying to ease her own trembling limbs.

Freedom from Stephanos might have been more costly than she expected. At least the women on Melos who sold their bodies were able to return to normal when the ships left. Her life couldn't return to the way it was. If she returned home now, penniless, her value would be nothing. A failure, and not just for herself. For her mother. And her sisters.

Melina had sold her body—something she swore she'd never do. She'd left her sisters, after promising her dying mother she'd care for them. And the dowry she'd hoped to gain for them was gone because now she'd have no proof of finding anything but dirt. The statue might as well be resting in the muck.

She didn't have enough time to try again, even if she could lift the entire statue. Her sisters were too beautiful to be ignored.

She struggled to breathe, feeling the same silt and water choke her that now clasped the marble.

Warrington leaned against the door in Ben's cabin and his brother sat in the berth. In hours they'd be docked. From a quick perusal of his brother, Warrington saw clear eyes. Now Ben yelped when he moved. A good sign.

But Warrington was more concerned about

Melina than he was of Ben. Melina had not been the same since the arm was lost.

'The quartermaster will bring the physician…' Ben said. 'Besides, I'm on the mend. Gid will see to the rest. Go meet with the Foreign Office. They'll need to know of your negotiations. And don't worry about me. Gidley knows how to take over my duties and he'll watch me as close as he would his own son.'

Ben's words brought Jacob into Warrington's mind. He'd still not be seeing him for a few days. He didn't relish the chore that would meet him when he arrived home. The voyage hadn't vanquished Cassandra from his memory. It had only raised more questions in his mind.

And he would help Melina find her father. But her body could put his obsession of Cassandra to rest. He'd made sure never to be in Ben's cabin again while Melina was there. Ben would have been able to take one look at his older brother's face and know lust crashed into Warrington every time he looked at Melina. But he would control it.

Melina might not care a halfpenny for him, but the darkness of her eyes and her hair called to him. And her body.

He'd watched her when he was on the rigging and his imagination had replaced the feel of the ropes in his hands with the strands of her hair across his fingertips. Immediately he'd thrust the thoughts aside—knowing that to let her invade his mind while he was perched in the air could be fatal.

She'd only walked on deck a few times. If she'd slipped or leaned against the mast, every seaman on deck would have been able to describe exactly where she stood when it happened. And unlike Cassandra, he didn't think Melina would have been able to describe each watching male and where he was standing while he viewed her.

Cassandra had been gently bred a lady and had the heart of a dockside whore. Melina, the dockside whore he'd purchased, hadn't yet learned the things she could buy with her body.

And he wanted to be with her. Over and over and over again—with only his body involved. No wondering who she talked about when she whispered with her maid and planned for her day of social calls—with detours.

'Andrew.' Ben spoke the word quietly.

Instantly, Warrington's thoughts returned to the room. Ben had called War by his Christian name. His brother watched him, lips pressed together, but the smile on his face had a rueful curve.

'You know—' Ben gave a soft shake of his head. 'The woman…'

'Yes, I do.' Warrington nodded. 'And she'll help me forget.'

'I agree. But when you clean out one trunk, don't fill it back up. Leave it neat and tidy.'

Warrington forced himself quiet while he heard the unasked-for advice.

'I don't—' Ben spoke softly.

Irritation jabbed Warrington, but he also understood his brother's concern. 'Ben. I know. I remember. Never. Again. In fact, I want you to plan a return trip to Melos for Melina. She and I have discussed it. She agrees.'

His brother's eyes widened. 'I can. Not immediately, but soon. The repairs we made earlier were only temporary. I have to get *Ascalon* ready to sail for the East India Company.'

Warrington knew his brother had contracted to carry goods for the company and he would be gone at least two years, perhaps as long as three. 'You've enough time. I already asked Gid how long the repairs would take and that gives you time to get to Melos and back again. Melina can return to her sisters.'

'The way you look at her...' Resignation showed in Ben's face. 'I will find the time to return her. Ships are a good thing, War. You get on one. You sail. A new horizon. A new woman.' Ben smiled and flexed his leg. 'Maybe some day you'll be tough enough to handle a true voyage.'

'Once my boots hit land, they'll not be back to sail. I'm not getting over any water deeper than a bath.'

Ben expelled a breath. 'Don't trip over your petticoats when you leave.'

Warrington pushed himself from the door. 'Wasn't me pretending injury so I could lay abed drinking and sending a woman on false errands.' He opened the door and gave a wave to his brother. 'I'll be at either the town house or Whitegate. See me before you leave, infant.'

'Goodbye, old woman.'

Warrington walked out, knowing his trunk had already been taken to his room and letting the sunshine caress his face. Even the sun felt better when not reflected from below by water and not filtered from above by sea air.

Then he thought of the concern he faced. Rage caused his steps to increase. Cassandra had not merely been happy to tangle his life while she lived. She mangled afterwards, as well. He slapped a palm against the outside cabin door so hard his elbow tingled.

His past ate at him, only it wasn't even his past. And it wasn't even in the past, but at his country estate.

Chapter Ten

Melina crouched on the oak-planked bunk in the cabin. The mattress had been replaced on the bed. The pallet gone. Now Warrington's trunk sat in the room, open. He stood in front of it, staring at the silk waistcoat and buff breeches, complaining that he had not brought someone named Broomer along so he could have cared for the clothing. Warrington had already taken out a gentleman's beaver hat totally unsuitable for the ship or Melos.

Warrington was not of her world. She'd seen silk before and touched it. Her father had worn it. She lived in the world of scratchy wool and rough linen.

'I do not like sailing.' She spoke low, knowing her words wouldn't carry though the wall.

'Makes two of us and I own half of the ship.' He gave her a half smile. 'But my infant brother could talk me into buying a bag of bees.'

She shrugged. 'He reminds me of Stephanos. Stephanos has a schooner and sometimes wears nearly the same clothes as the captain.' She gauged Warrington's face to see if he took offence at her dislike of his brother.

Warrington's chest moved as if he laughed, but she heard no sound. 'Ben doesn't take well to being on his back, alone. And he's superstitious. Though he'll never say so to you, he thinks you brought bad luck to the ship.'

'The only person I brought misfortune for was me and my statue.

Warrington turned from the trunk, preparing his razor, putting soap on his face and scowling into the small mirror. 'I'm pleased you forgave Stubby.'

'I've not—but he doesn't need to know that. He meant no harm.'

'Ben will stay on board a few more days, until he is walking better. Gid will see he has all he needs brought to him.' Warrington shaved as he talked. 'We three brothers have a town house in London. Ben will have to stay on *Ascalon,* making sure she is readied. Dane is at my country house, working with my man of affairs—taking care of the estates.'

He looked out of the window, as the ship sailed past warehouses for unloaded goods. 'I can't yet return to the country house. Whitegate is my ancestral home. My real home—though I've lived in the town house since Cass died. Now that I'm to be in London again, I have to settle a few things for myself. Things I couldn't face before, but now it's time.'

When he finished, he stored his shaving supplies and prepared to depart.

She kept her eyes to the window while he changed clothing. Each rustle of fabric echoed in her ears. He stood so close, she could see his arm when he donned the shirt. She bit down on her lip, trying to keep her awareness of him from changing her breathing or showing in the colour of her face. She wondered what he would do if she turned and watched. Probably continue exactly as he had been the moment before. But she could not let him see her interest and she could not give in to it. She swallowed, and tried to think of the sights she saw outside the window. But nothing beyond the glass had any appeal for her at this moment.

'You can turn now, Melina.' His roughened voice whispered at her ears, jarring her. She jumped forward, but couldn't move much or she'd have her face against the panes. 'I'm all tucked away.'

'The sights of the town are *neos,* fresh, for me.'

He gave a teasing grunt and she could tell he backed away from her. But she was also aware from his response that he remembered well it wasn't only the view in front of her that was new to her.

The clothing he'd worn while he sailed was tossed on to the floor.

'You are not taking those?' she asked, looking at the heap.

He shook his head. 'Gid'll see use is made of the scraps. I will never wear them again.'

She forced herself not to pick them up. Surely they could be sold for a few pence, but they weren't hers to sell. She would have to find her father and hope she was wrong about him. She'd planned to rail at him for leaving her mother. Now she would have to be kind.

She'd not wanted Warrington to know she had a father in London because she felt ashamed he had deserted them. But she'd told him anyway.

'Remember, Ben chose the town house fripperies and hired servants.' Warrington opened the door. 'It'll not be much different than the ship. But when the ship is repaired, you'll be here and able to go back to Melos, and care for your sisters.'

She took the satchel she'd brought, slipping the strap over her shoulder, and wrapped the shawl tight around her, then followed Warrington to the deck. She watched the port come into view. Already she could see the buildings and the people. The ship floated up the waterway, into England.

On deck, the shouts of orders and replies faded in her mind as she saw the city taking life in front of her. The people on the docks appraised the ship as if it were of no more significance than a mug of ale being put before them.

Waves sloshed, and somewhere in the distance, tar burned—from the odour, enough to coat Melos. The city stank.

Gidley waited, watching everything. His legs were braced for the ship's nudge against the dock. The quartermaster steered and Stubby coiled rope. One adjustment to a sail always meant another loosening or tightening would be needed somewhere else.

Gidley had already placed the huge rolls of rope on the outside of the ship, which kept the sides from knocking constantly against the dock while in port. He stood, brow furrowed and showing no pleasant emotion about the chance to leave *Ascalon*.

Preparing herself to be jolted, Melina was surprised when the ship eased in with little more than a brush.

Melina wished she could slip into this new world as easily as the ship had. She'd have to find her father. She put her hopes in a man who'd left her to starve the past few years. But surely he wouldn't feel the same if she stood in front of him.

Until she found her father, she was at the mercy of a man who cursed his wife's name and when he looked at her after he said the words, he glared.

Warrington had sent Stubby for a hackney as soon as the ship docked and ushered her inside the carriage before she had a chance to look around.

Melina used a fingertip to edge back the carriage window shade so she could peer outside. Warrington insisted she not make a spectacle of herself and keep concealed. Never mind she'd just shared a vessel with over thirty able-bodied seamen—now he told her she would have to go about with a chaperon. An odd world.

She would have hated waiting to begin her search, but the sights in London amazed her. Melina had never imagined such wealth and such vibrancy. She could hardly believe what she saw. No city could be more alive. With so much activity, she wondered if the city ever slowed, even at night.

Melina didn't know how the size of the city compared to Melos, but she imagined the whole of her island wouldn't hold London. And she felt smaller and smaller.

The front of Warrington's town house wasn't grand compared to many others she'd peeked at during the carriage ride, but a sturdy shape, and beyond any dreams she might have imagined while on Melos. Curtains billowed outside, through the open windows, and she saw a young boy, pail in hand, trotting from the back of the house on some errand.

She could imagine telling her sisters about the city and not being able to convince them of the size. No one could create such a picture with words. More horses and carriages than she knew

existed in the whole of the world. And people
shouting out, and sometimes the drifting smell
of baked goods pleasantly covering the more
usual odours caused by so many people so tightly
packed together.

When the carriage stopped, Warrington helped
her to the paving stones.

'If you think of this as Ben's home,' he said,
standing at the door, 'it will make more sense.
Dane and I have lived in it at one time or another—and we all move in and out of it. But
Ben stores his collections here.' He looked to the
house. 'Dane and I refer to it as *Seascrape*.'

The house was set among other similar dwell-
ings, close to the street, and three levels of windows, with a front that looked as fresh as if it had
been completed the day before.

When the door opened, a man stood there,
looking down. This giant of a man well out-
stripped any person she'd ever seen and he would
have been frightening if not for the humour in his
face. His upturned lips looked to stay in place at
all moments of the day and if he were ever moved
to tears, he'd still be smiling.

'Ah, my lord,' he said, giving a proper bow.
He wore breeches, one leg of the clothing hanging a hand width too low as it appeared to have
lost the securing button just below the knee. His
yellow vest had a shine to it and his cravat was
of the same colour. His brown woollen coat kept

his clothes from overpowering the sun, but not by much.

'Step inside. Step inside.' He moved back. 'We've made the house up pretty for when you and Captain Ben arrived.'

'He'll be staying on *Ascalon* a little longer than expected, Broomer.' Warrington stepped inside the door and gave his hat to the man. 'The ship needs repairs—and so does he. He's limping around, grumbling and groaning because a wave tossed him into a spar.'

Broomer frowned.

War nodded. 'It was close, but he's tough. And he looks to be mending good as ever.'

Melina followed him inside and the big man gave another bow.

Warrington spoke to the man. 'See to having us fed soon, but you're not to do the cooking.'

Broomer laughed. 'Can't blame you. But you can see Mrs Fountain's still working here.' He patted his stomach. 'I tell her she could make a dead rat taste good and she says she'll try it some day to see if I notice.' He laughed again. 'If she wasn't so scared of them little creatures, I'd be worried.'

'Does your sister still live in the area?' Warrington asked.

'She's doing work for that sewing lady you told me about,' Broomer said. 'My sister says everybody thinks that woman sews faster than anybody else. They never suspect two women are doing the fancy work.'

'Can you bring her here to meet Melina and fashion several dresses as quickly as possible, and find fripperies to match?' The corners of his eyes creased. 'Tell her we do not want Melina to draw attention.' He gave Melina a quick smile, and then turned back to Broomer. 'Garments suitable for a governess, I suppose.'

'She'll be happy from ear to ear to be putting together something for your woman.' Broomer gave another small bow to Melina. 'She will be honoured.'

Melina saw Warrington's face the moment Broomer called her Warrington's woman. His jaw had tensed first, then he had looked at her and the light behind his eyes changed. He'd not obviously perused her body, but he'd watched her face in such a way she'd known he was remembering her touch, then the side of his lips lifted in the smallest amount before he turned back to Broomer.

'I will pay your sister double if she can have something here by morning.'

With that the large man left and Warrington took Melina to the upstairs. He paused at the top. 'Sitting room.' He indicated to the right with his head.

He opened the door and she stepped inside.

The walls were blue. A painting hung above the fireplace. Mermaids.

'You can surmise who commissioned the art.' His brows rose and he seemed to be saying something other than his words. 'He's a collector—of a sort.'

A fish candle holder sat on top of a bookcase and a ship replica with what appeared to be silver masts graced the mantel. The staff leaning in the corner was the serious end of a harpoon. Two sofas sat angled to catch the warmth of the fireplace. A writing desk with good-sized seating for it sat near the window to catch the light. One overstuffed chair was in another corner with the table beside it holding an ivory-coloured object mounted on a stand.

Warrington followed her eyes. 'Tooth. Some kind of fish. My brother strangled it with his bare hands or something. Claims it wanted to drown a friend of his or swallow them both whole. Took it as a sign the day he caught it and said his luck changed.'

She nodded, even more certain she wasn't fond of Warrington's brother.

He shrugged. 'I suppose having a passion for the sea is no different than any other. Ben didn't choose it. I believe our passions choose us—unfortunately.' His look lost emotion. 'Horses. Gambling. Beautiful women. The trick is not to let them become too strong in your life, I suppose.'

He turned away, speaking. 'I'll show you the

bedchamber. We have two sleeping rooms on this floor. One is empty and the other is Dane's, on occasion. Two are on the upper floor—one I use and the other one, which has more of the watery mementos, Ben prefers. I believe he even has part of an old sail stored there. The room smells of stagnant water, in my opinion—though Ben says I imagine it.'

He turned to leave the room, then reversed his movements, facing her. 'Tomorrow, we'll go to the British Museum.'

'What of you seeing your children?'

He looked at her. 'I'll have them brought here or I will go there. Soon. I have not fully decided yet.'

She paused, measuring her words carefully. 'I would like to go to Somerset House. That is the place I sent letters to my father.'

'It will be no bother.' He gave the words no inflection, no importance, and turned. Taking her to a bedchamber, he paused at the door. 'We've had to move some of Ben's collection here. Dane and I keep moving them around to whichever room is unoccupied.'

When she walked inside, Melina saw what she assumed, and hoped, was the most extensive collection of mermaid paintings in the world. The captain did like his mermaids. Or what passed for them.

These were not virtuous sea creatures if one judged by the looks in their faces and the poses they chose. Each mermaid had long flowing hair, which didn't always fall in a modest covering, but more in an accentuating frame.

She kept her composure. 'I suppose they are beautiful.'

'That is not my first thought when I see them.' He looked at her. 'I'll turn them to the wall if you wish.'

'I am fine with them.'

'I do not have a single mermaid painting in my room. Not one. I have sensible art. Not rabid females.' His mouth was so close to her ear, she could feel his breath. 'I would like to show you.'

His hand slipped to her waist, weakening her knees. Her mind flashed back on the memory of his body over hers. Muscles. Male skin so much different than her own. A new world at her fingertips.

'I would have had the mermaids moved had I known I would be returning with you,' he said.

She fought for her voice. Too much newness surrounded her, and yet, none of it took her thoughts as Warrington's presence did. 'I did not know such paintings existed.' Nor such a man as Warrington.

He shrugged. 'I would say they don't anywhere else. I think my brother has found every one in the world and had the rest commissioned. One artist always has a painting to show Ben when he docks. Ben can't resist any painting of a naked woman with scales.'

He pulled Melina's hand to his lips. 'I prefer a true woman.' He pressed a kiss to her fingers.

She pulled her hand back, sliding her fingers along his. Without meaning to, she'd slowed her movements, her entire concentration on the feel of his skin against hers. Thumping footsteps sounded up the stairs—the movements were exaggerated on purpose to alert them of Broomer's arrival.

She turned her shoulders from Warrington so he couldn't see her face. The paintings could be more proper. But she feared even if an artist painted seaweed over the creatures, they would still be unsuitable. A small painting propped in the corner would be turned to the wall as soon as she was alone.

He put his arm around her. 'I won't have them near you if you wish. Or there is another chamber you could choose… One in particular would welcome you…'

She firmed her voice. 'I think this room is perfect for me. Perhaps the mermaids will keep wicked spirits away.'

'I would not count heavily on it, Melina. I think they would welcome any wickedness.'

She turned, needing to escape the sensations rocking her body, and he followed her from the room.

Broomer appeared in the hallway. He held his

hand up and gave a little twist of his wrist near his head. 'Mrs Fountain's hair stood on end when I said you'd be needing a meal, and pots began flying.' He patted his stomach. 'But from the smell of the beef, she's putting on a fine feed. It's waiting on ye.'

Then he ambled to the stairs and Melina looked at Warrington. 'He is so friendly and not what I expected a servant to be like.'

Warrington met her eyes and she saw agreement. 'Broomer left Newgate and landed on a ship to keep from starving about the time Ben first became an able-bodied seaman. Broomer hated every day of it, but they became close and Ben sent him here when they docked.'

He tilted his head. 'After Cassandra died, I couldn't stand the way the servants watched me at Whitegate. First I'd been ill and then I recovered to discover my father had died of the same illness. We had cholera. Things were not smooth at Whitegate. Then, about a year ago, Cassandra became ill, just as my father and I had. Cass died. I worried that the servants thought I had poisoned her. I came here.'

The light from a window at the end of the hallway illuminated his features, leaving shadows that darkened his eyes. She put her hand on his arm, rubbing along the smooth fabric of his sleeve. 'I was miserable after my mother died,' she said.

Nodding, he held out an arm for her to precede him. 'This house gave me a chance to step from the memories even if I could not forget them. Long ago, my father purchased the town house, saying it would be an investment, and I am thankful he did. I think even then he thought one of his sons would live in it. But we all use it.'

He stopped outside the doorway to the main sitting room. 'I was surprised the first time I walked in and the fish-women portraits graced the sitting-room wall.' He looked heavenwards. 'I could not tolerate them—felt I was in some sort of fish harem. The paintings had to be moved to the room you're now in.'

Warrington continued, 'I'd get a bottle of brandy and shout for Broomer.' He smiled. 'Ben had sworn his friend could be more enjoyment than any Drury Lane performance. He spoke the truth. Broomer would come to the sitting room and spout tales left and right. Never asked a question of my life.' He turned his head so she couldn't see his expression. 'Not even when I returned home one night with blood flowing down my back because a man I'd never seen before was waiting in the shadows to stab me.'

If he'd not moved slightly back, she might not have noticed the way a muscle flexed in his jaw. 'Why would someone wish to kill you?'

'Jealousy over my wife—though at that point she was dead and it didn't matter. But she was carrying my babe when she died. Perhaps…he felt betrayed.'

The air was silent for a moment. She had to keep him talking. 'Did Broomer go for the magistrate and a physician?'

Warrington shook his head. 'Refused. Said all he'd ever known a magistrate to do was lock up people if somebody else caught them. Said all a physician could do was make people die faster or slower and with more pain. I cursed him, sacked him and thought I might as well die. I gave in and let him tend my back.' He raised a brow. 'Don't ever plan a friendly chess game with him, either. He doesn't like to drag them out. I believe he has three boards set up in his chamber and I suspect if he were to find an opponent he believes is truly worthy of his skills, he'd stop at nothing to cadge them into a game.'

He paused, the silence so soft she could hear the sounds of carriages from the street.

'Make yourself comfortable,' he told her. 'I must arrange for a meeting concerning my voyage.'

Before he turned to leave, he looked at her, his voice thoughtful, and said, 'I do not know what my brother sees in mermaids. Anyone would prefer a goddess over a sea creature. They're much more enticing.'

Chapter Eleven

Warrington waited until the house became quiet and walked the hallway to Melina's room.

Conflicting thoughts battered him. He'd meant to stay from her and he praised himself because he'd kept out of her bed. But now he stood at her doorway.

He raised his hand to knock, but then he stilled and let his hand fall to his side. Melina couldn't refuse him. After all, he'd paid. And now he provided everything she needed and had ordered clothing for her.

The bed she slept in was soft, the pillows softer. The sheets even better. If she became warm, she could go to the sitting room, pull the bell for Broomer, and he would rise from his bed, ask her what she wanted and act as if he'd been waiting to be summoned, and go merrily back to his chamber after doing her bidding.

Or she could take a candle—not a tallow candle or a burning flame from whatever could be fashioned, but a beeswax candle—and peruse the collection of books in the library all the brothers had contributed to.

For the morning meal, Mrs Fountain would prepare her bread—hot, and dripping with butter—a rasher of bacon and chocolate, or tea, and even porridge, because Ben preferred the simple fare and Mrs Fountain always wished to please. If Melina were to ask for a different meal, Mrs Fountain would do all in her power to comply.

He doubted Melina would even suspect such luxuries were at her fingertips.

But she would know he was her benefactor and remember he was the man she gave her body to in exchange for passage. And now she lay in a room of his house, in comfort except for the hideous artwork, and she could not tell him not to lie with her.

Mrs Fountain or Broomer or the maids could say they had another position and leave. But Melina's father had abandoned her once, was likely to do so again, and the woman had no one or anything else. His fists clenched at the unfairness.

Granted, the first night he'd taken her body in exchange for passage. He'd been rewarded by his own inner guilt. She'd been a virgin forced to sell her body or go to the Stephanos man she spoke of.

And Warrington had once felt forced, as well. Forced to remain in a marriage. Forced by his own beliefs not to take a lover. Forced by the insistence of his own body to return to his wife.

He turned, hoping Dane had added some interesting titles to the books, but his feet would not take him from Melina. He searched within himself, trying to understand his need to see her and wondering why he could not shut off the craving he felt.

A clunk. A thump. He stood outside Melina's door and heard shuffling noises. Things being moved.

He rapped softly.

The door opened a crack and wary eyes peered out.

'Is something disturbing you?' he asked.

'Not if— Yes. They are… Those women all…' She changed her sentence. 'In the dusk, the features of the paintings are dim, but the whiteness around the pupils glows. Eyes stare at me.'

Inwardly, he smiled. He could imagine his brother relishing the eyes on him.

She stood there, peering around the door, the thin shoulder of her white chemise showing well in the bare light and the skin of her neck filled with dark hollows, but they were inviting valleys.

'The mermaids—they seem to get more evil the longer I am near them,' she whispered, perhaps so the women could not hear her.

He agreed, though he felt some loyalty to his brother's choices. And in the light, the women did have a certain appeal to a man's base side. 'I don't think they should be in public view, but in a man's private quarters…' He paused. 'I think my brother prefers mermaids because he knows he'll never find one and he uses them to keep—' He stopped. 'I can understand Ben's views, but yours take preference tonight. If he were here, he would feel the same.'

She laughed softly and the sound of it hit him in his stomach, a punch without pain. But with a certain power involved, taking some of his strength.

'Melina—' The night on the ship kept returning to his memory. He had wronged her. And he'd tried to stay from her to make it right in his mind. But he also kept calling himself a fool. She wasn't staying in England and he felt relieved. He didn't need another entanglement. He had Jacob to think of and Whitegate.

He lived in a man's world. Women brought tension. Goblets being hurled across the room, shattering. Servants upset. He'd truly been amazed at how well a house could run with only servants at the helm. A fractious woman could cause more upheaval with a misplaced smile than a general with a battalion of men.

He looked into Melina's face and gently shook his head. 'I'll move the paintings.'

'Warrington.' Her eyes darted down. 'I know…'

He didn't like talking to her with so much between them and particularly standing in a hallway of his house. Broomer could step up the stairs at any moment, probably stomping to alert them of his presence, but all the same—

He gave a soft push to the door and she stepped back, letting him enter without resistance—except in her face. She'd not braided the length of her hair, only pulled it tightly and put a ribbon around it. He'd never seen a woman leave her locks so free when she slept. He took in the dimly lit room and saw the backs of the art now propped against the walls.

The chemise, too full for Melina, hung on her. The garment sneaked into the recesses of his mind because he knew it was the one thing touching her skin the whole of the night.

'I made sure a dressing gown was placed in the wardrobe for you. He will not mind if you use it. Everything in here is for you to use as you wish,' he said.

She absently touched the tie she'd put in her hair, which caused a shifting in her clothing, pulling the chemise across her breasts. He instantly turned, not wanting more images of her lodging in his mind—causing a pounding ache that stirred from below and crept up to his chest until he could think of nothing else.

Reaching to the paintings she'd turned to the wall, he took one in each hand, carried them to the hallway and placed them facing the wall. Then he went back for more.

Passing her, he held two more paintings. 'This is the one way we haven't displayed them before.' He sat the two beside the others in the hallway and returned to her. 'This arrangement might be the best view of them.'

'You don't have to—'

'Yes, I do. They are not what any woman would choose to have around her and only one male I know cares for them.' A single painting remained in the room. 'Melina, take the wrap and wait for me in the sitting room. Let's give these immoral women's spirits a chance to clear out of the bedchamber.'

In moments she was covered and they walked to the other room. The familiarity of being in a woman's presence in such a mundane way stirred pleasant feelings in him. Caressed him.

Inside the sitting room, Melina curled into a chair and the candles he'd lit burnished her face, giving her features an otherworldly look. He stood at the door, but she didn't turn her face to him, avoiding his eyes.

'Melina, if you have any debt to me—*have* had any debt to me for passage or anything else—I release you from it.'

'It's not so simple. Not for me. I am in debt to you.'

'No, Melina. You are not. Not any longer. It's

fully paid. You do not owe me anything. I am obliged to you.'

He saw her gentle disagreement in her eyes. He couldn't take her again. If he did, he'd know she only lay with him out of repayment and duty. He would not go to her chamber. He'd already had his fill of a woman's dutiful coupling.

He took another chair and lifted it, sitting it beside her, not so close the arms connected, but close enough she could reach to put her hand on his arm if she wished, or if they both leaned together, their lips could touch.

Before he sat, he undid the buttons of his waistcoat and pulled off his cravat. He lowered himself into the chair, taking the neckcloth and folding it carefully, then placing it on the floor at the side of him opposite her.

'I should have lit a fire, though it's too hot,' he mused, 'because it would make more sense than sitting here staring at a cold grate.' He paused for a moment. 'Do you play chess?'

'No. I embroider. I embroider, and embroider, and embroider. When I am not mending or making clothing. Every night we sewed, or did some quiet chore if we weren't sleepy when darkness fell.'

'Sounds lively.'

'Sometimes we did argue for entertainment, I suppose.'

He chuckled. 'I have seen that happen in my own life.'

He wanted to take her to his bed. She'd go if he asked. But if he did, he'd suspect— No, he'd know she let him touch her in repayment and he did not want that. He didn't want her saying yes because she owed him. For that, he could leave the house and quickly find another pleased to toss up her skirts for quick, uncaring moments, and most happy see the back of him while she tucked the coin away. But he wanted to be with Melina.

'If you wish it—' Her words rocked into the room and he knew without doubt what she meant. Perhaps she could read his thoughts, but even the coal boy would know what a man contemplated when he saw Melina in bed clothing.

'I realise that.' Sadness tinged his words, but he didn't know if she could hear the emotion and wished he hadn't felt it.

He looked at her. She didn't accidentally open her dressing gown and lean in his direction when he spoke. The woman wasn't a jade.

And he could pull her from the chair and roll them on to the carpet and never feel the floor.

'Perhaps I—' He looked at his hands, fingertips touching, resting on his lap. 'I shouldn't. I think I might like you, Melina. And one probably does take advantage of friends, and all, but I fear if I do, it will seem base. Not like before. Before, we hardly had spoken. We were strangers.'

'Better with a stranger?'

'I suppose.'

'You only plan to speak to me tonight?'

He put his hand on the arm of the chair, palm up, inviting. 'Yes. I've not spoken with a woman much in so long. I'm surprised I miss it. I never saw a woman and said to myself, *Oh, she looks lovely. I might wish to spend hours talking with her.* But perhaps I wanted that more than I knew.'

She didn't move at first, but then put her hand in his. The touch, delicate and warm, pleased him more than a seductive rub. More than a teasing smile, or a planned accidental brush against his body.

'I shouldn't have spoken,' he said softly.

'No. I like your voice.'

'Are you comfortable?' he asked.

'I suppose.'

Warrington watched the fireplace as if he could see flames. 'You will not be amiss if you wish to go back to your room.'

She didn't move. 'It's all so new to me. Everything. This world. I had heard stories. Hours and hours of them, telling us what this land was like. But I still didn't know. All of it. I didn't know.'

'Tell me about your days on Melos.'

She began describing her mother, her sisters and her life.

He didn't have to prod himself to pay attention or stay awake. Her voice, filled with a woman's softness, entranced him more than any sound he'd ever heard. Even when she sat back in the chair and her pauses grew longer, and her eyes slipped shut, he kept watching her, soothed by her presence.

And a whisper inside himself warned never, ever to do this again. Never. He could not let his soul be shredded again by falling in love.

When he heard a clock in the dining room give three chimes, he woke Melina, took her by the hand and led her to her bed.

He kissed her forehead.

After he left the room, he moved to his own chamber.

He'd just kissed a woman's forehead. He didn't understand himself. But he did understand the simmering, pulsing need throughout his body. His temporary sainthood was leaving him. He was barely hanging on to his vow of celibacy.

In his chamber, he poured water into the wash-bowl and used both hands to dip his face into it. He dried, wishing he could shake his body like a wet dog and quiver away his desire for Melina.

His hands stopped on the flannel, resting. He could think of better ways to ease himself of his want for the dark beauty, and all involved her softness.

He could show her so much, but then, he could end up with another man laying claim to his child. The spectre of Stephanos rose up, and tore at

Warrington. He could not let Melina go back to Melos with his child inside her and he could not let a woman close enough to destroy him again.

In the morning, Broomer woke Warrington and barely gave him time to get his eyes open before the servant said, 'My sis brought the first dress and I'm asking her to stay until you take a look 'fore she leaves. I'm thinking you might want her to keep the garment.'

War raised a brow and left his bed.

'It's the colour of mud or boot scrapings,' Broomer continued. 'I asked my sister what she was thinking. She reminded me of you asking for something governess-like... She's in a fierce mood now.' Broomer shrugged. 'They're dressing Melina because my sister did bring some of those underneath trappings and you know how those take an age for a woman to knot up.'

When War saw the garment on Melina, he understood Broomer's statement. The gown was suitable for a stern governess, but it didn't hide her enough.

He turned to Broomer's sister, a woman close to Warrington's own height. Her eyes had the same friendliness of her brother's, but the dark blue dress she wore, and the long line of her neck, gave her a gently bred appearance—the exact opposite of her sibling.

'A pleasant gown,' Warrington stated. Those were the best words he could say about it.

'We will need a chaperon.' He spoke to the seamstress. 'To protect Melina's reputation.' Broomer's face jerked around. Obviously he'd noticed Melina was living in the house with no chaperonage. Mrs Fountain and Broomer were not talebearers, though. And for the day servants, they would not make note of a woman staying with him, thinking her a mistress of no consequence.

But to be in public with Melina was another thing. She would be noticed and that should have the appearance of propriety.

'I could certainly go about with you. If that's what you wish.' The sister looked taken aback, but agreeable.

He nodded. 'But some of the conversations Melina and I will have with other people—you'll need to make yourself scarce for those moments. I'll nod to you and then you can absent yourself for a bit.'

'Whatever is needed.' Her chin went up, sending out a message of complete agreement and perfect servitude. A woman who considered it a show of her loyalty to help accomplish a task and would consider it no challenge at all to do Warrington's bidding.

Warrington first had to give his report to the Foreign Office and then he took Melina to Somerset House. He stood in the centre of the room, looking up at the paintings lining the walls. Above eye level, he could see about three more rows of large paintings, under the windows at ceiling height. The paintings, all ornately framed, weren't arranged in a neat line, but more like a pleasing array of mismatched sizes of tiles covering a wall.

This wasn't the annual display of Somerset House, but he'd arranged for a meeting with the man who'd forwarded Melina's letters to her father.

He started at one side of the room and checked each painting, looking for Cherroll's name. Melina started at the other. Broomer's sister stood close to Melina and he realised, based on the women's dress, an onlooker might think Melina the chaperon.

After a few minutes, Melina called him over, pointing to a painting. The chaperon walked discreetly to other artwork.

'My father did this one,' she said.

At that moment, a man, with a precise cravat and a pace just as measured, walked up to them. Warrington turned. 'Mr Bridewater?'

The man nodded. 'Yes. I received your message. Please follow me.'

After they entered a small room with an ornately carved desk, Bridewater spoke. 'My lord.

I believe you went to university with my son, Marcus.'

'Yes.' Warrington nodded. 'The fellow could outrun a horse. Never saw anyone who could move as fast as he.'

Bridewater laughed, pointing them to chairs carved in the same manner of the desk. 'My boy never sat still. Could hardly keep a tutor for him. Never thought I'd see the day he finished his education. Soon as he did, he put his nose in an accounting book and now to get him running, you have to kick the legs from his chair.'

Warrington sat and noticed this room boasted a selection of paintings that would be hard to equal. 'I want to find the artist who painted a portrait my brother saw and also one that you have displayed. The man's name is Cherroll.'

Bridewater stared a moment and fiddled with a chain hanging from his waistcoat pocket. 'I suppose it couldn't hurt for me to tell you his true name.' He shrugged, stretching his arms out in front of himself, fingers interlaced. 'He paints under a false name and does not show himself in public as the artist. When he was young his family wanted it kept secret he painted and for some reason he still fancies the old name. Always, I handle any transactions for him. Any enquiries or post in the Cherroll name always come to me and I see that he gets it.'

Bridewater leaned back in the chair. 'He paints

all the time. Chases art like some men chase skirts or spirits.' He pushed his chair back a bit. 'Lived on some Greek island off and on for years. That helped his painting—because he's not a terribly creative artist and he lacks something. Painting a different culture helped get his work shown, but didn't increase his skill. He repeats himself— never stretches or grows. Never studies others.'

Warrington stood. 'How old is this man?'

Bridewater squinted. 'About my age, I'd suppose. But don't plan on meeting him, even though he's in London now. If he's painting, he won't accept a visitor.' He shook his head. 'Man thinks he'll be more famous than Rembrandt, so he wants to give the world all the art he can.' At that, Bridewater leaned his head back a bit and grimaced at the ceiling. 'Just wish he would push himself to paint better, not more.' He lowered his chin and looked at Warrington. 'You may know him. Lord Hawkins.'

Warrington paused for a moment. 'One of the Duke of Beaumont's brothers?'

'Youngest, or next, I believe. Never was any chance of him becoming duke. He's the old duke's third wife's second son, or some such. Married well.' Bridewater smiled and chuckled to himself. 'Though his father-in-law rather did know how to remind him who the funds truly belonged to. The father-in-law—not a man you'd cross. He loved his daughter and his coins. Tolerated Hawkins.'

Warrington and Melina stood, and Bridewater gave them directions.

Melina spoke as she stepped to the carriage. 'He's married again. Now I know why he did not return to us.'

Warrington sat in the carriage beside Melina, pleased at the feel of her so close beside him. The soft scent of new fabric of the dress clinging to it. He sat back against the squabs, which caused their bodies to brush again, and knew he'd only moved because he liked the feel of her beside him. He looked at her fingers clasped in her lap, and moved his eyes to her face.

Her brows were puckered, and his chest tightened in response. He knew what she was about to discover.

'We'll call on him tomorrow.' *This man who forgot about his daughters.* As soon as the thought formed, his own blackness slogged into his veins. He tensed. Jacob. The rest of it. Once he arranged the next days of his life, he could put everything behind him. Everything but Jacob, and start fresh. He would close away every unpleasant memory and go forward. His life would begin again.

But now he needed to prepare Melina for what she was to find when she met her father, and he didn't think there was an easy way.

Chapter Twelve

Melina rose from the table, uncomfortable with the amount of food left in front of her. The platter held more boiled carrots and parsnips than had been taken. Parts of three different meats remained—one dark and spiced, small game of some kind and her favourite, one with the lightness of chicken resting in a pool of herbed juices.

Warrington ate, hardly looking at anything other than his food, his movements slow, as if he didn't taste the meal in front of him.

He wore a dark coat and a gold-hued waistcoat under. The cravat at his neck drooped so it hardly stood out from the shirt. But when he moved his arm, the sleeve fell back at his hand. She could see the broadness of his wrist and the shape of the bone resting under the darkened skin. Hair spattered the back of his hand, hardly showing. Even the leanness of his fingers gave him a look of strength.

And if she doubted his power, she had only to let herself gaze at his shoulders or across his chest. He was born with command.

He'd not spoken during the whole meal. She'd not felt ignored because she had her own thoughts to consider. When she stood, he immediately put down his fork and rose. Grim eyes met hers.

'We should go to the sitting room.' Warrington stepped beside her, not touching, but close enough she could see a darkness of his jaw, hinting of stubble.

She paused, studying his face. He smiled—one he might have given a convict headed for the gallows.

She didn't move. 'What is it?'

'I was just thinking of…' He shook his head. 'I don't know. My wife. It's too late to ask her questions now, and even if it weren't, her answers… Why would anyone ask a question of someone who has repeatedly told lies—unless to see if the answer is so preposterous as to be laughable?'

He put a hand to Melina's back and shepherded her towards the sitting room. Two candles were lit to dispel the gloom from the drizzling rain outside. 'A man might ask a question of his wife and in his heart he knows the answer, but he wants to hear something to convince him he's wrong.' His voice was low, laced with ruefulness as if he couldn't believe he spoke. 'I suppose Shakespeare has written a play about it, or he should have. Doesn't matter. I wouldn't have liked it.'

When he entered the sitting room, he stopped, frowning. 'If you ever can't sleep, make use of the books we have. Dane's tomes on gardening are quite useful for nodding off.' Warrington stood in front of the large, chintz-covered chair, but he didn't sit. 'I know you can read English because you wrote letters to send to your father, and I believe I even have several volumes in Greek.'

Melina walked in front of the books. She ran her finger over the titles. 'I can't read Greek. Neither of my sisters can. I would not know how to read English if my father hadn't had trouble painting for a while and found it amusing to teach words. A new game and I was good at it. I even taught my sisters later—and when Bellona realised she could read English, she was enraged. Bellona then took the two books my father had left behind and found a French sailor who would buy them.'

Warrington didn't speak and he looked at his hands.

She wondered why he didn't face her—and why he didn't say what he thought. 'Continue.' She shrugged. 'I know you have more to say.'

'Your father has a large home, very old, very well kept—from his wife's family. When you see it, understand he…'

Melina let out a breath and turned from the books, keeping herself calm by force. 'You are telling me he is both wealthy and married. But since it is his wife's funds, I could understand him not sending much to us, but forgetting about us completely was wrong.'

Warrington stepped closer and took her hand. He led her to the sofa and pulled her beside him. He didn't release her fingers, but held them. 'I am trying to prepare you for the luxurious life he lives and I wanted you to know the money isn't his. And I don't think he is able to control it as husbands do with their wife's funds. The father-in-law was quite shrewd. The man profited greatly from the war with the colonies, and then the one with the little Corsicans—ensuring that England had the weapons they needed. And he only had the one daughter to pass his wealth to.'

'So my father had two families. He surely had enough funds to feed us. We did not need much, by English standards.'

Now he held her hand in both his, the warmth touching her, but not driving away the aloneness. She pulled back, feeling the anger towards her father that he deserved, but Warrington raised his grip to hold her wrists.

His eyes fixed on hers, and his voice softened even more. 'Your father hasn't recently married. He had two families, Melina.'

Melina couldn't speak. Her words burned in her throat.

Warrington continued, 'You have a half-brother near my age. And your father has daughters here. If we are to go to his house tomorrow, I know you will probably see them, his wife or their portraits. You'd find out. It's better to know before.'

She jerked free from Warrington. 'Yes. It's best you told me. I will have the whole night to hate him more.'

He stood silently, watching.

'How many children—here—does my father have?' she asked.

'Four, I believe. Maybe only three.' He paused. 'I believe one may have taken ill and died. I'm not sure.'

She heard her voice and the bitterness she couldn't conceal. 'Do they have the birthmark, as well? The one like we have.' She touched the mud-coloured bodice where the mark hid beneath.

'Not that I am aware of. Well, perhaps the son has a small spot near his ear.' He squinted, thinking. 'I'm not sure.'

On Melos, she'd never considered her father could be married to someone else. Maybe a mistress, but not a marriage. She'd seen the seamen dock. Many of them had sweethearts or family somewhere else, but her father had seemed different. He stayed for long stretches of time and he loved his painting. He hardly had time for anything else.

'He *had* to take his paintings to England to

sell.' She held her hand out, palm up. 'I should have known.'

'Not everyone has a wondrous family. Even kings.'

'I will tell him what I really think of him and the daubs of paint he calls *techni*. But you heard the man at Somerset House. They are not true art.'

He pulled her back into his grasp, and although his arm was around her, she felt no comfort. The coldness inside her blended with a hot anger boiling into her chest and arms and forehead, causing spikes of pain behind her eyes.

He didn't speak at first. 'The wife's father supported the family while he lived, but when he died, he left all his funds to a favourite nephew. Not a pound to his only child. The father trusted the nephew to allow the daughter to control the funds. The nephew inherited the wealth and made a great show of letting Hawkins's wife have freedom with her father's funds. I suppose the men made an agreement before the old man died.'

Melina shuddered. 'But *my* father would not care about who has the purse. As long as he has pigment and canvas, he is happy.'

Warrington turned sideways and pulled her chin so she had to look at him. 'Perhaps not. A man expects to control the purse strings since a woman's property becomes the husband's on marriage. When your father found out his wife didn't inherit, it's said he had to be restrained. His father-in-law had given Hawkins a grand slap.'

She stared at the harpoon and thought of the man she knew on the island. 'I would not be surprised if Melos was his revenge. If he stayed with us to punish the woman in England. Just enough to annoy but not enough to enrage.' She shook her head.

'I understand it better than you might think—parts of it, anyway. My wife, Cassandra... I think, even our son, Jacob, the heir she'd had for me, and perhaps even the little girl, were merely tools for her to use.'

'If you are saying you know what it is like when someone doesn't care for their children—still, it doesn't make me feel better. My sisters. My mother. He forgot about us.'

'My wife—forgot about me.' He dropped Melina's hand. His voice hardened. 'No, she didn't forget. She didn't care. She left when I was ill and came home carrying another man's child. And she begged my forgiveness—because it was going to be impossible for me to think the child was mine. I was sick, grieving for my father, angry at her for leaving me when I was about to die. I hated her, and yet I could not stop myself from wanting her. She was silken, soft, alluring—when she wanted something—and she wanted to be back in my home, as I had not heard a word from her in months and I severely curtailed her funds. Besides, how powerful she must have felt, knowing I hated what she had done, knew the child was not mine and yet I still desired her. But I had conditions on her return and I insisted she meet them.'

He stood and his words became soft. 'And I hurt the night she died... That was the worst part of all. How could I feel sadness when I was free from such a person? I should have gone out and celebrated. I *mourned* and was disgusted with myself for it.'

He turned back to her, letting his arm rest on the back of the sofa. His knee touched hers. With his arm still aligned on the back of the furniture, he reached out his other hand. 'Yet sometimes I think I miss her. That is the oddest part and makes me the most angry.'

He ran his forefinger along her arm. 'I tell you about my wife so you will know you are not the only one betrayed. That I have experienced disloyalty, too, and I don't want you alone in this.'

She crossed her arms around herself. 'My father is alive and he has no care of his treatment of us.' She shuddered. 'Not even a letter to see if we lived or died. Perhaps that is part of the reason I had to travel to England. If I'd merely wanted to escape Stephanos, I could possibly have found a French sailor from one of the vessels in the harbour. And I could have used them to send a message to the museum in France.'

'I would hope you are pleased you chose *Ascalon*.'

'*Malista*. Yes.' She looked to the rain-splattered window.

He stared at her, his mouth straight. He took her hand, his grasp overpowering her. He pulled her to stand in front of him and the room was silent. He touched her cheek and held her arms. 'I *am* better than the French sailors.'

Even though she felt no true joy, her lips did curl up. 'I said you were better.'

'Not with conviction.'

'You're an earl.'

His voice was petal soft. 'And, sweet, you're a goddess. You outrank me.'

Chapter Thirteen

Melina's fingers traced the delicate lace at the capped sleeves of the dress the seamstress had brought that morning. This gown was more colourful—only because the brown was darker and the ribbon bows at the sleeves were pink. The dress fit better, too, and the fabric was silk. Her birthmark showed at the edge of her bodice, peeking out, reminding her of her link to her sisters. She had asked the seamstress to make sure the mark showed.

When Warrington first saw her in the garment, he took a step backwards.

The step might have concerned her, except the look in his eyes could have lit a candle, and it caused an answering flame to spark deep within her stomach.

And she felt stronger, just from the way he looked at her. A woman might grow used to such attention. She walked towards him. He smiled.

Even the silk against her felt more luxurious when his eyes brushed over her.

Warrington hurried her to the hackney. He'd said a chaperon wasn't necessary, as they'd keep the shades drawn in the carriage and not be in public.

As the vehicle lumbered along, Melina could not help stealing glances at the street. The houses. She could not believe a world of so much opulence and then, sometimes, such sad people trudging along. And young boys dressed in tatters. Running freely. Without parents nearby.

The vehicle stopped in front of a home and she looked out. She had to gasp to get a breath of air.

'Is a king's home as big at this?' she asked, not taking her eyes from the grandeur. This creation was someone's masterpiece. Birds flew from a small fountain and a tree had low branches spreading out gracefully, like welcoming arms. Each blade of grass looked exactly as if an artist painted it.

'Yes,' he answered. 'And as far as I know Hawkins doesn't have a country house, only this one.' He moved out of the conveyance and reached back to lend her his hand.

'I would say it is enough.' She put her foot on the lowered platform from the side of the hackney and slid her gloved fingertips into his outstretched hand. 'I was impressed when I saw your home.

Five families could live in the town house. The whole of Melos could live in this one.'

'But Hawkins doesn't truly own it. His wife's family does.'

Melina stopped her footsteps and looked to Warrington, raising a brow. 'So could she toss him from it?'

'I doubt it would be that simple.' He put a hand at her back. 'Besides, it doesn't matter. A woman who wants to make her husband unhappy does better to stay at his side.'

She moved up the steps of the grand house— comparing the mansion to the rooms she'd lived in her whole life.

Melina stopped for a moment, thankful the knowledge of her father's life never reached Melos. At least, she hoped her mother never knew.

While she remained at the door, unable to move forward, Warrington stood beside her, one palm on the small of her back. He reached towards the gleaming knocker. He gave two quick raps.

She sighed, movement exaggerated. 'The poor man. Living in a sad state such as this. Nothing to do all day but the one thing he loves. He didn't travel to Melos for revenge. You don't leave riches to live as he did. He is truly mad for his art.'

He patted the small of her back.

When the butler opened the door, Warrington gave the servant a nod. Warrington's hand slid to Melina's side as he walked into the house. He moved between her and the butler, and she had no choice but to step with him. Melina noted the scent of paint. Even after artwork dried enough to be hung, it could be months before the lingering smell of the pigments left it. And she imagined in this house, the scents never completely left.

The entrance was crisp and even the plants she saw placed near the windows knew to grow straight and tall. Not a one leaned one way or the other, or dared a yellowed leaf.

The butler's face took in awareness of Warrington's commanding stride and his determined entry into the house. The servant's eyes narrowed.

Warrington gave the servant a card.

'Lord Hawkins is not at home,' the butler intoned, 'to anyone.'

'I must see him—about a painting of his.' War's voice—soft, a jagged caress of the words. 'I might wish to purchase it if he has it.'

The butler's eyes never changed emotion, but a muscle in his jaw tensed. He appraised Warrington, and Warrington moved his body forward, letting strength add volume to his words.

'I am *the* Earl of Warrington,' he said. 'Tell Robert I am here.'

The butler opened his mouth, but before he could speak, Warrington leaned in, shortening the distance between their faces to little more than a breath. 'You'd want me angry less than you'd want the artist upset.'

The servant stilled and the line of his jaw stiffened, and his eyelids dropped to half mast. She didn't have to look at Warrington to know how he appeared. She could feel the challenge in him from the tone of his words. The breadth of his shoulders gave emphasis to everything he spoke.

'Of course. Follow me.'

A stairway rose, with the hand-carved banister made to look like twisting ropes feeling cool under her touch. And candles. She'd never seen so many lamps at the ready.

The servant led them to a sitting room and marched away without looking back.

'I fancy hiring him right out from under Hawkins...' Warrington led her to a sofa and pressed a hand on her shoulder, increasing pressure until she sat '...except Broomer would have laughed had someone tried that with him. And he would have done something accidental—such as stepping on the man's foot and crushing his toes.'

He leaned in towards her, touched her chin and turned her face to him. 'You're his daughter. His flesh and blood. You have power, too. While it won't destroy an artist to have it known he has a second family, he can't relish his other children knowing.'

Her eyes moved to the walls and she saw the painting over the fireplace. Without thinking, she stood, her gaze locked on the artwork. Talons shredded her insides and she gasped. The painting above the fireplace. Melos. The houses with barns at the base. The olive trees. And shadows in the background, children playing. The shape of her mother sitting on a bench, watching the girls. She remembered that painting and the day.

Melina turned. Anger replaced the pain.

As she opened her mouth, Warrington spoke. 'Quite a good likeness.' His words flowed with a silkiness Melina had not heard from him before. 'I am impressed.' He tipped his head in acknowledgement. He captured Melina's fingertips.

The rich timbre of Warrington's voice broke into the fog in her mind. 'Painted your home on Melos quite well. I can hear the sea in the distance.'

'How dare he?' Melina could not take her eyes from the wall. He'd captured her world exactly, and she could see a woman in the shadows—a woman who watched three girls digging caves in the dirt with seashells. 'My *mother.*'

'I suppose some people dare anything.'

She shifted her eyes to the mantel and nodded in that direction. 'The one candlestick. The one candlestick—he could have sold it and had enough money to feed us for a very long time. I know it was difficult to get funds to us and he had to make the trek himself to know that it was done. But he'd managed enough before, even with a war going on.' She leaned in. 'Even with a war. He convinced the seamen he was French when he wished to. A penniless French painter who spoke sparsely because the words twisted in his mouth. A man hoping to make a few coins to feed his family. Neither side must have cared much about an artist.'

She sighed. 'I am thankful I did not know the truth then. I might have been tempted to tell the sailors on the man-o'-war my father was a spy. Except it would have hurt my mother. She believed him a great artist. She loved him.' She said the last words and couldn't stop the derision of her voice when she said the word *love*.

Her father walked into the room. Melina would not have recognised him had they passed on the streets of London.

Gone was the scruffy, unkempt look of the island. Now he had the look of a gentleman artist. The only thing unchanged was his turpentine scent from the brush cleaner. He had a cloth in his hands and kept scrubbing at daubs of pigment even as he looked at Melina.

'Your paintings must be selling quite well,' she said to her father, realising they were strangers. But maybe they'd always been such.

At first, he stared at her as if he knew he should recognise her, but didn't—then he looked to choke, and then he stared at Warrington and back at Melina.

'You.' Her father's voice filled with accusation. 'What are *you* doing here?'

His eyes—his eyes flashed something darker than when his work was disturbed. They showed the same emotion from the day her sister knocked one of the wet paintings into the dirt and that day had lasted for a fortnight.

He was her father, but not the same man from Melos. His hair, even more streaked with silver than before, surprised her with its perfect grooming. The points of his collar were starched and even the flowing covering he wore over his clothes had been cared for—even though it sported a palette of its own.

She wanted the tension in her body to fade, but she shuddered deep within her heart. The man she'd known on the island was gone for ever. He might have never lived.

Her father looked back over his shoulder and spoke to someone in the hallway who Melina couldn't see. 'Leave us.' He tossed the paint-splattered cloth to the floor. 'Why...' The words came out as if jerked from his soul. 'Why are you in my home?'

She could see the next words forming in his mind to tell her to leave, so she sat. Warrington stood beside her, staring at the other man.

'My muse will be destroyed for days because you have disturbed me.' Her father raised a hand, as if orating for a crowd. 'The stem is not quite right on the dog roses and the honeysuckle is life-less. But my *bee orchis* is perfect. It truly looks like little bees clinging to the stem and I have captured that.' He turned to her, smugness in his eyes. 'No. I will not let you destroy my work today.'

'I know your work is everything to you, Father. I have no quarrel with that.'

'You shouldn't, Melina.' His grey hair fell across his brow.

'Truly. I never cared painting came first in your life. *Mana* didn't, either. It was the natural order for us. The art came first to you. Always. But she should have been second. I hope you received my letter saying *Mana* died. She did not recover.'

His eyes flashed, perhaps guilt, but then he shuddered, shutting away the emotion. 'I knew she was to die. And it would have hurt me too much to see her suffer.'

Darkness clouded Melina's vision and stole her voice. The image of her mother, eyes hollow, cheekbones with only flesh across them, lying in bed, and the whole world around her falling into nothingness, flared into Melina's memory. 'It would have hurt *you*?' She controlled her words. 'How do you think it was for her? To be abandoned when she needed you most.'

'She understood. She told me to go.'

'She might have understood. I understood. You would not waste a moment on something or someone if it was not to your advantage. And she may have told you to go, but she wanted you to stay. It would have showed you cared.'

'My art is from my core spirit. It cannot be interrupted.'

'But…' she tilted her head to the side and forced her words calm '…think how much your work would have improved if you had had an added measure of grief to draw on. Now you have lost that chance for ever. Your work can never be what it could have.'

His cheeks reddened and his voice rose. 'That is ludicrous. I have felt grief. I know the emotion well and my paintings show the depth of the human soul.'

'No. They don't. They show the depth of your soul and it doesn't go very deep.'

He jabbed one finger towards her face. 'You are lying. You are not to speak so to me. I am your father.'

'Father?' She filled the word with derision. 'Father? What does that word mean? Tell me.'

'I gave you life. And you must respect me for it.'

'No. I do not. I may have respected you when I was a child, but then I knew no better. I esteemed *Mana*. The only mistake she made in her life was in caring for you.'

'I was the best thing for her. She was a Greek peasant.'

'Worth ten—ten thousand more paintings than you could ever create.'

'You have no true knowledge of art. You are here crying to me because you are weak. Did you not take care of her as you should? Did you not see that she had what she needed? Are you feeling in the wrong because *you* did not do what was necessary at the end?'

Melina's whole body shook. Her face burned and her fingers clenched.

An arm snaked around her waist, holding her. Warrington stood beside her. She caught her breath. 'We did all we could. And you did nothing but throw colours on to canvas a world away. That takes no true talent.'

'My painting is art. It was what she wanted. She knew the truth of art. She saw the value of it. You do not. You see nothing beyond your selfish spirit.'

'Selfish spirit? You left us without enough for food, and yet you live like this?' She waved her hand.

His nose went up and his lids lowered as he looked at her. 'It is not mine to give.'

'My sisters need funds,' she continued. '*Proika*. A dowry. They should not have to rely on scraping the earth and hoping rocks grow food so we can eat.'

'I do not give you funds because it is time you each learned to stand on your own legs, not toddle about like children looking for a teat. You should all have wed before now.'

'We have no dowry.'

'Bah...' He shook his head. 'Do not tell me the men of the island cannot overlook that. I am well aware of how they think. You three could each find a husband if you wished. It is only your haughty airs that keep you from it. When you get hungry enough, you will learn what I mean.'

She appraised him. 'We are better off without you. When you left us, I was angry. I thought we needed you. Now I see. We didn't. We were fortunate you left.'

'Melina.' Her father's voice sounded the familiar angry bark he used when disrupted. His eyes flashed. 'You know nothing of life. On the island—it is a different world than England. My marriage to your mother is not legal here and I have no call to support you, now that you are of age. And you have no right to speak so to me. A man has to have a woman. Especially an artist. We must have our senses fulfilled to continue to create. It's nature. And your mother is dead. My life on the island is gone from me.'

She paused and listened to her own words as she spoke them. Hearing her truth as he heard it. 'When I was a child, I had hoped I would some day visit England with you. I worked so hard on my speech and my letters. I am here now and it's not as I expected. You do not have to worry I think of you as my father. One cannot keep what one never had. So I will not miss you.'

Hawkins stepped forward. He stopped only an arm's length from her and he turned to Warrington. 'It doesn't matter who you are.' His words came out as a snarl. 'I will not have it. I don't know what she told you—and how she convinced you to bring her here. Say what you wish—I cannot stop you. But get her out of my home. You will not sully my house.'

'Melina—' Warrington said.

'Don't talk of this.' The man spat out the words and then stepped back. 'Get out. Now.'

Warrington leaned into Hawkins's face. 'You don't deserve her for a daughter and she deserves better.'

Hawkins stepped backwards, to the door. 'I want her gone.' The plain words bit into the room. Hawkins couldn't seem to stand still. He moved a step sideways, huffed a breath and then paced the other direction. 'Gone. Keep your distance from my family. I don't want my—' He turned to Melina. 'You are most distracting. You always were. I do not know why I ever painted you.'

He'd just given her one of his most severe cuts—she was not worthy to be captured on canvas.

Moving quicker than Melina thought possible, Warrington grasped her father's clothing at the neck and pulled the man forward.

'You will support your daughters.' His words were a command.

'No.' She lurched forward, tugging at Warrington's arm, but it didn't move. 'No,' she shouted again. 'I will find another way.' The statue. 'I want nothing from him. Nothing.'

She wrapped both hands over Warrington's sleeve, holding him.

Warrington stopped, jerking his head to indicate the painting. 'How much for that?'

Her father's eyes moved up and he looked above the fireplace. 'It's not one of my favourites. I can hardly stomach it.'

'Price?' Warrington demanded, voice slamming into the walls.

The muscles moved in her father's face. 'I plan to throw it in a rubbish heap.'

'Nonsense. It has small value. Even life has small value—sometimes. Such as yours—now.'

Hawkins waved his hand. 'You may have it. Burn it. It means nothing to me.'

Warrington released him. Hawkins fled the room. Within moments, a door slammed in a distant part of the house.

'Warrington.' She stepped forward, putting her palms flat to his chest, holding firm enough she felt heartbeats pounding through his silk waistcoat. 'Let us leave. I cannot bear another moment of the scent of fresh paint.'

He moved, taking the artwork under one arm,

and put his other hand at her back, walking her through the doorway.

Melina stepped into the hall and a woman stood just beyond the open door, staring. Her hair was pulled into a silver chignon. She wore at least four rings on each hand and each jewel outweighed the finger holding it.

She gave Melina a wavering smile. 'Hope you had a pleasant visit, dear. My husband rarely sees visitors this time of day.'

Melina caught herself before she said *I know.* Warrington touched the small of her back, nudging her forward. She took a step, snagging the hem of her dress under her shoe, making a small stumble. Warrington caught her elbow. 'Careful, sweet.'

'Do you need a cup of tea before you go?' The older woman stood directly in Melina's path, but her eyes showed only kindness.

Warrington gave a bow to the woman. 'My pardon…' his voice caressed the words '…as we must be on our way. We have…duties to return to.'

'I understand.' She smiled at Warrington and moved back. 'I hope your trip home is pleasant.' Then she looked at War, puzzlement in her face. 'I believe I was acquainted with your mother before she passed on. The Countess of Warrington?'

'Yes,' Warrington agreed and shepherded Melina out through the doorway.

Melina walked without another mishap to the stairway, but even though her steps were sure, her mind stumbled.

She'd just met the woman her father had married long before her mother and now Warrington had a painting—the only one she knew of that had her mother and her sisters in it.

She tried to get comfortable in the carriage seat, wishing the air didn't seem so thick and hard to breathe. Her father's rage hadn't really surprised her. If he'd acted any other way, that would have been unexpected.

Warrington handed her the painting, but she didn't look at it.

'Of course it's yours.' The calmness of his voice told her he'd been prepared for the fury. But then, he also knew of the older man.

'I suppose I must take it. I don't know, though.' She tilted the art to him. 'The house you see plain. But we are in the shadows. Fitting.'

'If you don't want it, I'll safeguard it for you.'

She held it in front of her face. 'I know the woman is my mother.' She let the artwork fall against her chest. 'I don't remember another picture he painted of her. He did one of each of my sisters, and one of me, but none of my mother. That should have told us something, I suppose.'

'At least he cared enough to capture your likeness.'

She grimaced. 'He said art with people in it sold better—an observer might feel something for them.'

The carriage jostled along and she tried to get the sound of her father's voice from her mind. 'I would rather have the stone I left buried on Melos than this painting.'

'I saw the arm you brought on board.' He looked at her. 'I think you've convinced yourself of the chunk having worth. It's the offering you wanted to give to your father to please him after he left you and your sisters. To show him you'd found something of the past. A value. Something from another artist.'

She put her hand to the small ledge of the window. The clashes of her feelings threw her into turmoil.

'You didn't see the expression on the face of the statue.' She pushed her mind to form the correct words, but wasn't sure she knew them. 'Simple rock became the same as my own skin. Rock—became flesh. The fingers. They—' She held up one hand, flexing, twisting her wrist, watching the movement. 'The sight of her—you could feel life—as if you could blink and look again, and her eyes had changed. The carving started as lifeless stone and then someone touched it, and it became alive.'

He caressed the strand of Melina's hair that had fallen again from where she'd tucked it. His fingers wove into the locks, making her breath flutter. 'Melina, you've more life in this wisp than anything made by man.'

Warrington turned, bringing his body closer to her, and lightly touched both sides of her face. The scent of shaving soap and crisp wool surrounded her.

'No painting or creation from things of the earth could ever reach out to a man as a woman's whisper against his cheek.' He gave a half smile. 'Truly, she could be someone he never wished to see again, but in the right moments he'd still be more impressed than with any art.'

'You are talking of simple lust. To feel art is different.'

He nodded, and by the slant of his lips she could tell he placed no store in it.

'Stone, Melina.' He straightened in his seat. 'Art compares little to life. When my son, Jacob, forgets himself and runs to me, showing me a stick that is nothing but a twig, but for some reason he thinks it is shaped like a bird, that makes any decoration in a house seem meaningless. And the reason the statue means something to you is because you hoped for her to rescue you.'

Melina remembered the agony she'd felt when her mother knew, even though she was sick, that her father wouldn't stay. 'Some believe capturing the likeness helps the person live on. True art,' she murmured. 'Not the captain's mermaids. Or probably even the paintings of my father. But when you look at a sculpture or a painting and you can see thoughts in the face of the person the artist captured… You know the pull of their heart. The dreams they have. You feel something.'

'Melina, I can feel the thoughts of the fish women.'

She shuddered. 'A different kind of painting— but it does speak to Captain Ben—although the things they say are vulgar.'

He smiled, eyes crinkling. 'True.'

'I care for the statue I found. It's as if she has the same heart I do and she's waiting to be freed from her hiding place.'

'The statue is still as you left it and it is cold and feels nothing.' He talked softly, and in the same tone he must have used with his son. 'Forget the marble. Forget your father.' He studied her, his own face concerned. If not for the painting in her hands, she would have leaned into him. Would have put herself against his chest and felt his compassion.

She shook her head, a lock of hair again falling across her eyes and tickling her. 'Father once said he wept when he saw beautiful art. And he had some small pieces. One a sculpture of a Madonna. One a miniature of a woman and a painting only about half the length of my hand—so small, and the woman looked so alive you could have recognised her had she walked into the room. Our home was plain, and to see those things…'

'I know what you're saying, but it's not the same for me, I suppose. The paintings at Somerset House. A nice way to spend the afternoon, admiring them. But…'

'The piece I left behind on the island. I care for her. Both her arms broken and now one lost for ever. Because I did not safeguard it.'

'It wasn't meant to be, Melina. Leave the woman buried. Let her rest.'

'Her face— My mother died before I found the bits of carving. When I dug down, scraping the dirt from the statue, I saw my mother's likeness look back at me.' She took in a shuddering breath. 'I must have this woman unearthed. She cannot remain buried. She should live.'

'It won't bring back your mother.'

Her eyes locked on his. 'Perhaps my grandmother posed for it. Or her mother. So long ago that she's been forgotten. And that is why the stone must be rescued. The woman cannot be left buried. She is so near the surface. I brushed the dirt free from her with my hands. She's ready to return into the world.'

Melina had tucked the statue back into the broken archway and covered her, hiding her. But she had to go back to Melos to save the woman. The thought of the likeness lying buried another hundred years was too much to bear. Melina couldn't imagine how long the art had been concealed. And how, at one time, someone must not have cared. She'd heard of a war fought on the island long, long before. She imagined the invading army must have knocked the archway to the ground. Or perhaps time itself. She could not be sure why anyone would leave such a work. But now Melina knew she needed to get the woman freed from her grave.

She had to escape the world her father lived in and return to Melos.

'Ben will take you to her.'

'I thank you. My sisters. I cannot abandon them as my father did. I cannot leave the likeness of my mother buried. And I will not tell them all the truth about our father. I would like to tell them he fell on a paintbrush and met a fitful end.'

'Be honest. They are not children.'

'Perhaps. Perhaps they can understand it better than I. Thessa, my middle sister, has already said we should forget him. Bellona, the youngest, truly hates him. She doesn't remember when he was kind, only the way he was at the last. And she'll not forgive him for leaving our mother when she was ill.'

She wanted the statue—whether it was worth all she imagined, or nothing. She'd found it and she wished to have an expert examine it. To tell her that her eyes were right.

The dowry—she'd thought it her only reason

to care for the statue. But, no. The stone woman had something in her eyes telling Melina she must be freed. Melina had to get her from the dirt. The woman had to be rescued in the same way a living, breathing person would. The same way Melina would have saved her mother if she could have.

The carriage stopped.

'Leave the painting on the seat. I'll make sure the hackney waits for us, Melina.'

'Where are we?' she asked.

'The British Museum. I wanted you to have a chance to talk with the man about what you've found.'

Chapter Fourteen

When they left the museum to return to Warrington's home, Melina fought waves of despair. The curator could promise her nothing. He could form no opinion. Of course, he would like to be the first to see the find, but he must inspect it and have the statue examined by others before he could even guess at its worth.

She stepped back into the carriage, Warrington following behind. Pulling the painting into her arms, she rested her chin on the gilt edge of the frame. 'I want to get London behind me. To forget my father's ways and find a way to take care of my sisters. I fear that when I go back, Stephanos will have already noticed them because I have left. I warned them many times not to go near him. He pirates for Greece. He plunders and gives the funds to the island, and to people who are planning to overthrow the Turks. If he is caught, it would be dangerous to be his wife.'

She held her hand out to brace herself on the window facing, and then looked over her shoulder. 'Before Father left, he told me Stephanos would make a good protector for me and I would be able to take care of my sisters. Yet he knew of Stephanos's trips at sea and the risk of being seen as too close to him.'

She half turned to Warrington. 'Father would never have emptied our mother's slop bucket. Or his own. They would have overflowed.'

'I am thankful for the pails, Melina. I believed I had learned my lesson. I would not let a woman's face or body move me should I not wish it. And on a miserable ship when I had no desire in me until I saw you, I was burning to get you to my bed.' His booted foot kicked the inside of the carriage across from him. 'On the blasted ship—I was back at the mercy of a woman's body again. Smelly slop buckets. Ridicule from the mates. And *you* turned out to be…not what I expected. I cannot trust myself to know a woman's true heart. True person.'

'Don't you feel you know me?'

He moved, taking in a breath in such a way he pulled from her. 'I'm not sure. And it doesn't matter, even if I knew. I cannot exorcise the past I helped create, but I must make sure my son has what he needs for the future. I want to go home to Jacob—need to go home to see my son. But I can't yet.' Warrington's eyes firmed on to something in his memories. 'I have to talk with Cassandra's sister. I want to know who the girl's father is. To see if he knows of the babe, though I would think he does. When Cass returned home, most couldn't have easily guessed she was with child—though I suspected the moment I saw her face. She'd changed. And the date of the birth was not something any of us wanted made note of.'

His hands curled into fists. 'I woke up one morning on *Ascalon*. I wished for the sound of Jacob's voice. Before too many years pass, he'll have a man's words. I'm going to lose my little boy whether I wish it or not and I was on a ship, sailing farther and farther from my own responsibilities.'

He brushed a moth from inside the carriage and it fluttered and found another resting place of darkness. 'I feel nothing for the little girl. I keep lingering here, finding reasons to stay. Because I don't want to return home and face a child who looks like my wife and looks nothing like me. I have to get her from Whitegate.'

'You can't leave a child with no parents.' She turned back to the window and indicated the street. 'I see the children here, and even though we had nothing on Melos, everyone had the same nothing. Some of the little ones here barely have clothing hanging on their thin bodies.'

'She'll have her needs met. But before I make any decision, I have to find the child's father. But

I can't leave her with him. He is the one who tried to kill me.'

She turned to Warrington's face, the dim interior of the carriage changing the brown eyes into obsidian.

'But you don't fear him now.'

'No. I'm careful in darkness, and besides…' He laughed and reached to his boot, pulling a short dagger from a scabbard sewn into the leather. When he held it up, his hand covered the hilt, but the blade was twice the length of the handle. 'Cassandra may be at rest, but she's not one to sleep quietly. When the man stabbed me, he approached from behind, a fortnight after Cass's death. I turned and grabbed his wrist, taking us down, and the weapon fell aside.'

He spoke his next words as if they meant nothing. 'I can't forget what he shouted over his shoulder as he ran. "Mind my daughter". The man stopped my movement with his words—words with the sound of the street in them.'

He stared forward. 'I've small scars about my body of no particular note, which I don't even think of, but I don't like the thin line on my back. A mark Cass left—even though it wasn't her hand holding the blade.' He touched the edge against his thumb, feeling for the crispness that let him know the blade remained razor fine. 'You can't toss aside a weapon that wounded you so easily. It's not a talisman to bring me luck. I saved it to remind me I survived. But I haven't yet.' His laughter barely reached her ears. 'Never, ever will I return to the abyss of my life before. Not again.'

His eyes locked on her. 'You must understand, Melina. I learned my weakness. Learned it well and I won't risk returning there—to that. I am meant to be alone.'

He let his legs stretch long and leaned his head back, resting against the leather squabs, eyes shut. 'My brother is watching my home and he knows of the attack. I hired two extra servants who have no other job than to make sure my country home is not breached. Cass used to say I imagined too much. How many times she told me.' He snorted and opened his eyes, staring at Melina. 'I never imagined my wife would find so many diversions to pursue. I never imagined she would have someone else's child when I was ill. I should have believed every suspicion I had and it still would not have touched the wicked truth.'

'Leave her in the past.'

'I can't. She left too much of herself behind.' He reached out, pushing back the painting from Melina's body and viewing the art. 'The shadows. What was real for me was only shadows for her. Moments meaning little. *What fools we mortals be.* That saying I remember. I had my golden princess and I put her above all else in my heart. I have had many nights to reflect on my foolishness.'

Taking Melina's hand from the side of the art, he pulled her knuckles to his lips. His kiss touched her and then he released her hand. 'Even when I look at you, Melina, I keep wondering if you somehow convinced me of your virginity when it wasn't true. I wonder if you secretly plan to go back to the island to see Stephanos.'

'I have been honest with you.'

'It really doesn't matter. I tried to turn lies into truths for so long, I don't know how to care one way or the other. I can never trust another with that child in my house to remind me what has happened. I'm sure whoever Cassandra dallied with—her sister knows. When Cass left my house, she lived with Daphne.'

He turned to Melina and his eyes had a raggedness she'd only seen in her mother's face before she died. Melina's fingers tightened around the picture frame as the carriage pulled to Warrington's house.

'I know I must find him.' His words were precise. 'I *will* find him. And then I will kill him.'

Warrington stepped from the carriage after it stopped, reached in and took the painting, and with his free hand he helped her on to the steps.

She saw no anger in his face—no emotion at all. His grip on her hand was light. When he released her fingers, he took a coin and tossed it to the driver and gave a wave to send the vehicle on its way.

'I've already sent a message to Daphne and Ludgate telling them I've returned and asking if they can spare a few moments before I go to my country house.' He walked ahead, unconcerned. 'It will be good to see them again.'

She thought of the words he'd said. She had no doubt he meant to murder the father of the little girl. And she could not let it happen. Except for stabbing Warrington, the man was no different than her father. Warrington would be leaving the child without either parent. He would have blood on his hands and another scar, which might be even deeper than the first and harder to ignore.

Chapter Fifteen

Warrington marched inside the doorway. Broomer gave them both a deferential nod and he had the expression of a perfectly trained butler. But the hair standing up on his head gave him the look of just having rolled from bed and he smelled of lilacs. When he took Warrington's coat, a lopsided grin broke out on the servant's face.

Melina moved up the stairs and Warrington followed. In the sitting room, he stopped, staring at the harpoon. He moved his eyes to the mantel, the room tinged with evening's shadows. 'Let me see how your painting looks there, Melina.'

She stared at the art in her hands. At first he didn't think she would agree. Then she placed the picture against the mantel long enough to take down the other one and exchange them.

An explosion of conflicting emotions rushed through his veins, taking him by surprise. Such a simple act she'd performed and it caused an ache in him. And ache for a woman's care in his world. For completion of the ephemeral dream he'd once had of having a helpmate. A woman who was another part of himself.

He could not let the feelings take hold in himself again. But when he saw Melina stand back from the fireplace and look at the likeness of her family, he ached inside. It was too late. He wanted the dark-haired beauty. But now he had enough control he could keep himself from folly.

'Warrington.' Melina strode to his side. 'You are not concerned that I am alone in your house and you've invited people who might see me?'

He let out a slow breath. 'No. Daphne knows of my trials. We've shared letters. Before Cass died, Daphne visited Whitegate to help Cassandra's spirits when she was going to have a third child. This one mine. Only the sisters seemed at cross purposes with each other. They argued. Cassandra locked herself in her bedchamber and refused to speak to us. Daphne left and Cassandra died a few days later. Daphne wrote to me of the sadness she felt because their last words had been unpleasant.' He huffed out a breath. 'I think my wife awaited the third birth with the same joy I had of the second.'

'Daphne was caught between loyalties,' Melina said.

'She tried to warn me before I even proposed to Cass. I perceived Daphne jealous then. I believed Cass wanted to marry me, not my title.' He turned to Melina and shrugged. 'Titles are handy things—if you don't expect too much of them.'

He moved close to the wall and touched the harpoon. 'Like this, I suppose. Nice to have at rare times. Completely useless in daily life.' He turned to her. 'And I have a child in my house. A child who means nothing to me but a memory of betrayal. My illness. My father's death. All seem tied in the little one's face when I see her.'

'Even your father's death? You jest?' She stepped within reach of him.

'No. I am tall enough that if I walk into a hovel, I will have to bend my head, but an imp no higher than my knee has conquered me, her innocent face a trumpet blaring the past. She makes me remember—when all I want is a new beginning.' He raised his brows and shook his head at the same time. 'I cannot return to Whitegate because of the child Cass left behind. When my wife was alive, I pretended the little girl didn't exist. But I can't now. And she reminds me of everything bad of my old life. And the suspicion I have that I still don't know everything that happened under my roof.'

'You tell me your wife had a child by another man. What more could there be?' She took his hand.

At first, he ignored her question. Instead, he pulled her fingers to his lips to brush a light kiss against her wrist. He caught the scent of her soap and his mind flashed back to the memory of childhood innocence and the sweetness of his youth. Before his mother died and his father re-married. When his life had held the promise of every difficulty being no higher than his knee. Before he realised the littlest-sized hurdle could be the biggest to overcome.

He shook his head. 'I tell myself I'm wrong—and perhaps I am.' He took her arms and moved her aside so he could leave. 'But I believe I'd not even suspected the evilness in my home until now. I believe Cass had a secret that died with her.'

'What?' Melina stood so close. He would not have had to take a step to pull her against him for comfort. But he couldn't.

He had brought Cassandra into his life. And the part that still confused him was that he didn't think she'd loved him, but she'd not hated him, either. He felt certain she'd not hated him.

He needed to be alone. To think clearly. Without memories haunting him or the lustre of Melina's eyes.

And now his hopes were fixing on Melina. A woman whose face caught the light with inten-sity. Melina had an allure of another world. He could not let an impossible illusion take over his life again.

He shrugged. 'I suppose I can feel another storm coming and it gives me unease. I've not put her to rest yet. I wanted to bury her memory in the sea. I came home—but then I realised I had brought you, another lovely woman. The child is still here. The scar. Everything is just as I left it, only perhaps bigger.'

He walked to the window, peering through the opening between the draperies.

'No platitudes?' he asked. 'No sympathy?'

'No.'

'I left Whitegate when Cass returned after her adventure and did not go back until shortly after the birth. I decided I didn't want a whole nest of other men's children popping up around me. I made my view clear—and I delivered my rules if she wished to stay. And she became faithful. Not by choice, I'm sure. A carriage wheel would not turn without my approval. Nor could she sneeze without my being made aware of it.'

He could see nothing but bare shapes in the dark. He pulled the curtains wide, but the moonlight was hidden behind clouds. 'I tried to go back to where we were. To start over. I tried every day. Every night.'

He breathed in the blackness around him, putting his palms flat on the panes, feeling the coolness, wondering what would happen if he let his strength go and he pushed.

'It's not her I hate. It's myself. I loved her. And I wanted her to have another child. This one mine.' His heartbeats almost made him unable to hear his words. 'She was a wanton of the first water, and after the girl was born Cassandra had to have another child for me. It was one of the many conditions I made for her to continue to live in my world. She loved the illusion around us and wanted it to continue.'

He turned. He wanted to leave the memories he'd pulled back into his thoughts. He already felt the shortness of breath and the darkness so thick he had to push himself to move through it. He had to leave the room. 'I hope you have pleasant dreams, Melina.'

Melina watched Warrington leave, seemingly unaware of the world around him except for the shapes he needed to avoid to keep moving. If ghosts were real, the spirit of Cassandra would have been walking along with him. She didn't believe in any kind of supernatural beings, except perhaps goddesses, but that didn't mean his wife wasn't still with him, as strongly as ever before.

She just wanted to touch him and comfort him. Putting her arms around him might not truly soothe him, but for that moment, he would know he wasn't alone with his memories.

Curling herself into a chair, Melina imagined the life he'd lived. She would have thought his wealth made everything simple. But it hadn't. Even now, as she tried not to think about the things of her past, she couldn't. And she'd not had Warrington's heartbreak. The betrayal.

Melina looked at the brown garment she wore
and knew Warrington had wanted the frock made
in such a fashion. Touching the sleeve, she ran
her hand over it. A soft garment, but still a hideous sack.

In Melos, even a grandmother would not make
such colourless clothes. If Melina wished to be
unseen, all she'd have to do was stand close to a
wooden wall. The strangling undergarment the
dressmaker had forced on her made no difference
because it didn't matter how much her stomach
was pulled to nothingness and her breasts were
pushed up, out and over, the brown concealed
everything.

She remained in the room, thinking about betrayal, until the darkness surrounded her with
the same pressure of the suffocating cabin walls
from the ship. Moving to the mermaid room, she
began pulling her clothes from her body so she
could dress for bed and remembered she was tied
into the underthings from the back. Squirming
and twisting did her no good.

With her dress left lying on the bed, Melina
went back to the sitting room. She opened the
desk drawer and found a penknife. Reaching behind her, she hacked the knife upwards under the
ties. This garment pinched and should be burned.

When she loosened the strings enough, she
wiggled free of the underthing and let it fall to

the floor. She smoothed out her chemise and put the knife back into the drawer.

Taking the damaged garment, she walked the hallway to Warrington's room and knocked.

A groggy 'Yes?' came through the wood.

Gathering her courage, she pushed open the door, peering in. Moonlight fell through open curtains, mixing light and shadows. The scent of shaving soap, and something that reminded her of trees with new leaves, lingered in the air. One pillow was on the floor, leaning against the bed. Warrington lay in the middle of the mattress, his fist clenched around tangled coverings. When she stepped into the room, he slowly opened his eyes.

'Broomer—you've changed.' He spoke without inflection.

She shut the door and moved to the side of the bed. She stood so close she could see the outline of his bare shoulder.

'This *thing*...' she tossed the corset over a boot stand '...is broken. And I do not want it repaired.'

'What is this *thing* you just tossed over my boots?'

'A noose for a woman's stomach.'

'They are ugly. Those nooses.'

'I can't breathe in it.'

'Then I am pleased you removed it.' His words were soft, reverent. The husky tones flowed into her skin.

'I worried about you.' She forced the words

out. 'You are alone, though you have brothers and a son.'

'You needn't concern yourself, Melina. Men are meant to be alone more than women. But I am thankful for your thoughts.' He rolled to the side of the bed near her, took her hand and brought it to his lips, brushing a kiss along the closed fingertips. He pressed his face against her knuckles while raising his gaze.

His lips parted and sleepy eyes watched her. Tousled hair fell across his forehead. In less than a second, she locked the image into her mind.

His eyes awakened fully. He moved again, the covers rustling, and he waited.

She pulled her fingers from his grasp. His breathing changed, almost stopping. She pressed closer to the bed, her legs touching the edge. He moved back, pulling the coverings and leaving an empty space between them. His eyes flicked to the bare spot and then to her. 'It's still warm,' he said.

He propped himself on one elbow—a tower of strength capturing her senses so much she couldn't blink. His fingers—still callused from his time on the ship—clamped over hers, tugging her forward. But the burning need in his eyes drew her into the bed.

She slid into the cocoon he'd woven with the air he breathed and with the beating of his heart.

He bent over her and the force of a wave crashed into her. He was muscle, strength and sinew.

'Aphrodite has risen from the night and captured me.' His words, roughened by emotion, rolled over her. He looked at her and pulled her deeper into his embrace. 'Is there a reason you've appeared before me? A reason you've graced me with your presence?' He stopped, his breath brushed her lips and her body pulsed alive.

He kissed her, a warmed brandy taste. Her hands reached out and the strength under her palms overwhelmed her senses. The power in his body caused her breath to hitch—and she wanted Warrington even closer.

He pulled back and she looked up, completely overtaken by his presence. 'I can resist you in the daylight,' he said, 'but in the darkness, I believe you aren't real. You're a spirit to tempt me and I am in your power.'

His eyes held emotions she'd never seen before and not known existed. Any goddess would have met her match with him. He was like no mythical creature she'd ever heard of. Perhaps one had been so wily as to escape detection and did not let himself be found in any tales, and now he was before her, more compelling than any imagined.

Warrington took one finger, touching the tie of her chemise, and with a tug he unfastened the ribbon and flared the opening. He only barely brushed against her, but she responded as if she had been stone before and he woke her.

His hands slid over her breasts, caressing, sliding down, covering her hips and reaching the hem of her chemise. Reverently, he pulled the garment over her head.

Her fingertips traced the wall of his chest and the pebbled nipples. She could sense the whole of him with the barest touch. He stilled, as though the sensations overwhelmed him.

She splayed her palm, feeling the hair flattened beneath. His chest seemed to go on and on and on and on, but it was only that time had stilled, magnifying her movements, letting her experience a treasure in the feelings.

He hugged her to him, tightening her against the ridge pressing upwards between them.

She ran her fingers over his shoulders, traced his neck and stopped at the tendrils of his hair, holding him. Her movements unleashed something behind his eyes, but it wasn't as if he turned from marble to a man—the opposite. Awareness left his face and he became controlled by passions and light and pulses.

'Let's forget the ship. Let this be our first time, Melina.'

He kissed her once again. All she could taste or touch or know was the overpowering awareness of his body. Her heartbeat had changed into pulsations—sensations beyond what she ever could have imagined.

He put his hand to her legs—her inner thigh—and up, into the centre of her pleasure. He touched her, stroked her, and the sensations became stronger, building, until they burst throughout her entire being. Something surrounded her and caught her and filled her with intensity and wrung it from her, bringing every possible pleasure she could feel together at once, leaving her stunned, and alive and unable to move.

Warrington pressed himself up, the covers falling free. He rose—not from the sea, but like the earth moving a volcano upwards until it blocked out sun and all the rest of the world. Her hands reached up to him, but she had no control over them. Nothing remained in her control. Not him, or herself.

He touched her legs, opening them, but she didn't truly feel his hand, the pleasure was too intense to belong only to one part of her, or to be felt in one place. He nuzzled his face against hers, whispering her name, and then he moved above her.

The moment his body united with hers—the warm rush of him—she bolted alive, pulling at his back, and pushed herself forward, wanting his touch to penetrate all of her.

And she knew when he lost himself in her. Sounds, simple heartbeats sounded as a thousand drums and even then the world became completely silent.

He looked down at her. She didn't know if a second, a minute or a night-time passed, when he whispered, 'Aphrodite.'

And then he rolled to the side and pulled her into the haven of his arms, but it was really no haven. Nothing could shelter her from the feelings he unleashed.

No person could have experienced what had just happened to her and not be changed for ever.

Warrington rhythmically touched the strands of Melina's hair, her head resting on his shoulder. Melina slept, but he had no weariness in him.

How many times had he left his chamber to go to search out Cassandra in the night? And not once had she found her way to his bed. After his illness, he'd been tempted to find a mistress, but he hadn't. Each time he'd sought Cass out after the betrayal, he'd hoped their joining would mean something more than his body's desire for relief.

Cassandra had never pulled him closer—even before Jacob was born. Her fingers rested against him, but they didn't move. Melina's deep gasps had startled him, but they'd also inflamed him, and taken his control. And her hands—clutched at him, gripping him as if she could not bear to let him go.

He shut his eyes. He'd not known. He thought

passion was from the body and had not realised it could begin in the deepest recesses of the heart.

Placing the lightest kiss on her head, he slipped his arm from under her shoulders and pressed the covers close. His movement caused her to roll towards him, and in the dimness, he could see her lashes touching her cheek, fluttering awake.

Her hand clasped the covers at her chest, and she sat up. He forced himself not to run a hand down the gentle ridges of her backbone, but to turn away.

Leaving the bed, he padded to his wardrobe and found his own dressing gown. He put it on and sat in the overstuffed chair.

'Are you not sleepy?' she asked.

'No.'

Melina sat on the disarray of covers, hair tumbling around her shoulders. Pulling the counterpane close, she moved forward on the bed until she sat near the end. She wrapped a hand around the foot post and rested her head against the smooth wood.

'Do you not sleep afterwards?' she asked.

'Usually.' He brushed back his hair. 'This is different.'

She shut her eyes, face still against the wood, bedclothes tucked under her arms, and he wondered if he dreamed the moments with her. But it wasn't an illusion. His mind could not have conjured something so perfect.

Melina was more beautiful than anyone he'd ever seen and the woman he desired more than any other. And his demons surfaced, asking him how many times his own heart had lied to him.

Chapter Sixteen

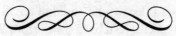

Before the day was out, Warrington intended to know who Cassandra had met after leaving him to die at Whitegate.

He dressed and left the chamber after telling Melina who would be visiting that evening.

He wanted to be alone so he could think with a clear head. But perhaps he'd picked the wrong room for solitude. In the sitting room, he stopped after one step on to the rug, looking down as if he expected to see shattered glass. He raised his gaze to the gouge on the fireplace.

The mantel was the most ornate thing in the house. Big, white, carved marble and one of the acanthus leaves had been broken off.

More than two years before, he'd been discussing changes at Whitegate's stables with Dane and a messenger had arrived to let them know Cassandra had had the successful birth of a baby girl. The chair had been replaced afterwards. One of

Ben's mementos had been broken—perhaps some kind of ship made of twigs. He raised his eyes to the tops of the curtains. His mind flashed on pulling them down from the walls but maybe he imagined it.

He didn't want to be told about that night, didn't want to know what others knew of it and didn't want it known he couldn't recall the fury. He was thankful he'd been miles from Whitegate and wished he'd been far from any other seeing and hearing person.

Now, when the raps at the entrance alerted him of guests, he walked to the head of the stairs. Broomer wasn't in the house to answer. He'd been sent on another of the special errands he excelled at. The maid of all work bustled from a doorway below, a cleaning cloth in her hands, and rushed to the vestibule to answer the knock.

Warrington stepped back, knowing the servant had been instructed to show the guests directly to him. He waited for them, thinking of a spider's carefully constructed web, and how fragile it was. Success or failure depended on the whims of nature.

Daphne's yellow day dress swirled around her as elegantly as if she glided into a ballroom when she greeted Warrington, her hands outstretched. 'Did you have a grand adventure?' Daphne asked, mentioning the reason Warrington gave for his travels. Her husband, Ludgate, entered the sitting room, his crutch working in tandem with his leg. He stood slightly behind her, watching the welcome.

Daphne had Cassandra's colouring. Cassandra's features. But on Daphne they'd taken a wrong turn. Her azure eyes, pert nose and full mouth were spaced too close to each other—giving her a full forehead and long jawline, which had made her face seem wide. But now, with the thinness in her cheeks, her features blended together. Age favoured her, except for the way the shadows around her eyes seemed to make them shrink into her face.

Even Ludgate had a paleness Warrington didn't remember, but then it had been years longer since the two men had seen each other.

Warrington grasped Daphne's hands, lifting one to kiss the air above her glove.

'I would find another word to describe our voyage besides *adventure.*' Warrington released her. 'Ben can make hell sound like a paradise. He put the hook in my mouth, slowly pulled me in, and I didn't know what was happening until salt water splashed all over me. The dousing was warm, but all the same, a rude awakening.'

'Oh, it could not be so terrible…' Daphne's voice chided, and she reached briefly to pat his cheek. 'A sea voyage. New sights. New lands. Surely you have some good to say of it.'

Small brackets framed her mouth—ones he'd

never noticed before. But he'd not seen Daphne since right before her sister's death. Daphne had returned home after the women's tiff. He'd sent his brother Dane to break the news of the death because he'd not wanted to tell her in a letter. Dane said she'd collapsed and later Warrington had received the missive telling him how troubled she'd been because the last words the two women had spoken had been harsh.

Pushing the memories aside, Warrington chuckled. 'I assure you, it was not a grand adventure. You will not again get me on a sailing ship unless it is at gunpoint.'

Daphne continued into the room, walking past him. 'You jest.' She spoke lightly, but her voice had an edge. 'You want to make it sound difficult so men who travel will appear brave and strong. I dare say you quite enjoyed it.' She pulled at the strings of her reticule, twisting them around her finger, sliding free and then roping them around her hand again.

He heard the forced gaiety. He supposed Daphne still suffered the loss of her sister.

'Of course.' He put warmth into his words. 'I slept every night and dreamed of the novelty of getting stranded at sea in a longboat, with Ben's smelly feet sticking in my face, and I would awake to discover the scent of bilge water in my nostrils. Bilge water. Imagine a swamp so distasteful animals will not even drink from it and that is perfume compared to the sloshing liquid in the hull of a ship.'

Ludgate barked a laugh and nodded to Warrington.

Daphne, back straight, looked deeply into Warrington's face. 'You've darkened in the sun. And you look strong enough to lift a horse.'

His smile warmed, but inside, regret sliced him. Daphne had inherited the heart for both the women, but her presence made his palms sweat.

'I had to experience the whole of sailing, according to Ben,' he said. 'Steering the vessel wasn't so bad. But after working the sails, my arms ached as if I had lifted the masts. The first time I climbed the ratlines, my heart pounded in my ears so loud I could not hear the instructions shouted from below. When I put my feet back on deck, I acted as if I could do it over and over. I didn't worry I'd end up swimming if I fell, but missing the water and damaging the deck. If I did, Ben would insist I scrub my blood from his precious ship.'

She moved to the sofa and turned back to him. 'I'm just thankful Ludgate wasn't along—the three of you would have surely overturned the boat.'

The caring in her eyes comforted him. He'd known Daphne so long and they shared truths that bound them. She'd loved Cassandra, yet she saw her sister's flaws just as he had eventually.

He shrugged. 'Never again. Ben's the mermaid hunter, not me.'

Ludgate's laugh bounced from the walls. His crutch wobbled and he followed his wife to the sofa. He used the wood as a balance, lowering himself to sit. The tool had been a part of his life since a childhood accident where he'd fallen from a roof. Ludgate seemed no more aware of the stick than he was of his own fingers. In fact, he used the aid as another extremity.

'Been thinking of investing in a ship myself— though I don't have a brother to sail for me, of course,' Ludgate said. 'Wanted your opinion.'

'One.' Warrington held up a finger. 'Don't.'

Daphne leaned forward, her voice a whisper. 'So dangerous. I cannot imagine.'

'Truly, I am pleased to keep my feet dry. Don't know how I let myself get talked into it.' Warrington made himself comfortable on the facing sofa. He shook his head. 'We saw no mermaids and everyone looks like a sea monster after anything longer than a fortnight from England. Except, of course, Ben. He kept himself dandified. He is more at peace on *Ascalon* than he will ever be on land.'

Warrington paused. Of course, he was pleased to see Daphne and Ludgate, but this visit had none of the familiarity of before. He felt as if he were talking with two people he had just met at a dinner party and didn't quite know if he liked them or not. Ludgate kept looking around the room and Daphne's jaw appeared clenched. Perhaps she suspected he had a question for her.

'You surely favoured some of it?' Ludgate asked.

Warrington smiled. 'It will take a bigger man than Ben to get me from land again. I've had enough sea air—everything still tastes like salt to me.' He made a face as if he had a mouthful of ocean water.

Ludgate chuckled. 'Can't be that terrible if you two youngsters can tolerate it.' He balanced his crutch across his knees.

'We barely survived. Had a fire when the ship rolled a bit and the bail of a lantern slipped loose from its mooring. The liquid flamed about. I didn't expect when I departed on the journey I'd be bobbing around in a wooden bowl coated in a resin to keep it watertight—resin that just happens to be easy to ignite, especially with a lantern dashed on to it. Nothing matters once the fire starts—but putting it out. If I had any chance of liking the sea, it burned to ash in the blaze. After that, I decided if I had the need to sail again, I'd reside at Newgate for a while. Same luxuries—without the chance of drowning, or burning to death.'

'It cannot be as bad as that.' Ludgate patted a rhythm on his crutch. 'Adventure at sea.'

Warrington shut his eyes. 'Misadventure at sea. Not even a good place for ships to be.'

Daphne shook her head, ear bobs dangling, a teasing gleam in her eyes. 'I think Ludgate should go before the mast if he wishes. Then he would truly know if he enjoys it. Maybe a short trip first, of course.'

'No trip at sea is short unless you go gills up.' Warrington nodded. 'The first day is not terrible. The novelty. But the suffering grows with the days. Your clothing turns to a board from the salt mists drying on the garments. Your face burns from the wind and your hair tangles over your eyes. You listen to the everlasting groans of the ship—the vessel complains, as well.' He put an arm along the back of the sofa, trying to relax. 'Ben didn't even consider it a concern when a wave slammed him into a spar and nearly knocked him over the side.'

Daphne leaned forward, eyes wide and her glove touching her cheek. 'He is well?'

'He will be. I'd rue the day I bought the ship with him, but better for him to be sailing on a vessel he knows than risking a rotted one.' Warrington grimaced and stood, walking to the decanter.

He wanted to get the ugly part of the conversation over. He did want to know who had fathered the child in his house and not just because the man had knifed him. He was curious to find out if one could gut a worm.

Before, he'd not truly blamed the man. Warrington understood, in some deep recess of himself, the man's betrayal. The need for a woman's body could be overpowering. But time had cured that empathy. Now the cur was going to pay.

Warrington filled them in on the details of his journey. By the time the conversation lulled, Ludgate had a jug-bitten look in his eyes and Daphne's face kept pinching when she looked at her husband.

Warrington could feel bile in his mouth, knowing he'd soon be able to say the name of his wife's lover. He no longer cared if the man were a footman, a cit or a king. Death treated all men the same.

He tapped his forefinger a slow heartbeat on to the base of the goblet while Ludgate rambled about some tailor's choice of a button. The man had never been so eternally boring before and he refused to meet Warrington's eyes.

Ludgate knew... Ludgate knew who Cassandra's lover was. Of course he would have to know. She carried on her liaisons under his roof. Warrington's gaze locked on Ludgate's face and anger slammed Warrington's body. Ludgate. Could it have been him? But, no, Warrington had seen the man who attacked him. And one thing he knew, knew positively—he would have recognised his brother-in-law. And the man who ambushed him didn't limp or speak the same as Ludgate.

Warrington sipped his brandy, and just wondered if—if perhaps Ludgate could have had something to do with the stabbing. But he wasn't murderous—he practically swooned if his tea was too hot and couldn't even reprimand his horse or command his servants.

When Warrington rose to lift the decanter to refill Daphne's glass, her eyes darted to her husband. Her words were slow. 'Maybe we should—'

'Nonsense.' Warrington wasn't letting them leave. Let his foxed friend ramble all he wanted. Warrington would garble and warble along with him, right up until the moment Daphne conversed on one particular subject.

Warrington poured the wine for Daphne and more brandy for her husband. 'Please stay longer, Daphne. It's so rare I have guests.'

Ludgate talked on, the liquid in his glass sloshing as he mumbled and sipped. He'd discussed the construction of the frame over the mantel and the way the wood had been carved, and now he compared that to the pictures in his house.

Warrington watched Ludgate's brandy nearly spill. Who else would think of the skill to make a picture frame? Apparently Daphne had heard her husband expound on artistry many times. Her stare was fixed on the wall and she looked to be asleep with her eyes open, entranced in her own recollections.

Warrington didn't for one blink think Ludgate could not know about Cassandra's loose corset ties. Ludgate's valet probably knew about the playthings. The sisters talked. Servants talked. Even the wind carried tales when two people whispered and breezes blew their words into another's ears. Secrets didn't go to the grave. They couldn't lie still.

Warrington asked Daphne about her dog, a little hairy creature smaller than a man's boot. She placed great store in the dog and War kept the conversation going while he eased his way to the pull. When the servant peered in, Warrington pointed to the near-empty wine glasses and the woman left immediately.

When she returned, she brought a decanter, filled, and sat it beside the first. Warrington gave a firm shake of his head and indicated for the maid to put the liquid near his brother-in-law. It didn't take long for Ludgate to put his glass down, prop the crutch at his side and cross his arms. His head bobbed a bit to the side and his half-closed eyes fixed on the tooth decoration. Then Warrington saw the lowered jaw and heard the heavy breathing. Ludgate slept.

Daphne followed Warrington's gaze. 'He's going to be aching tomorrow if his head hurts as I think it will.' She sighed, looking at Warrington. 'But he'll get over it. He always does. I suppose we should leave.'

'Daphne, I have something important we must

talk about.' He tapped the edge of his glass. Her eyes narrowed.

'We must go.' She stood, reaching to wake Ludgate.

'No, Daphne.' He stopped her movement with his words. 'This is vital. I need you to tell me about Cassandra.'

The emotions behind her eyes blazed, but he couldn't decipher them.

'I'm sure your memories are as strong as mine,' she said. 'I read her letters again from time to time and I miss her so. Really, I can't talk about her. Makes me too sad.' She stood.

'Who's Willa's father?'

Daphne's jaw dropped and she stumbled, almost falling back to the sofa. 'Warrington—this is not proper conversation.'

'Daphne.' His voice brooked no argument. 'I need to know.'

She grasped her skirt in both hands, shaking her head.

He put his glass on the side table and stood. He reached out, moving forward and securing her elbow. 'Daphne, this is about a child's life.'

She turned back to him, eyes flat. 'We won't talk of this. I lost as much as you. Nothing will ever be the same.'

'That may be. But I need to know who Willa's father is.'

'Why, you, of course.' She pulled from his

grasp, but he grabbed her fingers before she could jab Ludgate awake. She jerked her hand from Warrington's and pounced on Ludgate, pulling him up while handing him his crutch.

'Time to leave.' She bit out the words.

Ludgate wobbled and Warrington instinctively reached out to give him assistance. Warrington felt a stab of guilt while he helped his friend down the stairs. Warrington hadn't thought of the trouble Ludgate might have walking should he drink too much. Loading the sotted man into the carriage was no easy task. Ludgate mumbled his gratitude before sliding back into the squabs and closing his eyes.

Daphne avoided Warrington's gaze when she rushed into the conveyance and shouted to the groom, 'Home. Now.'

Warrington turned back to the house, angry with himself, but more displeased with Daphne. She knew. He could not blame her for wanting to keep Cassandra's confidence if she'd been alive, but this was a different matter.

Then he wondered if a spider ever built two webs at the same time. A good practice.

Chapter Seventeen

Warrington walked to Melina's door and knocked. Melina peered out, a question in her eyes. He took her by the hand and she squeezed his fingers. He led her to the sitting room.

'They've left. Daphne claims not to know. But it doesn't matter if she doesn't tell me from her own mouth. Perhaps I only asked her to see if she would speak of it.' He stopped near the fireplace, and stared at the chip in the mantel.

Melina didn't sit. She put her hand on his fore-arm.

He gave a long blink and nodded. 'My illness before Cass left—I have not been able to get it out of my mind. Something about the watchfulness in Cassandra's eyes before I became ill. Suddenly she was at my elbow every moment, watching me. Even putting a palm to my forehead.' His lips twisted in mockery of a smile. 'She'd never shown such care for me before. Not long afterwards, my stomach began to revolt, my heartbeat changed and I could hardly think of anything except how ill I was. Cassandra's concern vanished and so did she—with my son. To protect his health, I was later told. I wondered if she'd tainted our food.'

When he'd finally regained his strength and reviewed the household ledgers and accounts, he discovered that Cassandra had struggled through his illness at the *modiste*'s and the perfumer's, and even the stationer's—and she never neared ink because it might stain her hands.

'Because she didn't care for you, didn't mean she wanted you dead.' Melina squeezed his arm.

'It certainly didn't mean she wanted me alive, either. My father died of the same sickness I had.'

In the days she was gone, Cassandra became visible to him in a way she'd never been before.

She never let herself be alone. In her quiet moments, the maids would work with Cassandra's hair or fingernails, or somehow change a dress she liked, and he would be aware of the gossipy hum of conversation. Not only did Cass know of every movement in society, she knew if the stable master fancied a household servant and who'd bedded whom.

Cassandra held no past, only the present moment. She'd never had a portrait or miniature of Jacob done and the knowledge plunged regret into him. He'd not asked for a painting, either.

Pulling himself from his memories, he spoke

again. 'I found nothing in her chamber to indicate she wished me ill.'

His eyes reflected the past. 'Even now, I cannot believe she would do such a thing. I tell myself I must be imagining it, and after the knife attack, I felt some relief, because she couldn't have planned that. No matter how much I say Cassandra cannot rest in peace and would continue her mischief in her death, I know it's not possible.'

He put his hands on her hips, holding her, and she didn't know for sure if he steadied her or himself.

'I could not go back,' he continued. 'But I could not leave her be, either. If I put her from me, she would have other men's children. If I kept her near, I wanted her in my bed.'

He turned and seized a near-empty glass from the table and raised it as if making a toast to the memory. 'At first I saw her in a halo of sunlight and the world bloomed with the hint of her rose perfume. Now I hate the stink of roses.' He turned his back to Melina, took a drink, thumped the glass back on to the table and continued speaking. 'I don't believe my recollection of her appearance is tainted—because as I think of her compassion, I see nothing. Her heart beat for herself.' He uttered something from deep within that she couldn't decipher. 'She had very little care for our son, I suspect. She only kept him with her because if my father and I died, then Jacob would inherit and, likely, Dane would oversee things. She thought Dane much more gentle of heart than I was. He'd never shown her his true distrust. And I assure you, when he saw her put to rest, he could not keep the smile from his face. I had him by the throat before I knew it. We both understood the other, though.'

Warrington touched a marred spot on the mantel, tracing where the stone no longer matched the rest of the leaves. 'I've had long enough to mull over it. With me dead, Dane would not be near enough to scold her sweethearts. She could be in mourning, cloistered with a bevy of suitable friends to ease her grief.'

Melina saw him pour more amber liquid into his glass and the bobble of his throat when he took another sip. She could feel the brandy's warmth in her own body while she watched him. No woman of sanity would poison a man who appealed to the eyes as Warrington did. Even in his stained shipboard clothing she had been aware of him. He had the form of a lean Hercules. No, much better. She tilted her head to the side. 'Don't soak your memories with brandy and make things worse.'

'I've told you my wife could have poisoned me. You know she had another man's child and you think I'm making things worse?' His voice lowered. 'If she had shot me while I slept—would you have told me I must have snored and disturbed her rest?'

'You could think of it every day for the rest of your life. It will not punish her. You will only torture yourself.'

He moved back to the decanter and filled his glass, a challenge in his eyes. 'At this point, if a valet nicks my face shaving, I'm certain he is thinking how lucky I was to lose such a wife and that caused his shaky hand, and I blame Cass for the cut.'

'You admit it?'

He nodded and gave a slight shrug. 'She did enough while she was alive that I can feel justified blaming her for every storm cloud in the sky for the rest of my life. I saw Ludgate and his shaking hands and his movements. He didn't act like himself, nor did he once look me in the eyes. He knows I didn't father the child.'

He drained his glass. 'It just jabs at me she has the last word. I cannot see the little chit without remembering. Yet, the child is innocent. Unaware of her circumstances. Born to my wife in my marriage. My property. To care for. And I can hardly bear to be in the same house with it.'

His lips firmed and his fingers clenched on the glassware in his hand. He walked to the mantel and stared at the picture over the hearth. 'I've grown so distrustful I *did* wonder if Daphne would truly tell me everything. Perhaps she is more like Cass than I imagined. So earlier I sent Broomer to watch outside their home. He has coins and instructions to be quite friendly to any servants who might be leaving or entering the house. True servants—not ones like Broomer. Ones paid to be invisible and often so good at it their masters and mistresses don't realise they are watched. And the employers often don't understand the hint of information given in front of one maid is often shared with another who might have heard something else until a whole story is pieced together.'

A clattering sounded at the entrance and Warrington turned, listening.

'I know the way,' a female voice carried up the stairs. 'I lost a bracelet and I had it when I was…' In moments, Daphne rushed into the hallway.

'I considered what you asked. And I…' Daphne spoke as she crossed the threshold in front of Warrington. Her gaze stopped on Melina, froze, and Daphne took a step back. Her shoulders dropped, and her voice came out dazed. 'Perhaps we should talk privately.'

'Melina is as much aware of the thorns in my past life as I am.' Warrington walked to Melina and introduced her, not by the Hawkins name. 'She needed passage on *Ascalon* and I agreed to help her locate lost family members here in England.' His hand went to the small of her back, and then to her waist, holding her beside him.

Daphne took a deep breath and registered the situation. The edges of her lips dropped before she spoke. 'If you don't care for her knowing, then I suppose I don't, either.'

She paced to the mantel, making the space seem smaller with her flurried movements, her hands clasping and unclasping. Warrington stayed at Melina's side. Daphne faced them both.

'Warrington…' Daphne spoke cautiously, at first, and threaded her fingertips together. Then her words rushed out. 'I know Cassandra wasn't always as demure as a wife should be. When you were ill, she came to my house and I took her in. She was afraid for Jacob's health. But…' she shrugged '…you know how she was…'

'You cannot simply give me the name of the man?' Warrington's voice slashed the air.

Daphne strode to the window, and stared out, her back to the room. 'After all I'd done for her. I took her in—and I believed every word. I knew her. She spent more time thinking up lies and missteps than most people spend awake. She lied, but never to me—never—I believed. She hated your father. Hated him. I understood. He was a tyrant. But you'd been so good and she came to me when you were sick.' Daphne turned back to the room, her eyes narrowed and lips pinched. 'You were sick. I hadn't expected that. She left you and pranced right into my house like she owned it.' Her voice became shrill. 'I was supposed to just hand her my handkerchiefs and lend her my maid, and wait until her hair was done before I dared leave the house in the morning, taking her here and there in my carriage.' Daphne crossed her arms. 'Always expected me to put her little world back together. And her...'

'So who do you think she could have met?' Warrington's voice slashed out the words.

'Half the town of London for all I know.'

'Thank you for making me feel better, Daphne.'

Her face changed, softened. 'I didn't mean to say that. I truly didn't. She did things and then regretted them.'

'Then she had many regrets.' His lips twisted into a wry line after he spoke. 'I need to know who the man was. Is there a servant you have now who could help me learn who her last lover was?'

'How are you so certain he was her *last?*' The words tumbled from Daphne's lips.

'Fine, then. Is there anyone who could help me make a list of her last lovers? I can hire an expert in mathematicals if you think I might need help with the numbers.'

Daphne shook her head, rapidly. 'No. No,' she said, a blush sweeping her cheeks. 'I didn't mean that, and I'm certain she—' Her voice became brittle. 'I'm certain she couldn't have had but one affection. She slept half the day and we went to the shops until they closed.'

'I'm only interested in learning who the man was. You can't convince me you don't know. You knew her better than anyone and you would have sensed what she was about. And don't concern yourself about hurting my feelings if he is someone I trusted. Right now, I cannot look at a man in London without wondering if he bedded my wife.'

Daphne spoke, compassion in her words. 'You did care for her, though. I watched you dance with her as if the clouds floated at your feet.'

'I don't wish to talk about how I felt for your sister when I first met her. Our feelings were never simple. After she had another man's child in her belly—after it was too late for me to ever look at her the same again—she told me what a mistake she'd made. She said she hadn't even cared for his touch. I believed her. I knew it to be true by the way she smirked about the agonies she caused him by threatening to expose him. She was full cracked, or evil—or both.'

Daphne's face twisted and she didn't speak, just stared ahead.

'Who did my wife share company with when she left me on my deathbed?' Warrington asked again.

She shook her head and clasped her hands in front of her, but her words snarled. 'I don't want to talk about it any more. I believed you loved her. You're no different than my sister.' She speared a glance at Melina.

He left Melina's side, taking a step towards Daphne. His words were stone hard. 'Yes, I am different. I was faithful to Cassandra—against my better judgement. I am a widower now and I am free to do as I wish.'

'An earl doesn't dally with the servants.'

He stood directly in front of Daphne, towering over her. 'Daphne—you could close your eyes to my wife prancing around with another man while I lay ill and you dare find fault with my behaviour. Nor can you disparage Melina. She has the peerage in her family history.'

Daphne scowled disagreement. 'You and Cass were made for each other. I was going to tell you, but now I won't. I couldn't tell you before because I didn't want you to know that I knew. I knew, but by the time I found out, it was too late.' She turned, her skirts flying around her feet as she rushed out.

Warrington went to the door and kicked it shut, swearing. The slam caused Melina to jump.

'So I misjudged Daphne, as well.' He whirled to face Melina. 'She's a traitor to our friendship. She knows who I'm searching for. I cannot believe she would not tell me. Well, perhaps I can. She is Cassandra's blood.'

'She loved her sister long before she cared for you.'

'And Daphne always protected Cass. Everyone in her family protected Cass. And to listen to my *wife*—how I hate that word... To listen to Cass she was misunderstood and never given her due. She didn't even believe she should have to share the stars.'

Sighing, he made a sweeping motion with his hand. 'It doesn't matter that Daphne won't tell me.' He walked to the decanter and arranged the glasses neatly, and didn't refill. 'Just wait with me, Melina, and let me have the silence to collect my thoughts. Before the night is out, I expect to have my question answered.

He sat on the sofa, his body in a relaxed pose of his arm along the back, his feet apart and his fingers tapping.

Within an hour, clumping footsteps sounded on the stairs.

'Broomer's not one to tiptoe.' Warrington's face changed, hard and dark. 'He's not much of a butler, but that face of his can smile and words just tumble out of people. Me included. And he can break bones and describe the snap like a musician describes the sound of the pianoforte. A good man indeed.'

Warrington walked to the door and Broomer bounded into the room, stopping by grabbing the facings.

'I don't know if it's the truth...' Broomer's words tumbled out, between his gasps for breath '...but I've been told every servant in that house believes it's one man who was dallying with the fair-haired woman.'

'Speak.' War near bit the word in two.

'Ludgate.'

The small lines at the sides of Warrington's eyes tightened and his face moved forward, as if he needed to hear the word again. 'Ludgate?' he repeated. He reached to his boot and pulled out the knife. 'Ludgate was not the one who dropped this at my feet.'

'Can't explain that.' Broomer's breath slowed to normal. 'But around that time, enough crockery was flying in that house to keep the servants sweeping up for weeks. The man sleeps with his door locked, *if* he stays at the home. They're married, but they keep out of each other's sight most of the time. Was a rare thing for them to go out together like they did tonight. The maids considered it odd.'

Warrington stood perfectly still. 'I won't need you again just now. I'll see you are rewarded for your efforts. However, do not drink overmuch until after we have discussed this again. I suspect you may be needed.'

Broomer smiled, gave a tilt of his head and then the most proper bow. 'Whatever your lordship needs done.' Then his large form turned and he left, each footstep soft.

Warrington strode to the door, but Melina caught his coat sleeve in her hand, moving forward, putting herself in his view.

'Leave it, Melina.' He tried to shake her away.

'I'm going with you. You won't kill him with me present.'

His voice held irony. 'I would not bet a farthing on that. I fed him drink until he was sotted.

Then I mistakenly helped him down the stairs so he wouldn't go head first.'

'At least wait until daybreak.'

Melina felt the cessation of movements in his body, so sudden it seemed more of a jerk than stillness.

'Enough. It's a singular betrayal, Melina. And duelling is outlawed. I see no reason to break two laws. One would suffice for this matter.'

'Murder.'

'I prefer to think of it as justice.'

'And should you be hanged, how will Jacob feel? Proud that his father died by a silk rope instead of a hemp one like the common folk?'

'I don't expect to be punished any more than I have already been.' He pressed his lips together and then seemed to pull words from deep inside himself. His eyes flashed a look, a different kind of anguish than she'd ever seen in anyone's face. 'Broomer will happily attest to the fact I never left the house if I need him to. He'll send for a physician and say he sat at my side, praying for the man's quick arrival. Broomer will have two plans, or three, by the time his foot hits the last stair tread. He is extremely loyal and knows his way around, through, under and above the law. He also knows about justice.'

'Justice?' she gasped, tightening her hold on him.

He pulled free and took both her wrists. 'Melina. You should not know of this. It is not your concern.'

'You are my concern. You have already suffered enough because of your wife. You do not need to have more problems.'

'Don't you understand?' His hands tightened on her wrists. His hair fell forward, brushing at his brows. 'It is not merely my wife who betrayed me. It is the whole lot of them. Cass. Daph. And Ludgate. All.' He dropped her hands. 'Ludgate. Cassandra despised him. I know she did.' He swallowed. 'But now that I think of her, I wonder if any soul lived she didn't hate.'

'Don't let her hurt you now she is dead.'

He put his back to her. 'Daphne and I have had a family affection since soon after Cassandra and I wed—or so I imagined. We were both in her thrall.' He stood in front of the painting he'd retrieved from Melina's father. 'We were both wronged. I had heard nothing, ever, at the clubs of Ludgate stepping outside his marriage. And when he strayed, he certainly did not look far.' He whirled around. 'I will hear no more kind suggestions. Do you understand that I need vengeance for Daphne as well—and against Daphne? How could she not tell me?'

'She couldn't want to speak the words that her husband bedded her sister.'

'I can understand that. But I will take him out of her life.'

'You will regret it.'

'Possibly as soon as Ludgate breathes his last. But at that point I can make no changes. Now I have regrets he is alive. So I am to be plagued with so-called regrets. At least this one will be of my choosing.' His eyes narrowed. 'Daphne. I don't know now whether to hate her or pity her. Cass betrayed her, as well. Nothing can coat the blade of a knife thrust into a person's back like family blood. The added twist of someone you've known your whole life—who you've shared whispers with and dreams with... And they betray you. With no care. Like Cass did with me. And I know it. How we planned for our son before Jacob was born—but the plans were all mine. She listened and agreed—probably planning her next liaison or slippers. Daphne told me once how she could close her eyes to Cass's selfishness because she'd never seen her any other way and had loved her from childhood. Daphne's eyes aren't closed now.'

His body racked back against wall and his face turned upwards, before lowering again. He grasped Melina's shoulder. 'And she knows. She must have known since before the birth of the babe. She had too much anger to be unaware.'

He let out a long breath. 'Nothing will happen to my old friend tonight, Melina. That is a solemn promise you can believe. I want him sober.'

Chapter Eighteen

Warrington sat in his sitting room and could not keep his boot from tapping the desk leg.

He felt as if he'd spent the night drinking. He should have named his demons. They'd lived so close to him for so long. And they had not grown smaller. He fed them well.

And now they tortured him and Melina had spent an hour talking, trying to convince him of a higher ground, and the merits of forgiveness, while he watched her lips move, knew words flowed from them and tried to devise a way to make his point with Ludgate.

Before Jacob came into the world, War had stayed at Cassandra's elbow. Awed. She grew even more beautiful.

With the second one, he'd had to shut it from his mind and he moved into the town house. Ben had been at sea and knew little of the true events. Dane moved to the bachelor house with

Warrington and each night they visited clubs and sometimes attended soirées, where Dane played the bashful rake while Warrington tried to forget he was married, but couldn't.

Melina rose, walked to him and took his face in her hands, her palms cool. She engulfed him in the scent of cleanliness. He didn't know how anyone could smell so innocent and pure. Perhaps it was the new fabric mixed with her soap. And he was surprised she didn't complain of wearing the formless sack. He thought a plain dress would keep her from tempting him so much. A foolish plan that could never have worked.

'You've a son.' Her voice soothed. 'You no longer have to let Cassandra's memory rule your actions. Let her rest or not. But you don't have to punish Ludgate because she couldn't honour your marriage. Think of Jacob. Is this the father you wish for him to have?'

'Melina.' He took her fingers from his face and let them fall from his grasp.

'My father doesn't care for me,' she said, giving a twitch to her shoulder. 'He doesn't have feelings for my sisters. And I can't believe he loves his other children. I've known all my life that we are not as much to him as art. He's told us often. *My gift is my purpose. My gift must be above all else.* You at least care for Jacob. Do not let him grow up with tales of how his father attacked someone because of an unfaithful mother.'

'He'll surely hear the stories of Cassandra.'

She stood in front of him, face earnest, fist clenched at her breast. 'But she'll only be a wisp in his memory. You are his father and he needs you. And he needs more than ever to be able to look up to you and respect you. Do not let him feel he was born of two tainted parents. At least give him one he can know is noble.'

'I don't want him to have two *tainted* parents. I hardly know him, Melina. My son. And I think of him above all else. But I let that whore be his mother. For that alone he should hate me.'

'I dare say he'll get older and find plenty of other reasons. I could probably name ten.'

Warrington's mouth opened. 'Your honesty is not appealing.'

'Stubborn. Forcing Broomer, a servant, to dishonesty. Bedding a woman and bumping her head into the wall, trying to—'

'Bumping your head into the wall?'

'On the ship. You near knocked me out.'

'You should have told me.'

'No…' She waved a hand. 'You were quite intense. And there was the whiskers…'

He stared at her. 'The circumstances were not the best. I told you I am not that bad of a lover.'

Melina wobbled her head. 'If you say so.'

'You do not have enough experience to know. A woman's first time is never quite what it should be.'

She shrugged. 'You say that to yourself.'

He looked at her eyes. 'You witch.'

She blinked.

'You insult me to take my mind from him.'

She touched the back of her head, fingers probing. 'It's still tender—*odyniros*.'

He pulled her into his arms. 'I didn't mean to hurt you. Not in any way. And I did not bump you into the wall.'

She squeaked her disagreement. 'You were consumed in the moment then. Just as you are mired in memories now. Don't kill Ludgate. You don't want to. You want to kill Cassandra. And you can't.'

He pulled her against his chest. She could feel the cloth of his waistcoat and the movements of his coarse breathing.

'You are a witch.' He whispered the words against her hair.

'I don't think you like nice people.'

'Whose side are you on?'

'The children's. And I've never met them. But I know what it is like to have a father you do not respect. And to be without a mother. I'm old enough to understand it, but I don't think they are.'

Strong arms held her and he rocked her briefly, surrounding her in the scent of warm male.

He stopped the rocking movement and leaned back, watching her face. 'Melina—do you have any fond recollections of our time on the ship?'

'Perhaps.' She looked at him and the heat of her memories weakened her limbs.

His eyes changed and he examined her with such intensity—the same way an artist would study a subject to be painted.

He pulled her into his grasp, holding her tight, but before she could gather herself, his lips closed over hers, overwhelming her with a storm of feelings as strong as any winds or waves from the ship. The swirl of his tongue slipping into her mouth tumbled her thoughts so strongly, she could not have remained standing without his support.

The next kiss to her lips was the merest brush. 'Goodnight, Beauty.' He backed away, staring at her, and she didn't know who or what he really saw.

Warrington had stayed from the house in the daylight hours and returned through the servants' entrance so he could find Broomer. Broomer said Melina hadn't stirred, except to ask about the earl, and the servant hadn't been able to tell her what he didn't know. From the spark in Broomer's eyes when given instructions, he still relished a challenge. Warrington gave him one.

Now Warrington sat in the glow of only one candle on the small table by his side. The painting of Melina's family showed murky in the dimness. Tonight, he would have preferred taunting eyes of black-hearted mermaids.

The thumping steps outside the door alerted

Warrington. Broomer had his own ways of getting a job done.

War pulled the blade out, the movement releasing the leather scent from the scabbard, and he flicked the steel back and forth through the flame.

Ludgate walked into the room, crutch under his arm. Broomer pulled the door shut behind them and leaned back.

Ludgate paused, his eyes taking in the room. He turned and saw the exit blocked. His fingers tightened on the crutch and his free hand went across his body and clasped the wood as if he needed even more help to stand. 'I knew you would find out.'

Silence and the flickering of the candle filled the air between them.

Ludgate spoke again, his words gruff. 'I know you're aware.'

'Broomer. Leave us and lock the door with the key.'

Without a word, the big man opened the door and left.

Warrington looked to the flame. 'Had I suspected you, I would not have been so slow to find out who bedded my wife. I held her responsible. No one else. But you betrayed me, as well.'

'If you had cared for her, you would have searched sooner.'

He held the blade tip in the flame and his fingers tightened on the handle. He kept his voice conversational. 'I suggest we not get in a match over who cared more for my wife.'

Ludgate spoke, each word measured. 'She was a woman no man could help but desire.'

Rage boiled in Warrington's body, causing a twitch in the knife blade. 'You should not mention your lust for her, either.'

Ludgate stepped back. Someone outside rattled the doorknob. Warrington ignored the sound.

Warrington didn't speak and he could hear Ludgate's breaths from across the room. 'Don't be in a hurry to leave.' He used the blade to snuff out the candle.

'I didn't know she'd return to you. She told us you were dying.' The words sounded through clenched teeth. *'She said you were dying.'*

'Makes it all the better, doesn't it? I'm breathing my last breaths on my deathbed. You're ploughing my wife.'

'Light a candle,' Ludgate commanded.

'I don't like the sight of blood.'

'Warrington. It's over. She's gone.'

'Not entirely gone. Willa, you know. Little girl, about so high.' He held out the hand with the knife in it to indicate Willa's height. He was certain Ludgate couldn't see the blade well, but that Ludgate's heart was pounding every shadowed movement into his mind.

He heard Ludgate bump back against the door.

'You didn't find any irony in the fact that she

named her Willa Marie,' Ludgate said. 'Marie is Daphne's middle name.' His voice rose. '*My wife's* middle name and my full name is Robert *William* Ludgate.'

'I didn't know.'

'Oh, I assure you, Cassandra knew. Daphne knew.'

Warrington touched the blade tip to the extinguished wick, scenting the room with smoke, and pressed the string down into the melted wax. 'Cassandra would find it humorous. Like a final dusting of face powder to get just as she wished. But I want to know why you set a man on me. A man to kill me—when Cass was dead. It makes no sense. You don't want the child—'

Again, the doorknob rattled hard. Warrington kept his eyes on Ludgate's form. In seeing Ludgate's slumped shadow, he knew the man wouldn't challenge him.

'Open the door,' Melina called through the wood and she pounded against the door.

'Leave us, Melina.' He bit out the words.

'No,' she said, and he heard a push against the door and her words rushed. 'Daphne is here.'

'Bloody hell,' Ludgate's voice rang out. 'I have an elderly aunt, as well. I hope you didn't forget her invite.'

Warrington kept his words soft. 'Trust me, Ludgate. Still not as bad as watching your wife present you with another man's child. I didn't invite Daphne. I don't know how she found out.'

'She watches me like a gaoler when I am in my home. Sends servants and wastrels to follow me about. I can get no peace in my house and rarely visit it.' Ludgate's voice held the brittleness of an eggshell. 'That's why Cass had to return to you. Daphne was suspicious and her mind was wavering.'

'Fancy that.'

The door rattled again, then abruptly stopped.

'She's gone for the key, I suppose.' Warrington stood, the cool knife hot against his fingers. 'I cannot understand why your wife might be upset to have her husband sleeping with her sister. Perhaps Daphne is overly sensitive.'

'I was insane for Cassandra.' Ludgate grumbled out the words, and his crutch top slid to his chest and he held the oak in front of himself, in a protective stance. He whispered, 'My senses left me.'

'But Cass returned to me.'

'I kissed the ground when she left,' Ludgate said, lips snarling. 'I realised—as soon as it was too late—that Cassandra was not quite what I expected. She put me on a string—in my own house. I had to dance at her whims or she threatened to tell Daphne. And Daphne found out anyway. I'm certain Cassandra couldn't rest until Daphne knew.'

'Cassandra had her own sense of enjoyment. I've had enough of games to last my lifetime.'

'You're ten years younger. You've a blade in your hand and I can hardly stand upright without support. I expected you to be more sporting than that.'

'I was…' Warrington paused. 'Your daughter lives in my house.'

'And if you've a wish to be rid of her, I'll see she's cared for. It doesn't matter either way to me. I almost died when I discovered Cassandra was with child. Daphne cannot have children and… Daphne's not what you think, either, Warrington. Daphne wanted me murdered and for you to get the noose for it—because you forgave Cassandra. I know I have no excuse for my behaviour, but even before I strayed, the two women showed a different side to you. *Both* of them did.'

Instead of a rattling sound behind Ludgate, this time the door opened, knocking into Ludgate. He used the crutch to catch himself and remain upright.

Melina rushed in, a key in one hand. Daphne followed, holding a lamp. Daphne's lips were parted, but her jaw was locked in place.

No one spoke and Warrington waited.

Melina tossed the key on to a side table, grabbed the lamp from Daphne and then moved to the sconce on the wall, lifted the globe and lit the candle. He saw her hand quiver when she touched the flame to the wick. Then she moved to the next one and the branch of candles beside Warrington's chair. The room glowed with light.

'Much better.' Melina sat the lamp base down with too much force. The sound bounced in the room. 'You must see to kill each other.'

'I can manage in darkness.' Warrington met her gaze. She had the same despair in her eyes that he'd felt for years. He couldn't move for the space of several heartbeats. Then he looked to Ludgate. The lamplight accentuated the wan colour of his face. The man looked twice his age.

'We should be leaving.' Ludgate grabbed Daphne's arm. 'I think Warrington and I have discussed enough for one evening.'

'No,' Warrington commanded. 'We haven't.' He switched the knife to his other hand, holding it upright by the tip, in a pitching stance. 'You had some ruffian cut me.'

Ludgate's eyes narrowed. 'I did not. I felt shame for what I did to you. But I had no reason to kill you. And I would not send someone to murder you. A man your size. I would send two, and one with a pistol at least.' Ludgate ran a hand through his hair. 'I wanted no more to do with you. It would not be beneficial to me in any way and I have enough to live with. Your death would not make my life easier. An earl murdered—oh, that would not be noticed, questioned, discussed… You think I want to spend one more moment on the events of the past—no.'

Daphne pulled her arm from Ludgate's grasp while she turned her head to stare at him. 'Warrington. He said he wanted you dead. He blamed you for Cassandra's death.'

Ludgate let out a strangled gasp and turned to Daphne. 'I did no such thing.'

She gave a twist of her head. 'You boasted. You laughed about having your child under his roof.'

'You are mad, Daphne.' He turned back to Warrington and both his hands grasped the crutch. 'I did not. If I would have killed anyone, it would have been that…' his words stopped, eyes locked with Warrington's '…woman.' His voice lowered. 'She didn't care for me. I was a game she played.' He looked at Warrington. 'If it were possible for her to love anyone, she possibly cared for you. She did marry you and she returned to you. She didn't have to. I would have given her funds to go anywhere she wished. I told her.'

Warrington gave a twist of the knife, turning it point down, and jammed it into the tabletop. The sound of the blade vibrating caused Ludgate to jump. Daphne didn't move.

'Daphne—amazing, isn't it—how much you truly favour Cassandra.' Warrington put his hand on the handle. 'Just now. When you spoke, I saw the image of her in your eyes, your face. And when you looked at Ludgate…'

'Cass and I were sisters. We should look alike.'

'And you and I were both wronged.'

Her shoulders tensed and her chin quivered. She breathed through her teeth, then spoke without opening her mouth wider. 'You had plenty of time to get used to Cassandra's ways. You should have made her remain faithful, but when you didn't… You should have gone after Ludgate.' She indicated her husband with a quick nod. 'He betrayed me. With my sister.' Her hands were fisted and she stared at Warrington. 'You should have kept her under control. But you didn't force her back home the moment you recovered from the illness. And I cannot forgive you for that. I told the man who attacked you not to kill you. I told him to limp when he left and not let you see his face, and what words to say. The fool. Both of you. You'd not even searched for the child's father before. I wanted you to get so angry you had to find out. And then discover Ludgate. I was going to tell you myself last night after I left Ludgate in the carriage, when I was positive he wouldn't hear. But then you had *her*…' she jerked her head towards Melina '…with you and I knew you wouldn't leave her side long enough to do justice.'

His ears heard, but he didn't want them to. 'Daphne—I treated you as my own family.'

She gave a careless shrug. 'I treated *you* as my own family.' She gave a lift to her skirts to keep

them from hampering her movements. 'I truly
did.' Her lips turned up and her eyes glittered
when she gave a regal toss of her head. 'Truly.'

'Did Cass poison my father? Me?'

She shrugged, looked around the room and
then levelled her eyes at Warrington. 'How could
I know for certain?' She pressed a hand to her
hair. 'All I can say is that I didn't do it. I would
have been assured of the correct amount.' She
glanced into the distance. 'It is not that hard to
do, I assure you.' She shook her head. 'You can
see her plan. Jacob would be the next earl. She
didn't like your father at all. Not at all. An illness
sweeping the house. Who would think it poison?'
Daphne walked out of the room, moving as if she
had not a care in the world.

'I know I wronged you, Warrington.' Ludgate
stared at the open doorway. 'I wronged Daphne,
too.' He stood silent. 'She is not the same since
I wounded her. She hides it in front of others,
mostly.' He turned to Warrington. 'But you cannot live always in front of others.'

Warrington shook his head. 'It feels that I have.'

'Daphne believes she was betrayed by all
around her. Everyone. Me. Her sister. You.'

'I did nothing to her.'

'You took Cassandra back. Daphne received a
post from her sister, telling her the joyous news
that Daphne would be an aunt—for the third
time.' He stumbled over his words. 'I no longer

fear for her sanity. It's buried under layers of hate. I fear for my own.'

He touched his cravat and, when he raised his hand, his fingers jerked. 'These things take time.' Leaving the room, he mumbled, 'But there will never be enough time for this to heal.'

Warrington reached for the knife with his right hand, jerked it from the wood and tossed it into the fireplace. Melina touched his back. From behind, she slipped her arms around him. He covered her hand with his.

'My wife's love could be harsh in so many ways. It would have been better had she hated me.'

Melina rested her head against his back. 'Now you can let her go.'

He took Melina's hand, brushed a kiss against it and stepped back. He sat on the sofa and stretched his legs out and his stare focused on the candle. 'I no longer feel anger at the trouble Cassandra caused me. I only feel anger that she caused so many others to suffer. Ludgate has his own troubles. You're right. I'd prefer to strangle Cassandra and it would undo nothing.'

He gave a long blink and looked at her. 'When Cass came home, I raged. She had to agree to my terms and they were not easy ones. Cassandra was no innocent victim. I suppose it didn't matter to me earlier who the father of the girl was because I already knew who the father wasn't. It wasn't me.'

He leaned his head against the back of the chair, his face towards the ceiling. He shut his eyes. 'And I can be thankful that Jacob and the girl will not have to grow up living with their mother's penchant for finding trouble.'

Warrington turned his head to the side and opened his eyes, watching Melina. 'I wish you'd seen none of this, Melina. When Ben finishes his next repairs, I'll see that you get passage home and I'll make sure that whatever is needed for your retrieval of the artefacts to be taken care of.'

Melina kept her irritation hid. He talked too calmly of sending her away. She didn't ask that he throw himself on the knife blade, but he might *look* nicked.

'I will be happy to see my sisters.' She blew out one of the candles.

He stood. 'I believe Broomer needs my company. I'm sure he has a tale to tell me and maybe a song he heard at Drury Lane. He's not fit for polite company sometimes, which makes him all the better for me.'

At the doorway, he looked over his shoulder. 'I'll not trouble you tonight, Melina. I know you aren't of the same cloth as Daph or Cass. I knew who Cass was, but until tonight, I believed Daphne someone else entirely. I thought her a sister.' He shook his head. 'Lies. Everything. Lies.'

Chapter Nineteen

That night, Melina had slept lightly. When she woke in the early hours, the stillness of the house seeped into her skin. She slipped from her bed and crept to see if she could find Warrington.

At the doorway to the sitting room, she stopped and saw candles lit on each side of the room, but only one candle glowed in each branch. Warrington sat where the light from the window would have flowed over his shoulder had it been day. Instead, shadows danced over his face.

His eyes were shut and his head sagged to the side. She supposed he and Broomer had swallowed enough ale to drown themselves. His fingers were clasped together and one leg was sprawled out, the other bent at the knee. He still wore his frock coat.

'Melina.' He spoke without opening his eyes. 'Don't stare so.'

He moved only slightly, upright, but not as relaxed. When he looked at her, he took in her body. She could feel his eyes as she watched his face. The instant his eyes lowered to her breasts, she felt the heat ignite in her. His gaze slid to her waist, and lower, leaving a fiery heat trail that moved inward.

'Again, Aphrodite has risen from the sea.' His voice unfurled. 'Arisen from the shells and stands before me. A vision. Her hair falling over her shoulders. Her eyes reaching into the soul of everyone she sees.'

'You're foxed.'

He shook his head, but his eyes remained on her, apart from his words. 'Yes and no. If I am drunk, then you must blame yourself. Because it's your appearance that has addled my senses.'

'Is that all?'

'Yes. There is not enough drink to wash my memories from me. I tried it once and it could not be done in three days. I would have had to swallow enough to destroy my whole mind and I didn't want that.'

She didn't speak. He kept her there without a word, only the presence of his being holding her captive.

She turned to leave, reassured he was at his home, safe.

'Stay, Melina. You truly do owe me that much if for no other reason than I helped you escape from this Stephanos you detest. But I cannot stand the notion of a man touching you.' He gave a humourless laugh. 'I do not want anyone you do not desire touching you. Even myself.'

'You need to be alone.' The wind outside picked up, reminding her of the night's gloom. But perhaps the true darkness was in his eyes.

He breathed deeply, moving back in his chair, sitting straight and clasping his fingers in his lap. 'I should have drank myself to sleep tonight and prayed to dream of shipwrecks.'

'There's still time.'

'Sweet Melina.' He laughed. 'You so guard your speech.'

'Perhaps.'

He softened his voice. 'I hope not.' He turned his face back to the dark window. His gaze took her in. 'If you were to think of poison, my dear Melina, or wish my death, I would be indeed fortunate to get a second chance. You determined to set sail on a ship of strangers and did. You would not run if the deed were not accomplished. You would try a different route.'

Melina felt a chill at her toes that crept up, but she hid her shiver. 'I have *never* even seen poison.'

'You have yet to marry.' He brushed his hand across his knee, picking at the doeskin. 'My wife killed my son's grandfather. My wife— How do I tell my brothers that our father is not here because my wife didn't want him around any more?'

'I have met Ben. If Cassandra's ways were so obvious—if it could be suspected that she would do such a thing—you know he would have told you. Did you suspect, before you became ill, she might try to murder your father?'

'Do not ask such a question.' His eyes, dark, locked on hers. 'I know you are trying to make a point, but to even suggest I could have imagined such a thing and allowed it to happen is intolerable. And along with my father's death on my conscience, I have her spawn with Ludgate to keep.'

'He said he would care for her.'

'I may not think much of the child, but I do not trust him to find a home for her.'

'I'll help you.'

'You've never even seen her.'

'It doesn't matter. She's a little girl. An orphan, in a sense. My father left me to starve and has no wish to see me. She shouldn't suffer because of something she had no control over.'

'Happens all the time. Though I'll pay her way.'

Melina spoke softly. 'Then let me take her back to Melos. She should have a family. I will treat her as a daughter.'

Warrington shook his head. 'My problem. My responsibility. I will see to it. Broomer can locate a couple willing to raise her as their own. I will examine his choices. You already have sisters to concern you.'

'You would send a servant for such a duty?'

'I would send the best person for the task. And that is Broomer. He knows what goes on in the world outside the peerage because he doesn't always have work inside the house and finds his way among the streets. When he talks, people think he is a simpleton and they don't notice how much he listens. I didn't at first. I've already told him that the little girl might need someone else to care for her and he knows of a place where she might find a home. When she and Jacob arrive here, she can meet her new family.'

'She does have a name.'

'Yes. She was named for her father. Thank you for reminding me. But I had not forgotten.'

'Perhaps you should forget. Remembering only serves one purpose—to cause you discomfort.'

He shut his eyes. When he opened them, he turned his head from her. 'That is one thing I will change. I will make the people who take her agree to give her a new name. Something they choose. Perhaps it will give them closeness to her.' He pushed himself up. 'This isn't her fault. I want the past behind me, and even if she doesn't know it, so does she. She deserves a chance to begin anew.'

He opened a desk drawer, pulling out a bottle of ink and paper. 'I'm sending Whitegate's butler a note. I never took my father's room after he passed. Cass and I had living quarters of our own, smaller but comfortable. Now I want my things moved to my father's chambers. While Jacob is here, the changes can be made. I'll return with him.'

Melina wanted to touch him, but didn't. She wasn't sure if she wanted to caress his jaw, feeling the skin, or slap him to try to shake him from his feelings.

'You're not accepting and forgetting, you're just pushing the reminder where you cannot see her,' she said. 'You still have the rage.'

'I do have the anger.' He dipped the pen in ink and wrote as he spoke. 'I just found out for certain that my wife killed my father. For nothing. No true reason. The only person she really had reason to kill was me. But I know she didn't like my father. Didn't like his wife and didn't like his controlling so much of our lives.' He dipped the pen again and continued writing.

Melina turned her back, feeling like a goddess. One who had come to earth only to discover that men were mortals and could not accept a peaceful world when they had opportunity.

'It is only what is inside you keeping the pain alive for you.' She did not face him, but her voice was loud enough that he could easily understand her words.

'A person who has never been burned cannot know what it is like to have the experience of fire consuming the skin and the way it lingers. The deeper the burn, the longer it takes to heal and to forget the pain.'

'You plan to live the rest of your life alone?' she asked, feeling each word jar into her heart. And she would live the rest of her life with the memory of him remaining in her mind and she'd wonder if he'd ever put the betrayal behind him. She doubted he could. If she thought he would, she might proceed differently. Because she would never forget the Earl of Warrington. And she didn't even know his given name.

'I think it best.' He didn't look up from his writing.

She stared at the bent head and didn't believe he was unaware of her. But she was being dismissed. Just like the child he thrust from him.

The wind pushed against the house. But it wasted its time. The house was Warrington's. Immovable. Closed tight. And very dark.

Warrington's head jerked up and his eyes narrowed, but he listened. The noise wasn't only the wind, but someone at the door.

Warrington stood. 'Sounds like someone trying to break inside.' Grabbing a lamp, he hastened to the stairs.

Broomer had a flintlock at his side, but he'd opened the door to Ludgate. The frail man stood at the threshold. He looked to the top of the stairs. 'I must speak with you privately.'

Warrington waved an arm, sending Broomer

on his way, and gave a nod to Ludgate. They moved back into the sitting room. Ludgate followed and stood just inside the door. Melina saw scratch marks across his jaw. He clasped something hidden in his hand and he paced in place, the crutch tapping along beside his leg.

Ludgate collapsed on to the sofa and pulled the crutch to him, resting his forehead on the wrapped top of the wood. His eyes were closed. 'I am so sorry, Warrington. So sorry. I had no idea.'

'I am making sure Willa is cared for.' Warrington's voice cut the air. 'You do not have to concern yourself with her ever again. In fact, you will not be allowed to.'

'I am not talking of that.' His head moved when he spoke. The sound of Ludgate's breathing drowned the sound of the wind outside.

'I saw…' He paused, finding words, holding a bottle. 'Daphne was too quiet when we returned home. Daphne is…no different than Cassandra in her own way. When I first heard of your back being hurt, I wondered. But Cass was no longer alive. That left only Daphne. I thought she might try to kill me, but never you. And I had never suspected the illness in your house anything but a fever until tonight. I only suspected Daphne of wanting me dead. Nothing else.'

He raised his eyes. 'Arsenic poisoning can look like cholera. Daphne had a bottle of the poison. I rarely live in the house, but tonight I did not leave.

When she stirred in the night, I listened. I pried a bottle of arsenic from her fingers. Meant for me and I knew it. She said…' He paused. 'She'd decided since you weren't going to kill me, she'd have to do so. Especially after I told her I would send her to the country because I believed she knew of Cassandra poisoning your father and did nothing to prevent it or to discourage her.'

Ludgate gulped out the words. 'She killed Cassandra. When Daphne returned home Cassandra died shortly after. And when I confronted Daphne tonight, she told me. She said they called the powder their guarantee of a happy marriage.'

'But why didn't Daphne kill Cass before Willa's birth?'

'She didn't expect… They were together every day and she didn't believe at first that the child was mine. I assured her it could not be possible. She didn't think her sister or I could betray her so. When Cassandra left, the baby came too early. Daphne knew the child couldn't have been yours and it had to have been conceived earlier. She knew the dates. And the girl's name was a slap. But Cassandra wouldn't see her. When Daphne received the letter from her sister telling of the chance of another child, Daph visited without telling Cassandra first. She said she had emptied a bottle of the Fowler's Solution medicinal she found at your house and put the poison in it, then told the lady's maid to be sure that Cassandra was given Fowler's Solution as it would ease her discomfort. I didn't know the truth until now, but I suspected. I've hardly stayed in the same house with Daphne since the little girl was born because she made my life a nightmare. I didn't suspect she wanted you to kill me, and when you didn't, she went for what she called the marriage powder. *Till death do us part,* she said. She claims it is why the vows are written such.'

'Will you tell the magistrate?'

Ludgate shook his head. 'No. I am the only one who heard her words. She can easily lie that she said nothing. That I did it. The footmen and butler have her contained now. She's still raging—at me—for the betrayal. I don't want her hanged. I will see she is confined to Bedlam. It is only my word and hers, and I do not want this to become known. I told the servants she has lost her senses and it is the truth.' Ludgate spoke quietly. 'The little girl should not have the spectre of this following her. The truth is bad enough, and what if it is embellished even more? Do whatever you want with the child and send an accounting to my man of affairs. The funds will be paid. I don't care.'

He left, then stopped and looked back. 'But I would place the little one in a home where she can never find out about her true birth, one with a lot of spiritual guidance. She will need it.'

Chapter Twenty

Warrington had stood at the window an hour, waiting for the carriage, watching the place the town coach would first become visible, before he saw Dane, riding Chesapeake. The carriage was next.

Warrington strode to the front entrance, stepping outside as the vehicle stopped.

'Father,' Jacob squealed, opening the town-coach door. A woman's arm reached for him, but missed, and the child scampered out.

'Careful,' Warrington shouted. Jacob dashed to the doorway and threw himself against his father's legs.

'You're back,' Jacob shouted. 'I knew you were back. I knew that's why Uncle Dane said we must come to London.'

Warrington could see the same family traits of his brothers in Jacob's long-limbed stance. He had the jaw that could jut into the same stubborn pose.

'Yes,' Warrington said. 'Did you behave for Uncle?'

He nodded his head. 'We fished. We rode. We did everything.' He stretched the last word out, making it take longer to speak than all the other words he'd said.

Warrington knelt to one knee in front of his son. 'I brought you black rocks from an island we visited, and some shells I'm sure you've not seen before, and a hat made by a wise old woman who said the boy who wore it would grow tall and strong.'

'I'm tall and strong now.' He flexed his arm and made a muscle. 'Uncle says I can carry a sword soon—then we'll fight.'

'Oh, I look forward to that.' Warrington grabbed his son by the shoulders and gave him a quick pull against him. Jacob somehow always smelled like porridge. He let him go, thankful his brother couldn't see his eyes.

'Can I have a real sword?' his son asked.

'Soon.' He stood and deep inside himself he was pleased Jacob wasn't old enough yet to heft the weapon. Jacob stayed at his father's side.

Whatever else Cassandra had done wrong, she'd done one thing right and given him Jacob. Although he was sure that if she'd known how the future would turn out, she'd never have let Jacob be born. If only for spite.

Dane had dismounted and given the reins to

the coachman. Then he helped the nursemaid from the carriage. The servant brought out the little girl. The older woman almost stumbled over her skirts as she moved down the steps, but Dane steadied her.

Dane's boots clicked on the walkway as he strode to greet his elder brother. He and Dane could not be any closer in age or likeness unless they were twins. But Dane made his own light and danced through shadows. He just preferred to keep his nose in a book, or a ledger, or a garden.

No one ever mentioned the slight—very thin—scar running from in front of the ear to the base of his cheek, but Dane would complain of it itching. An occurrence that only happened around females who could offer sympathy.

Dane stopped at his brother's side, reaching out to shove Warrington's shoulder. 'When you were late, I was sure you and Ben had a fight and had fallen overboard. I was going to send out a search for you next year, or the year after. Whenever I started missing you and had run through your funds.'

'I had a wonderful time. Would have stayed longer, but knew you'd have my house tumbling down if I didn't return—and I missed Jacob.' Warrington strode around Dane, leading his son into the house.

Broomer walked out from the servants' quar-

ters, giving a huge bow to Dane. Dane handed
his hat to the manservant.

Broomer gave another bow and took the hat,
holding it in both hands as he left the hall.

Dane's easy smile of welcome stayed on his
face. Then he saw Melina at the top of the stairs,
stilled and immediately his gaze darted back to
his brother, questioning.

Warrington made sure his face showed nothing. He introduced Melina. 'She'll be taking care
of the children when the nursery maid needs
help.' Warrington looked at his brother, giving
him a brief nod. They moved together up the
stairs, Dane at the end of the group.

Warrington saw Melina's smile when she saw
the little girl.

'You must be tired from the journey,' Melina
said to the nursery maid. 'Let me take the little
angel.'

With a stoic face, the maid handed the girl into
Melina's waiting arms.

'I'll help you get them settled,' Melina said,
leading the older woman into the room Melina
had prepared for the children.

Dane watched, unspeaking and unmoving.

Warrington kept his hand on Jacob's shoulder,
keeping his son near, and led Dane in the direction of the sitting room.

Once they reached the larger chamber, Warrington smiled at his brother. 'Hope you do not

mind finding somewhere else to stay. The children and the nursery maid will need rooms. The governess is in the other room.'

Dane's brows rose. 'Not at all. Not at all. I'm sure I can find someone who cares about me who'll give me a pillow and scraps from their table.'

'Aunt Adelphinia is always asking for you to spend more time with her,' Warrington said.

Dane turned to him, face solemn. 'Exactly what I was thinking. I so love playing whist with her and her friends. It brightens my evenings.' He grinned. 'But truly, War, you would not believe the tales those genteel ladies tell. They delight in shocking me.'

'You're easy to shock.'

Dane shrugged. 'True. And did you have all the adventures you dreamed of on the journey? You were gone longer than expected.'

'Only because we found an inviting island... full of lovely ladies...' He let his face reminisce on glorious sights he never saw. 'You need to go with Ben next time.'

Dane's head bobbled and his smile was smug. 'Oh, you'll not catch me that easy.' He paused. 'So the trip—as bad as I said?'

'Worse... Your brother...' Warrington grumbled. 'Put a captain's coat on him and he thinks he's Captain Cook without possibility of demise. I would insist you go with him on the next voyage, but that would surely increase the danger. With the two of you on board, the ship would sink. It was perilous enough this time.'

Dane watched him, waiting.

'Ben banged himself up sliding around the ship in a storm. But he's healing.'

'Papa,' Jacob interrupted, looking at his father. 'I have a boat. I brought it. Nurse is keeping it for me. I want to show you.'

War brushed Jacob's hair from his eyes. He was looking as ragged as the cabin boy. Warrington nodded and Jacob darted out through the door.

'And the, uh…' Dane tilted his head to the left, in the direction Melina had left. 'The woman—you brought her back because we have no suitable English governesses to teach Willa the ways of our country.' His eyes twinkled. 'Instead, you find a woman—I'm sure you noticed—and install her in your house.'

'We will not be discussing it.' He sat on the sofa and looked at Dane. 'And you will keep ten paces from her at all times—and keep your head down when she enters a room.' He grinned at his brother. 'Perhaps you should just leave now.'

'I will visit Aunt Adelphinia. She says I am her *favourite* nephew.' Dane spoke lightly, but he moved to lean against the unlit fireplace. 'And is the mighty Captain Ben returning home before he sails again?'

'He had to stay on *Ascalon* to make sure the repairs are being completed and to prepare her for the next voyage. As soon as the ship is ready, he'll sail. But he will make time to see you and tell us he's leaving.'

Dane nodded, lips pressed before he spoke. 'I believe I'll have to speak with Ben. You might not want to discuss the woman, but I'll wager he will.'

'Captain Little Brother will tell you Melina did spend some time with me. I took care of her when she was ill as I didn't wish for any of the randy seamen to push themselves on her. And he will find great joy in telling you how he made up senseless errands to keep her busy so I could not enjoy her company to the fullest.'

'Ha. If you had that woman near you, then you had enough time to find some comfort.'

'Doesn't signify. She's here. As far as Jacob will know she is merely another servant. I've certainly dressed her in sacks.'

'Those shapeless rags she is wearing do not hide all of her.' Dane teased with his eyes.

Warrington nodded, picturing Melina's form. If he had found Melina before he met Cassandra, things might have been different, but he hadn't. And he had Jacob. Warrington needed to be a true father and he'd already brought enough turmoil into Jacob's life.

'Have you heard from our stepmother?' Warrington asked.

'Yes. You received a letter from her.' Dane paused, moving the fripperies around on the mantel the way one would move chess pieces. 'I did open it. I sent her the funds. And a firm response. From you. You were a bit angry. Much more so than I would have been. You bluntly told her she must stop the wagers.'

Warrington nodded. 'I'm not as understanding as you are.'

'No. You're not. But I'm her favourite, too.' His chin jutted a bit, in the traditional family pose.

'You didn't like it any better than I did when she sold Mother's jewels.'

'I didn't relish it, but it made little difference. I didn't like her from the moment she called on her dear friend Adelphinia to see how she was faring over the loss of her mother. As if anyone who truly knew Adele would call her that.' He shrugged while he spoke. 'You also should be aware that you sent a man Broomer knows to our dear stepmother's house. The man is quite skilled at wagering and is to teach her not to lose so grandly.' Dane grinned. 'I am Broomer's favourite, too.'

'A favoured dung heap is still a dung heap.'

'As long as it is preferred above the other dung heaps, I am pleased.' Dane scratched at his chin and moved beside Warrington so that their boots almost touched. 'You're very close to the favourite, though.'

'I cannot believe I let you watch Jacob.'

Dane laughed. 'Don't worry. I pretended to be you. Stern and aloof.' He plopped himself down on the sofa. 'Now tell me what the trip was really like.'

Warrington began to talk, but his mind stayed on Dane's words. Stern and aloof. Just the way his own father had been.

Melina woke well into the morning. She'd had trouble falling asleep and hadn't slept soundly.

She'd spent the evening with Willa, instantly finding the child endearing.

In the night, she'd heard Warrington's laughter echoing in the house and the raised voice of his brother, telling some bold tale. Warrington had his own way to keep his shadows at bay.

And she wanted to find the place Cassandra was buried and take a hammer to the marker. This woman she'd never seen. A ghost with far-reaching tentacles. A woman who had everything she could have wanted and could have needed, and found her joy in destroying others around her.

Melina dressed slowly, knowing she would be leaving soon and never see England again.

She'd never see Warrington free himself of Cassandra. She'd never know if he could truly have a reprieve from the past.

A knock sounded at the bedchamber door and she hurried to open it. A draggy-eyed Broomer stood there, his waistcoat buttoned askew. 'Miss. You've a caller. An older woman. A real lady. Not one like that Ludgate's woman.' He shook his head. 'I'd have shot *her*.'

He plodded down the stairs, his words fading. 'I put this one in the sitting room because she had a peaceable face. Tired-like. But if you shout, I'll be there with the pistol.'

Melina found her father's wife examining the harpoon, her face only inches from it. She had her braided hair wrapped into a bun and lace ringed the neck of her peach dress. Her eyes were serene, but she had to have known something of Melina's life or she wouldn't have been standing in the room.

Melina could see no lack of strength in the woman in front of her. In fact, the woman reminded her of the stories she'd heard of the mythical Greek heroines. Even the scent Lady Hawkins wore fitted her, not a flowery delicate one, but more bracing, almost the same as the resin the men used to coat the ship.

'Interesting…' The older woman gave her a warm smile when she turned to Melina. 'I've never, ever been near so much of a sailing collection in a home. The seashells are amazing.' She pointed to the collection at the sides of the fireplace.

'Yes. Warrington's brother selected the objects.' Melina's eyes roved the room. 'Few women would choose a tooth, a weapon or a broken ship's bell.'

'Even the blue curtains hint of the water. This man has a fascination. I am impressed.' She touched the tooth. 'I don't believe I've ever been in a room an ordinary man planned—though I have been to Carlton House. One can't consider that an ordinary man's creation, though.' She looked to Melina, her eyes saying she expected Melina to agree.

Melina smiled and nodded. She'd never heard of Carlton House.

The woman's mouth quirked up. 'Like you, I cannot imagine a woman who would appreciate the decorations, but they are interesting.' She stood solemnly, and interlocked her fingers in front of herself. 'You're my husband's daughter, aren't you?'

Melina raised her chin in agreement, not seeing anger in the woman's face, but a searching perusal. 'How...'

The woman touched above her own breast. 'I saw the mark. My husband's sister had one on her arm. She's passed now. And one of my daughters has a smaller one on her back and one has one on her scalp, which is hidden completely by her hair. I doubt my husband is even aware of his daughters' marks.' She examined Melina. 'You have the same nose and perhaps profile of my daughter, as well. My husband doesn't know—

but I saw the painting of you. I always made it a practice to see his showings.' She shook her head. 'He never thinks to ask what I do when he paints. I truly think he doesn't know the world exists at that time for other people.'

'I did not mean for you to discover…' Melina felt she'd betrayed her father. Although she didn't think he deserved kindness on her part, she didn't wish to create problems.

The woman rubbed her right hand against the rings on her left, which she wore over her gloves. 'When I saw you in my house, I near had an apoplexy. It took me a day to think about it before I truly accepted that you were in England. I decided to find you. All I had to do was get in one of those dreadful hackney carriages and say I wanted to go to the Earl of Warrington's home.' Her eyes, wreathed in wrinkles, deepened into smugness. 'And to know about my husband's other life—I was fairly certain years and years ago. More than a decade, I would suppose.'

'You spoke to him about it?'

Her eyes flashed anger. 'I saw no reason to speak my doubts if he would not speak his deceit.' Her ringed fingers fluttered again. 'No. I saw no need to talk to him about this. I could not confront—accuse—and demand confession. He would have professed innocence—and other than hiring a man to follow him on a sea voyage, I had little chance of proving my suspicions.

I was content to wait, knowing the truth would surface.' She pointed a gloved finger at Melina. 'It does, my dear. Remember that and it will help you sleep better at night.'

'Why did you suspect?' Melina hadn't expected the woman to be so calm about something that should have caused such intensity.

'Too much secrecy. Too much contentment to be from England for long spells. And when I first viewed his painting of you, I saw it at a sideways glance and assumed he'd painted my daughter with a different hair colour. But why would he paint her years younger than she is? Then I saw the shoreline behind her. The sea. Hmm.' She touched a gloved finger to her cheek. 'He told me, and yet, he didn't know he did.'

'You were content with it?'

She shook her head. 'Absolutely not. But it makes little sense to move from a man who is hardly at home and seems to care little when he is. Why make a change when there wasn't a need. My secret, you see. He left for the island. I waved goodbye with a stoic promise I would try hard to survive while he was gone—and cherished the imagination of storms at sea. If he never returned, I would toddle along as always, wearing a lovely shade of black for a while. When he did return, I toddled along as always, wearing a lighter shade of black, for myself.' Hurt flashed behind her eyes, but was replaced with a wide, innocent blink. 'He does not touch me. I told Lord Hawkins my physician diagnosed a serious female complaint for me—and described ghastly lesions, bloody flux and being treated with leeches. I showed him a handkerchief covered in blood.' She shuddered. 'The poor maid had fallen and broken the mantle of a lamp, gashing her hand. But he didn't know.' She patted her silver hair. 'My children—I love. My husband—he is like a picture on the wall to me. I have him for display on occasion.'

Melina smiled at the thought of her father reduced to a painting. 'I was furious. I never suspected him married to someone else.'

'The question probably did not enter your mind with as much insistence as it entered mine. I had months and months to think of nothing else.'

The older woman took a breath, and her eyes darted to the side. This time, Melina could see the struggle she used to keep her voice light.

'Do you mind telling me the particulars?' Lady Hawkins asked. 'Why you came here? Your mother? Other children?'

'I have two sisters and my mother died. No brothers.' Melina looked to the window. 'I needed to come here to see if I could find a way to fund a dowry for my sisters.' She smiled, her gaze locked to the wall. 'Our lives are not the same as here. I cannot believe what I see. The *plouti,* gold and silver—for *buttons or spoons.* Even the servants have fine clothing.' She thought back to the island and the contrast.

The older woman appeared to shrug off the talk of wealth. 'How much dowry do your sisters need?'

Melina told her.

She tilted her head back. 'That's all?' She smiled. 'My dear, I will quietly see to having the funds for you. I think I could arrange it within a few days.'

Melina shivered. To think, she could be on board a ship for Melos—with a dowry for both sisters.

'What will my father think, spending the funds?'

The woman put her hand to her cheek. 'Oh. It was such a horrible injustice to both my husband and me when my father died and left all his funds in the care of my cousin. And my relative, he is such a strange young man. He will not listen to a word concerning the accounts unless it is from my lips. I could throw every pence into the ocean and he would simply say, "It's what your father wanted".' She smiled at Melina. 'You know, I think it never occurred to my husband who might have suggested such a spurious arrangement to my father before he died. It was at a particularly rough time in my life, when I'd just seen a painting of you, my dear.' She reached out and examined her gloves. 'I do feel I owe you.'

Lady Hawkins stood. 'I must get home, although my husband will not even notice I'm gone. He painted well into the night and woke early to catch the light. He found inspiration again—and the rest of the world is lost to him.'

Melina rose, and the woman moved close to her, looking intensely at her.

'I can't help but see my own children in your face.' She shook her head. 'And I never really thought to see you standing before me.' Her features eased. 'I didn't know how I would truly feel if I saw you, but you're a lovely woman.'

She looked at the harpoon again. 'I'm sure the painting session will be nearly over when I return home. But...' she touched her hand to Melina's '...should you encounter a problem, I'd be pleased if you send a message to me. I will help you as my own daughter—quietly, of course. I'm not ready to explain the truth to my children. They have been sheltered, I think, from their father's true nature. I would like as little upset as possible in the flow of my life.' Her eyes had a malevolent glint. 'I do like taking my husband's secrets and keeping them from him.'

'I understand.'

Her face softened again. 'I would be pleased if you consider me a friend.' She hesitated in the doorway. 'In some deep part of my mind, I must have wondered since he returned with the painting of the three girls playing in the waves. That one.' She looked to the wall. 'Their faces were obscured.' She winced. 'Such a painting was not his usual style. And when I saw the portrait of your face…and then the mark…' she touched above her breast '…like my own daughter.' Her eyes wavered. 'You were no longer a stranger to me. You were a part of my family. I only ask that you keep our ties private.'

When her father's wife walked out through the door, Melina knew she had no reason not to return to Melos. She could take funds back to her sisters and buy the statue. But now the island felt lonely to her in a way she'd never noticed before. She would be returning to a gaol, locked alone with her heart—and dreams too secret to mention aloud.

Warrington had distanced himself from her and she knew he wouldn't even let his thoughts linger on her. They were still taken by another woman.

Chapter Twenty-One

Melina sat in the children's room, which for some reason smelled like linseed oil—possibly someone's idea of a good cleaning solution. She felt an intense need to be near the little girl who had no true father and whose mother had died.

Willa chewed her doll's painted shoe. The nursery maid slept, lips parted, in a chair beside the window.

Melina didn't know if she should wake the woman up and tell her it was the children's bedtime, or put the little ones to bed herself and let the nursemaid wake naturally.

Quietly, Jacob walked to his sister and snatched her doll from her arms. Willa lunged at him without a cry and her teeth went for his leg. He jumped aside, his hand at her hair, restraining her. All done in silence.

'Give the doll back to her,' Melina commanded. He did, shoving it between her mouth and his leg.

'She bites hard,' he said. He stepped back, staring at his sister. 'Don't you, Ratface?'

'Jacob. Your sister has a name. Use it.'

Willa took her baby and hit him with it, and he grabbed the doll's arm and held on. Willa tugged the other direction. He pulled at the doll once and then released it. 'You can have her back, Willa, Lady Ratface.'

He smiled at Melina.

'Jacob. It is nearly your bedtime and you must behave if you wish to stay up any longer.' Melina stood.

He shrugged. 'Willa likes it.'

Melina kept her voice stern. 'I do not. Do not do it again. The two of you are not to fight. Brothers must be kind to their sister.'

He nodded. 'I am. She likes hitting me with the doll and I like calling her names.'

Warrington opened the door and walked in, making all the noise of a spirit, but Jacob saw him.

The boy jumped from the floor and whirled to his father. He gave a bow and schooled himself into the manner of an Englishman. Warrington reached out and tousled Jacob's hair, laughing when the child used both hands to straighten it.

'I need to show you the picture I drew. It's of Uncle's ship,' Jacob said, then scrambled to pull a paper from inside a book. He unfolded the drawing and handed it to his father. 'You can have it,' he said. 'I'm drawing another one.'

'Thank you.' Warrington took the picture, pulling it closer to his face. 'We must save it. Tell your nursery maid to start collecting your best drawings. I will have them bound into a book and we can look at it together.'

Jacob smiled. 'I'm going to sail with Uncle— Captain Ben, when I am bigger.'

He gave his son a pat on the shoulder. 'We'll see.'

Willa became aware of the conversation. She kept the doll's foot in her mouth and ran to Melina's knees.

The earl's face didn't flicker as he looked in their direction. Instead, he took Jacob by the hand and left the room. Melina could hardly believe the difference in Warrington. He'd not spoken to her privately after the night Ludgate had appeared. Perhaps she was more like the earl than she realised, seeing not the person, but the appearance, and she'd been misled.

Warrington hadn't burst with smiles on the ship, but now he acted colder, and this man's hands would not touch a slop bucket now. She had no question in her mind concerning that.

Willa ignored Warrington much the same way as he avoided her. But she had to be restrained from toddling to Broomer if he walked into a room where the little girl was, and even though the servant acted put out by it, Melina could tell he exaggerated the irritation to please Willa and he made silly faces at her when he thought no one noticed. He'd even given the nursemaid a little carved toy for Willa.

Now Willa sat, pulling at the dress on her wooden doll, the plaything's stoic expression a complete opposite of the little girl's. Willa had a fan, a full-sized one, and waved it over her doll, hitting the toy's face often as not.

Melina stayed with her until Willa fell asleep on the floor. Lifting Willa, Melina placed her on the bed. The nurse woke at the movement, and mumbled that she'd finish getting the little girl to bed.

Melina went in search of Jacob, but truly she knew she looked for his father.

Warrington sat on the sofa in the sitting room, in his usual relaxed pose of his eyes half-closed, legs relaxed in front of him. His cravat hung loose. Jacob slept beside him, looking as if he'd fallen over, and he used Warrington's lap for a pillow.

'I'll get him to bed,' she whispered.

'Nonsense. Sit with us and watch a fireplace with no flames.'

She hesitated. 'It's late.'

'It's getting later and then it will get early and become a new day.'

The melancholy air of the room touched her, but she stayed.

'I hope you remember your time in England well, even if you might now think it is filled with the worst of the world…' His voice rolled smoothly into the room, curling around her the way the flames would have wrapped around burning coals had the fireplace been alight.

'I will remember you.' She walked behind him, putting fingertips on his shoulder.

He reached up and clasped her hand. 'I hope it has not all been difficult for you, Melina.'

'The world has been so different from what I am used to. I miss my *adelfi*, my sisters, and the plainness of Melos. Each day is the same as the day before. And the sea—I liked the sea. Even the smells are different here. The scents there are from the earth and nature. Here, they are from the people cooking and bringing horses about.'

'I will give you a dowry.'

She shook her head, feeling lightness in her next words. 'There is no need. My father's wife has promised to see that we have what we need.'

The uplift of one brow was all the acknowledgement he gave her.

'I've arranged for Broomer to travel with you back to Melos.' Warrington's voice was a husky murmur. 'He'll get you home, safely. Threaten Stephanos or do what is needed. I've told him every woman on the island is as lovely as you.

He asked how soon he can leave. I've instructed him to gather his things.'

Melina looked forward, and saw not what she'd seen before, but the world through Warrington's eyes. And knew she was not in it.

Warrington lay in his bedchamber, trying to force himself to sleep. The brown sacks he'd dressed her in didn't work. Nothing would. His weakness hadn't left him.

Nor was her presence easing his memories.

Something inside gnawed at him, reminding him of the time he'd thought he would have the dream of a loving family. He'd wanted the world he saw reflected when one looked at the portraits of a man, his wife and children, carefully arranged, and all around them tidy.

Clawing desire burned in him, and not just desire for her body, but for a world where feelings were pure.

Warrington pressed his face into the pillow, trying to smother the thoughts torturing him.

At least Melina seemed to care for the girl. She patted the child's back when she held her and he didn't think she even knew she did.

He'd stayed away from Melina and he could feel her presence in the house every moment he kept inside. And when he walked outside, he could hardly wait to return.

He could attend a few soirées, Drury Lane, and

he'd surely be able to find a woman with some appeal. The way he felt, he doubted he could find one who *didn't* have enough to tempt him into her bed. He could go to Almack's and find someone he didn't find attractive, and perhaps then he could believe himself safe to bring her into his home. A woman he might have no true passion for and who could not blind him with her body and beauty and dancing eyes.

But before he left, he wanted to—

But if he did what he wanted to do before he left he'd not need to leave the town house.

He rolled himself out of bed and wrapped on his dressing gown.

Warrington went to the door and knocked, then opened it.

'Melina,' he whispered.

She sat up on the bed and he could tell she wasn't fully awake. Her face looked as puzzled as Jacob's would have.

'Come with me for a moment.' He reached out, taking her hand.

When he pulled her to her feet, she brought the covers with her. He took them from her hand and pushed them loose so they slid to the floor.

He saw her open her eyes wide and shake her head, and she moved back.

'Come with me,' he whispered again. 'I wish to talk to you without children or servants about.'

'It would be as easy as closing a door.'

Her feet didn't move when he took her elbow. He increased his grip.

'You're right,' he grumbled, getting her to the hallway. 'I'm awake now, though, and by coincidence so are you.'

He slipped a hand at her back, to guide her to the sitting room. Touching her was the wrong thing to do. He remembered how she felt when he embraced her, skin against skin. And he didn't need any reminders since he couldn't get the thoughts to recede from his mind for even a half-second. But he didn't know if he could let her go again if he touched her.

She moved to the window. Not sitting. He wondered if she didn't want to sit in his presence, afraid of getting too comfortable.

'I would have thought you would lead me to your bedchamber.' Her words were tart.

In the shadowy dimness, he could tell her hands were clasped together.

Apparently, growing up in Greece had robbed her of the awe she should feel from having the attention of an earl of some funds. And he was certain his mirror hadn't lied. He was not an ogre. Hell, he was better looking than Dane and Dane had a scar on his face and women practically fainted at his feet. But this was Melina. So different than what he understood. He crossed his arms.

'It is silent in here for someone being awoken

because someone else had to urgently speak with them,' she grumbled and he heard the rustling of her movements. 'I'm sure the nursemaid thinks we often meet secretly in the night. She smiles in such a way when she tells me to have pleasant dreams.'

'If she thinks we're together, then I certainly hope she believes it is of great frequency.'

He moved to stand beside her at the window. They were as close as two people could be without touching.

'I shouldn't be in a part of your life. I'm to be gone soon. Now I am watching your— Willa,' she said.

'You can call her my child.' His voice held bitterness. 'She and I are stuck with each other for the moment. I realise she is my child, by possession if not by birth. Ludgate doesn't want her and never will, I am certain of that.'

'And how could he have marched up and demanded her?'

'He could have asked for her the other night. Or he could have told me earlier, by post for his own safety. Or through Cassandra when she was alive. My wife, who'd not even written to see if I lived or died while I was ill—though I understand. It would have been laughable for her to express concern when she so obviously felt none. When she returned, she knew I couldn't possibly think the babe was mine. Particularly as I refused to touch her and did not return to her bed until after the girl was born.'

He patted the back of the sofa. 'When I no longer see Willa around to remind me, I can put all this to rest. Maybe now that I…' He paused. 'I now feel such anger for Daphne, too. More than Ludgate, I suppose. Had she come to me and spoken openly—it would have been different. But she paid a man to taunt me—as if I had not had enough. That must have been something she and Cass learned as children. They were so determined in it.'

He moved to a crystal decanter at a side table and released the stopper. He filled a glass with brandy. He didn't put the stopper back into the neck, but instead absently clicked the crystal against the rim. He finally let the stopper fall into the top and slapped it down with his palm. He swirled the liquid, then took a drink. 'Choices.'

'For Jacob, and for yourself—let it go.'

'I would have done so long ago, if I could. I'm trying. Tomorrow I have a couple arriving who might take Willa.'

She gasped. 'Are you sure they are good people?'

'Broomer would not mislead me. Three years ago, they heard of a street woman who had a child she could not care for and they took the boy in. With no recompense from the mother.'

'Perhaps they wanted…someone to help with the *ergo,* the work.'

'Perhaps. But Broomer said the boy is well fed and clothed, and has turned from a scampering street urchin to a whistling child who is being schooled.' He walked back to the mantel, and stared at it. 'I'll be glad to have the girl gone. The last image of my wife. The last ghost.'

'You aren't getting rid of the last ghost. That one is inside you.'

He nodded. 'I can't take a knife and cut it out of me. Or I would. I would rather have thoughts of you instead of memories of her. But I cannot forget what has gone on before.'

Chapter Twenty-Two

Melina stared out of the nursery window, looking into a day that would have been better served
with rain, instead of the fading fog and wet air.

When the couple arrived, Melina noted that
Warrington's carriage delivered them. They
stepped out. The woman adjusted her bonnet, her
skirts, and gave the man a hopeful smile.

Melina heard little clinks behind her, of Willa
playing with a doll and the feet tapping together.

Melina could barely look at the little cherub
face, feeling like a Judas. She could not be a Judas.

Even Willa seemed to sense a difference and
Melina felt a tug at her clothing. Willa stood,
looking up, with one arm cradling her own baby
tightly.

Melina gathered the girl up and took the doll
from Willa's hands, holding the girl snug. She
used the baby to give Willa's cheeks loud kisses.
The little one immediately laughed—her face

showing she'd forgotten about everything else in the world but her doll.

A few minutes later, a maid entered the nursery.

'Miss.' The servant stopped just inside the doorway, giving a smile in Willa's direction before her face turned serious and she looked at Melina. 'His lordship has called for you.'

Melina tensed and walked to Warrington's sitting room, giving one last glance at Willa while she stayed behind with the servant.

Warrington stood in the doorway, leaning into the frame. He wore a dark waistcoat and frock coat and had no lightness about him. Tightness lined his face. Sleep hadn't been kind to him. 'They're here. Broomer will bring them when I ring for him.'

He moved from the doorway and stepped back into the room, letting her cross in front of him.

'I saw them arrive,' she said.

'Do they pass your inspection?'

She gave a nod and halved the distance between them. 'I do not want Willa to feel abandoned.'

'Perhaps she will feel like she has a mother and father who care for her—like a true family wants her. She needs a family. You know that.'

She looked at him, hoping for a sign of his compassion for Willa.

He gave the slightest shake of his head, standing straight. 'I don't feel any warmth for the child. I don't. She will grow into her mother's image. I do not want that face in my sight for the rest of my life. This is the only way I can rid myself of Cassandra.'

Melina turned back to the window and stared at the horizon. Willa did deserve a caring family. Melina reached out and pulled the bell.

When the couple entered, Melina noticed the serviceable dress of the woman, but around the neck, she'd embroidered a row of flowers—the same ones Melina had once stitched on her sister's handkerchief.

The man, Sinclair, a furniture maker by trade, bowed. He stood thin, too thin, and wore dark clothing. After her introduction, his wife almost vanished behind him.

'This is Melina. She's been assisting in Willa's care,' the earl said and guided Melina to sit on the sofa.

'I hope you found the trip comfortable,' Warrington addressed the Sinclairs, moving behind Melina.

'Yes,' Sinclair answered. 'My wife is not one to leave the house often except for Sunday Services. I've promised her I'll bring her to Drury Lane before too many more months pass.'

The woman looked at her husband when he spoke and seemed scared to meet Warrington's gaze.

'You have a boy?' Melina asked.

'Yes.' The man looked to his wife, guiding her to sit. 'Today, he's with my wife's mother. She lives with us.'

'Do they get on well?' Melina asked.

'Very well,' the man answered, sitting straight. 'When Thomas is not helping with my work, he's asking his granny for a story. I do not know where the woman comes up with the tales she tells.' He smiled, and his shoulders relaxed. 'Sometimes, she tells of clumsy knights and dragons who have blackened teeth from their burning flames. All her dragons have blackened teeth, except the one who cannot muster a puff of smoke. That is the one Thomas must hear stories of over and over.'

'Why do you want Willa?' Melina leaned forward.

'My wife wishes for a daughter.' He shot a glance at her and then turned back to Melina. 'We would not mind to have another boy in the house. It would be nice for Tom to have a brother. But a daughter...' He patted his wife's hand. 'Alice would like to have a little girl to keep her company and so she can show her things a woman needs to know for a home.'

'Willa's timid.'

Sinclair turned to his wife. 'So is Alice.'

Melina stood. 'I suppose you should see Willa and she should have a chance to meet you.'

She hurried from the room and returned, slowly tugging Willa by the hand. Melina smoothed down the tufts of blonde hair too wispy to be braided. No woman could turn her back on a doll so fair. And her little woollen dress, the plainness only contrasted to show the beauty of the child.

When Melina sat, Willa stayed near her and leaned against Melina's legs. She burrowed against Melina and her eyes had a sleepy droop.

'She's quite behaved.' Alice spoke, her eyes locked on Willa.

'Not always.' Melina brushed her hand over Willa's hair again. 'But she truly is a good-natured child.'

Warrington's foot moved, tapping several times back and forth, but he didn't speak.

Melina continued, 'Willa does get irritable when she doesn't get her nap, according to her nursery maid, but she will drag you to her bed so she can be tucked in. And she does like to beg attention from her brother with a bit more force than she should use.'

She brushed down Willa's hair, again feeling the baby skin of her cheek, and looked to Warrington. He appeared more interested in the painting over the fireplace than in the discussion.

'She likes porridge—but not cold.' Melina spoke the words to the woman.

'Tommy is the same,' Alice said. 'I have a place at the back of the stove where I sit the pot. It stays warm there.'

Melina nodded. 'Do you plan on taking in other children?'

Sinclair shook his head. 'We didn't plan on Thomas, but once we heard about him and met him, we decided he should have a home with us. He's a good lad and my wife thinks another child would be dear. Tom's six, but she's already worried about him growing up so fast.'

Melina talked more with the couple, aware of Warrington sitting beside them, occasionally moving his boot, or rubbing away a speck on his clothing or a mote from the nearest surface. He looked to have no more attention for the conversation than he might if the cook explained how a chicken was plucked.

Melina rose, pulling Willa up with her. 'We will be sure to let you know of Warrington's decision. But he is still a bit undecided on letting her leave.'

His eyes darted to her. His jaw was locked. His decision was plain to see in his black stare.

He spoke a few courteous words to the Sinclairs as he walked them to the door and left, still talking to them.

Melina hugged Willa tight, but the cherub pushed away, and Melina lowered her to a standing position.

When Warrington returned, he had Willa's nursery maid with him. The woman picked up her charge and left the room.

'I would like to speak to you a moment, Melina.' Warrington shut the door and then walked to her. He put both hands on her shoulders. 'They are good people. The kind of people who should make up the world.'

'But not right for Willa. I want to take her back to Melos with me. I will be a good mother.'

His fingers tightened. 'They are already parents of a son. They are more right for her than either you or I. They can care for her without knowing what has gone before. They will be good family for her. You will start a family of your own.'

'And Willa can be my first child.'

'No. If you want what is right for the child, you can see the family she will have. She will be here where she can grow up surrounded by those fripperies women like so well. Not on an island that is used as a harbour for ships full of men who've left their morals behind. Willa can have two parents who will have the same love for her they have for their other child. I will see that she has no financial needs. The man does well in his business and he would do well by her should I not send a coin their way, but I will make sure they have no concerns. I will convey a message to them in the morning asking them to let me know when they are ready for Willa.'

Melina wanted to tell him to go to the devil. Wanted to hit him. But it would do no good. She walked from the room. *Cassandra*. Melina hated a woman she'd never met.

Hours after the Sinclairs left, Melina crept to Willa's bed, watching her sleep. The child should have two parents.

Melina pulled a chair near. She'd worried herself about the little girl, but now she felt calm. More at peace. She'd approached Broomer secretly, asking for all he knew of the couple, and he'd told her what decent people they were. He'd told her of his life and how he'd only had one parent, and how he'd wished for a father. She understood why Warrington relied on him so. The man, with all his loudness and size and capability for violence, still had the heart of a boy who longed for the love of a family. She trusted him, as well.

She knew the hour past midnight when Warrington walked in without knocking.

'Have you been hiding from me to punish me?' he asked.

She shook her head, then realised he might not see the movement in the darkness. 'I just had to think. To understand.' She felt spears of anger, but she tamped them down. The hurt ran deeper.

Fingertips touched her shoulders, rubbing gently, sending calming shivers into her body.

'You've been through a lot, Melina. You've slept in a room where the mermaids were.' His fingertips closed over her shoulder. 'I've actually had a fire lit this time. Come with me and we can watch flames instead of unlit coal.'

She rose from the chair and he followed her out of the room.

'It's not easy for me, either, Melina,' he said, sitting.

She sat at one end of the sofa, he sat on the other—his shirt open at the neck, no waistcoat and his hair ruffled a bit, as if he'd run his fingers through it. He looked to have been in bed, then left it and dressed again. His elbow propped on the back of the sofa and his legs sprawled in front. 'I want to go forward.'

She didn't answer.

'Jacob is my child. And he looks…' He smiled. 'Poor child, I suspect he looks exactly as I did at the same age. And I have seen him plan mischief and seen Ben in his face, as well. I will never let him near the sea.'

He leaned forward, moving so his elbows rested at his thighs and his fingers were loosely clasped in front of him. 'I know there is a chance you might have my child in you. I could not let you go if you had a babe that was mine. I could not leave it for another man.'

'I could lie to you.'

'Will you?' His face turned to hers and the firelight flashed one side bright.

She knew she shouldn't have said those words. He'd had enough lies with his wife, but if she'd not said them, he would have wondered anyway.

'I don't know. With a dowry, I could marry before the baby would be old enough to know otherwise, but I would be like you, I think. I would always be seeing your face in the child.'

'I would hope you would not feel quite the same way as I do concerning that.'

'No.' She moved sideways, so she could put a palm flat on his back, feeling through the clothing to the skin, and through the skin to the beating heart beneath. She'd had to touch him. Had to feel him.

'A little higher and you'll be touching the scar.'

She ran her hand over his back and could feel the thin ridge running a slice across his shoulders.

'It doesn't mar you enough on the outside to matter.' She let her fingers linger. 'It's the betrayal you feel.'

'I suppose.' He lowered his face, letting his head rest against his hands. 'I'm thankful that I will no longer have to worry about the past, yet the knowledge I have doesn't rest easy with me.'

He breathed and the movement calmed her worries.

Melina ran her finger to the side of his face, feeling the cheekbones and trailing down the roughened jaw. 'I wish you could have been sculpted. I would like a likeness of you to have with the one I found. To keep for ever.'

'You have an imagination.'

'I don't need one when I look at you.'

He leaned back, letting his arm lie along the back of the sofa, and his other hand touched her. Swirls of warmth swirled inside her caused by the circling of his fingertips along her shoulder. 'I am the same with you, Melina. I would have liked to have been a pirate, hunting treasure, and when I found you on Melos, I would have taken you and kept you. I would have left any jewels, or rocks, or carvings behind. Because I wouldn't have needed them, if I had you.'

She moved into the hollow of his shoulder, hoping that she could always hold his memory alive enough to feel his touch.

Chapter Twenty-Three

At first light, Warrington sat at his desk, penning the letter to Sinclair. The sooner Willa started her new life, the better she would be. She was young. She'd forget soon.

He wondered if his memories would fade, as well. He only hoped they moved to a part of him that didn't feel rage.

He dashed the words across paper, wishing he'd not been blinded by Cassandra's appearance. She hadn't minded if she'd destroyed him, or his entire family.

He touched his fingertips to his forehead. He'd been so ill. And when he heard she'd taken Jacob, he'd been grateful for his son to be safely away. Never knowing Jacob would have been in the most precarious hands of all. His mother's.

He held his own hands out, looking at them. They were as guilty of his father's death as if he'd brought a viper into the house and it bit his father. He didn't deserve someone such as Melina.

Warrington put his pen in the holder and left the room, feeling a gnawing sense in his stomach. His whole world had changed—thanks to Cassandra. She'd taken his father from him and put a child in his house who didn't belong. He went to the nursery to see his sleeping son.

'Jacob,' he called out when he opened the door. He saw Jacob's face, thankful Cassandra had never considered Jacob a chore. 'Put on some trousers and a rough shirt. Chesapeake is missing us. I'll send Broomer for him.'

Jacob rolled out of bed, moving with a slippery speed.

The boy stopped, bare legs showing from his nightshirt, and his eyes alight. 'I bet I ride fast now.'

'No. We'll not race.'

'Fast walk?'

'Perhaps.'

Jacob gave a confident nod of his head, fully agreeing with the statement. He turned, running to get his trousers.

Warrington strode to the library and waited, only to have Melina walk in. Her hair in a glossy knot, a rushed glow to her cheeks, and he felt desire—even when she wore the hideous tea-coloured gown.

She carried Willa on her hip, looking overloaded by the weight. Melina didn't look at his eyes. Guilt plunged into him. She blamed him for not keeping the girl. The child still wore her night rail and dropped her head to Melina's shoulder.

'Jacob rushed in wanting me to help find his cap,' Melina said. 'He thinks you are taking him riding. Don't you want to wait until after he eats?'

'He will not shrivel into nothing if he is late eating and he'll make up for it when we return.'

'Me go,' Willa said.

'No, Little Doll.' Melina turned to leave the room. 'We're going to find some ribbons for your hair.'

'Make sure the nursemaid has the child's clothing packed,' Warrington said as she walked away.

Melina's back stiffened. She didn't move. 'I will gather the things Willa needs.' Her voice could have had razors attached.

Willa's arms flailed and she pushed against Melina. Her voice rose. 'Go.'

'Not now,' Melina answered, voice still edged, and then it softened. 'Later, though.'

Melina let Willa slide to the floor and stand, clasping her hand.

'Papa.' Jacob ran in, rushing past Melina and Willa. 'I found my cap and I washed my face. I'm ready.'

'We'll see if cook can find us a biscuit, or something, before we leave.' Warrington turned back, getting the message on his desk for Broomer to take—the one he'd penned saying Willa could go to the Sinclairs. He'd give it to the servant now, before any more time passed. The sooner this was finished, the better for everyone.

Melina looked at the paper, leaning forward, and he knew she saw the name on it. She grasped Willa's hand and hurried her away, as if the child could read and understand the words in his hand.

Jacob chattered along beside him, having no more cares than how fast he could ride a horse.

Things could have been so different, but he was tired of looking at the past. Tired of breathing in the memories every moment. Of wearing the past like a cloak around him.

He'd been so besotted with his wife. Besotted. He didn't know how the word had started. But he'd been sotted for sure. And now he was the same for Melina. Getting her from England would surely cure him. He could feel the burning need inside himself for her, but he could not give in. If he did, he risked her returning to Melos with his child inside her.

And he had to keep moving, moving away from her while she was in England. If he touched her again, he would ache all the more when she left.

She wanted to return to her world. Take the dowry. Care for her sisters. Find her precious rock. And as soon as the little one left the town house, he would go to Whitegate with Jacob.

Broomer and Ben could take care of Melina and see that she returned safely to her island.

Now he would keep moving and not think again until miles separated them. He trudged from the house, calling Jacob to hurry.

When they returned from the ride, Jacob slid from Nero's back before Warrington could dismount from Chesapeake. The boy dropped to a crouch when he landed, before sitting on his bottom. Then he tumbled forward to his knees before he pushed himself up, laughing, oblivious to the dirt he'd gathered.

During the outing, Jacob had sung, talked about his preferences in horses and the biggest spider he'd ever killed. He'd boasted about seeing rabbits in the flower garden and how upset Dane had been when the deer visited and ate some of the plants all the way down to stems. Now he begged to feed Nero.

'Let the others care for them. It's their job.'

'What is my job?' Jacob asked, looking up.

'To be my son. To learn from your tutor when you are back at Whitegate.'

Warrington reached out, wrapped an arm around Jacob's waist and picked him up sideways, then shook him. 'I must shake the dirt off you before you get inside.'

Jacob squealed and struggled to get free. 'Let me down.'

Warrington released him. 'Didn't help much.'

Jacob brushed down the front of his shirt. 'Cook says I'm handsome and she calls me "your lordship". She keeps tarts hid just for me because I'm a lordship. And she says I'm getting bigger every day because of her tarts.'

'Perhaps you are, your lordship.' Pride flowered in Warrington's body when he looked at Jacob. He could not have asked for anything more in a son.

War reached out, putting his palm at the back of Jacob's head and giving him a nudge forward to the door.

When they reached the children's room, he took Jacob inside, where Melina and the nursemaid sat with the little girl.

Melina was sewing a dress so small it could only fit Willa's doll while the child played with Jacob's soldiers.

Melina raised her eyes—the eyes he'd miss—and he saw her own sadness pool in them. She put down the dress and rushed from the room.

The nursemaid watched Jacob and frowned. 'Have you been rolling in a hayfield? I think your hair is turning into straw.' She stood, reaching out for him. 'I am scrubbing that dirt from your knees. I expect the horse came back a lot cleaner than you.'

'Papa and I rode a long way,' he told the nursemaid as she turned to get the pitcher. 'Papa even let me get off Nero by myself and I didn't get hurt.'

'But you did manage to get dirty.' The older woman sighed.

'I stumbled when I landed.'

Warrington heard them talking and he left the room.

He moved to the room with the harpoon, planning to write instructions on how he wanted his will changed. Jacob would be cared for because of the entailed properties, but the girl could easily be forgotten about. He didn't want that to happen.

Hearing a rustling noise, he looked up. Willa had followed him, hair tousled, and dressed in a blue that mirrored her eyes. Drool glistened on her chin and she had one of her half-boots in her hand. She should not be toddling about on her own with the stairway so close.

Half rising, he planned to summon a servant, but the little girl sat, trying to put her boot on. It wouldn't hurt to watch her for a moment.

As he wrote, he heard her chatter again and looked up long enough to see her struggling to climb into the overstuffed chair. In moments, something rustled at his feet and he knew she'd given up on the chair and was exploring under his desk. A sharp, clamping pain hit his leg.

He jumped back. Standing, he pushed down his stocking and saw perfect indentations of teeth on his leg.

'Willa.' He raised his voice, then reached underneath the desk and snatched her out. 'I've horse hair on me, I'm sure. And last I heard, it tastes the same as dog fur. You shouldn't like it.'

Her bottom lip trembled and a sniffle looked to turn into a crying bout.

'Pardon,' he muttered, pulling her to his chest, and patting her back. 'I didn't mean to frighten you.'

Her eyes were wide and she stared at him as if she watched an ogre. She'd not yet made up her mind about tears. He jiggled her as he paced the floor, the same as he'd done with Jacob. 'You nearly drew blood. You must not like me and I understand.'

Her lip stopped wavering and she nestled against him. 'I don't mind that you don't like me. I wouldn't if I were you.' Bending forward, he leaned to put her back on the floor, but she clung to him, her fist tight on his waistcoat.

'No,' she said.

Willa had had no choice in the matter of her parents. Maybe neither of them should suffer any more for Cassandra's sins.

'Poppet, I wish you a pleasant journey and the best of life.'

'Horse,' she said.

'Not today.'

'Horse.'

'No.'

'Horse.' She looked at him, eyes hopeful.

'Some day, when you are older, I'll see that you have a horse of your very own.' He held her back from himself and put her on to the floor.

The wail shocked him. He didn't think he'd ever heard her cry.

He scooped her up, his arm tucked under her bottom, and her face was near his. He patted her back and took a few steps, hoping to silence the wails. Her tears dwindled quickly.

'Willa, you're going to get something special. A mama and a papa both—all in one day. Very soon. I have already sent the letter.'

She reached for his neck.

'No.' He paused, moving his head aside. She grabbed the cravat at his neck to hold herself firm. She tugged his neckcloth and the softness of fine hair tickled his chin. She smelled like Jacob had when he'd held him—a bit like soap and porridge and life.

She'd be all right. He knew she'd do well. The Sinclairs would be best for her.

'You'll like your new family. They're pleasant people,' he said to her. 'You'll have a new brother, and a new place to live, and a new papa and mama both.'

'Papa?' He heard the wavering voice at the door and turned. Jacob stood there, his eyes unsure. 'We're getting a new papa and mama?'

'No.' He rushed out the word. Shocked his son could think such a thing. 'Just Willa.'

'Here?'

'No. Of course not.'

His son stared, eyes searching Warrington's face, unsure. 'Why?'

'Willa's moving to live with her new family. You'll understand when you get older.'

This time, the eyes he saw staring back at him were his son's and he could see his own likeness in Jacob's face. His own eyes. Accusing.

'You're giving Willa away?' Jacob asked, his lip jutting out.

'We'll talk about it later.'

'If she did something bad, she didn't mean to.'

She burrowed against him and he felt trapped between the two children.

He knelt down, never taking his eyes from his son, and stood the little girl on her own feet. 'She needs a mother.'

'Why does she need a mama?' Jacob asked. 'I don't have one.'

'Boys only need fathers. Girls need mothers.'

'We can put trousers on her and cut her hair, and she can be my brother and we'll keep her.'

He saw Melina move into the doorway.

'Explain to Jacob,' he told her, knowing she'd heard the conversation.

Her eyes didn't accuse. They looked troubled and saddened.

She took a step towards Jacob. She dipped her chin and her words were gentle. 'I had a *mana* when I was growing up. It's something little girls need.'

'Why?'

'We do. Like you need your papa. Think how lost you'd be without him.'

'He went to sea with Uncle Ben and I had the tutor and I was all right. He showed me how seeds grow and everything. The stable master took me for horse rides. Uncle Dane told me stories about Romans and knights. We even saw a shooting star. I asked Uncle Dane, if Papa didn't come back like Mama didn't, would he keep me and Willa? He said he would.' He sniffed in a large swallow of air and stood as straight as his soldiers. 'Uncle Dane would keep us.' His jaw jutted out. 'I want to live with Uncle Dane or sail with Uncle Ben.' He ran from the room.

Warrington heard each word and they went into his heart. They were true.

He went after Jacob, brushed by Melina, and he could hear Cassandra's laughter.

But he was not keeping the girl. He'd already given her away. He had told them he would send a carriage for them on the next day.

Melina heard the steps in the hallway and knew Warrington was in his room. She sat in the blackness, feeling no need for light. Warrington had left after talking to Jacob and not returned until night.

The dark walls suited her well and one face kept floating through her mind. Warrington. Every servant in the house slept, but she doubted he did. And she needed one last moment with him. She wanted to hear his voice. To feel his scent cover her, and the skin that remained hidden from all the world to be hers to savour.

She stood, wearing her chemise, and crept to his bedchamber, standing. He opened the door after she called out, but kept his eyes on a miniature, examining it. He turned the painting so she could see it.

'My father—he lived for my mother.' His voice barely reached her ears. 'If one of his boys displeased her, he would not hear of it. We could have stolen from the church and he would have not been so angry as he would have been from an irritation to my mother. And rightly so. If she had a fault, it was in loving us to distraction.'

He brought the miniature back into his view and put his arm around her, hand at her waist. Her heart beat faster and she felt like a part of him. She let her cheek rest against his clothing. In those seconds, she changed. When he breathed, she felt the movements inside herself. But also, she could feel his restraint. He was not to be hers.

'And yet,' Warrington continued, 'almost the first woman he saw after the funeral, he began to court, thinking it a secret. Less than a month after my mother's death, he told me he would be married as soon as the proper mourning ended. He was bouncing in his boots. He was so happy and could not keep the news to himself.' Warrington moved the picture to his side. 'I vowed…'

Warrington tossed the miniature to a chair. He expelled a breath. 'Yet I lost my father because I was no different than he.'

She touched the softness of his shirt at his chest, feeling the heart beating beneath.

'I never told my father, not once, how I hated the moment he told me he would remarry. Instead I told Dane and we moved to the town house so we would not have to see the blissful courtship. I didn't move back until I wed. Whitegate is large, yet it wasn't big enough for everyone. I'm tired of living in my memories, Melina. They are getting old and worn, and making me feel the same. Like leather rained on and then baked in the sun.'

'I don't think you can simply close them off.'

'I know I have done the right thing with the girl and I will make it up to Jacob, somehow.'

'Don't think about it. Now it's done.' She pulled him close.

He squeezed her. 'You feel… You feel like…' He paused, swaying her on her feet. 'I can't think what you feel like exactly, but it warms up old leather nicely. Gives it new life.'

She let herself melt into his body and his

scent—fresh gardens and the brush of strength. She wanted to be able to close her eyes and slide into the memories of his arms long after she left. And secretly, she hoped there would be a child. She would let Warrington know—after a while. After her heart did not ache so.

She shut her eyes, imagining her own sisters who'd lost their mother and been willingly deserted by their father. 'I think of my family. The ones gone and the ones left. And I can't leave them, either. My promise to my mother…'

He leaned in, wrapping her in his arms, and when he spoke, his voice was at her ear. 'I've thought of nothing but family all day and you dream of yours. Let us take a walk from them and leave them for a moment. They will still be there for us when we return.'

Melina knew she would like nothing better and to be held by Warrington soothed her completely.

'Let me pleasure you.' He touched a tendril of her hair, brushing it back, but his finger returned to linger on her skin.

She looked up and desire stirred in every part of her just from being in his arms. She yearned for the touch of his lips against hers. She pulled back enough so she could tiptoe up, pressing her mouth to his, and feel the strength of his response.

He took her mouth with the same ferocity of needing one kiss to stay alive. One kiss to have another heartbeat.

She no longer stood on her own feet. Warrington held her, his fingers splayed against her back, keeping her aloft.

He moved, or she did, and that merest movement of their bodies, constrained by clothing, and yet freed to feel every whisper of touch, tumbled her into a world where passions conquered all concerns.

He pulled back and she opened her eyes. She'd never seen the expression on his face before. It was too strong for her to take in and too deep to turn from. He picked her up and deposited her gently on the bed.

Warrington pulled his clothes from his body, shedding them with no care for where they landed, but when he lay beside her, he undid the chemise ties, unwrapping her with the care of touching a wisp he didn't want the breeze to blow away.

She felt rich, pampered, treasured—valuable as marble carved by a hand guided from the heart of the greatest craftsman.

'Melina,' he whispered and said nothing else. No question or words. Just spoke her name.

And the sound of it from his lips filled her the same as an outpouring of love.

When he lay beside her, she ran her hands down his body and up again, trying to memorise every surface. Trying to soak in each fibre of him. Wanting to hold the feelings within herself for ever.

He touched her hip and their eyes were close enough to see in the darkness. He bent his head to her neck and his hair grazed against her, the scent of his skin lingering with the locks. Pressing her to her back, he lay beside her and pulled her against his body. He burrowed his lips into the hollow of her neck, his teeth brushing her skin, and his fingertips marked her heart, and all of her.

When he trailed his fingers down her stomach, reaching into the gentle slope, pressing her soft curls, touching the folds, finding the peak, she couldn't think any more. She gasped, lost in the swirls, the pulses of his touch, and she couldn't regain herself until he completed the feelings for her.

She felt him, holding their bodies close, moving them together, in a rhythm of lovemaking, while his hands caressed her, bringing her to the height of her passion again, crashing them together and taking all the power from her body. She relished all the sensations of him.

This would be their last night together.

Chapter Twenty-Four

Melina sat on the floor, dodging the edges of Willa's fan as the little one worked to keep Melina's face cool. They'd just finished breaking their fast and Melina hadn't seen Warrington since she'd left his bed at dawn.

'Melina.' Warrington's shout from outside the children's bedchamber penetrated the oak door.

'Oh, Little One...' Melina exaggerated her facial expression '...it appears someone is in very serious trouble. Warrington sounds very, very angry.'

Willa laughed.

The door burst open and Warrington plunged into the room, holding a letter. 'The Sinclairs are not taking her.'

Melina looked up. 'They are not?' She pulled Willa into her arms. 'That is terrible.'

He threw the letter from his hand. The paper

fluttered down. 'They wish for her to stay with her mother.'

She brushed her hand over the baby-fine hair and pressed a kiss to Willa's head. 'They must be mistaken. If they are addled, it is best for Willa not to be with them.'

'They received a letter, amazingly with mine. And they sent it to me along with their change of heart. The missive is from a woman they believe is Willa's mother asking them to not take her one and only precious little girl. The only baby she might ever have. That this woman wants her and needs to keep her. She loves Willa. The letter made them think I was forcing her—you—to give the child away.' He paused. 'Blast it, Melina. No one would be better for her than the Sinclairs. They are a good family. You should not have meddled.' He stood over her. 'And stop hiding behind the child.'

'I am not. We were playing.' Melina let Willa move to the floor.

'You were playing. With the child's life. You are not her mother and you should not have written to the Sinclairs. You have no right to do such.' He took a deep breath. 'She could have had two loving parents.'

'She has two loving parents.' She stood. 'Me. And Broomer...'

'What in blazes...?' His voice hurt her ears and he looked as if he had just spit vinegar. Willa's lips trembled.

'*Skase*. You'll frighten her.' She gave the baby a quick hug.

'I should be scaring you.' He lowered his tone and ran his fingers through his hair, pushing it back from his face. 'What do you mean, Broomer and you?' He leaned his head forward as if he could not hear correctly.

'He and I have discussed it. He would like to be a father and feels he might never get another chance. I already love her. We do not want to part with her and we both agree that two parents would be best. He is going back to Melos with me—and he will stay. He will keep me safe from Stephanos and be a kind father for Willa. And she will have my sisters for aunts.'

'I forbid it.'

'You cannot stop us.'

'You *cannot* take Willa without my permission. She is my legal daughter. And Broomer is my servant.'

Melina looked at the window, then turned her gaze to Warrington. 'I would not say Broomer is your servant. He has left. He has agreed to work for me, at no cost, because you were tossing aside a dear child. Broomer and I want her. If you choose anything otherwise…' her voice rose '…then you are a beast. You are less than a man. You are worse than Stephanos. You are worse than Ludgate.' Her fingers fisted. 'You must do the right thing and give her to us. Broomer and

I will live on the dowry money. And you do not have to send us a single pence.'

His brows furrowed. 'Are you planning to wed him?'

'We have no notion of it, but the people on Melos will readily assume he is my husband, and it would be best if Stephanos thinks I am married.'

He took a step back. 'You are completely daft. And so was I. I trusted you and Broomer and you both made plans behind my back.'

'Yes. You are fortunate to have two such caring people in your life. Or, should I say, to have had two such caring people in your life.'

'I cannot believe you would do this. Again, a woman misled me.' He glowered. 'And I will *not* let you take the *Ascalon* back to Melos.'

'I have already had Broomer make arrangements with Captain Ben. On the ship. Your brother said he will have no trouble sailing *Ascalon* to the island, as you have already given the command, and he knows it is what you meant. And you might have trouble finding him to give him any changes, as Gidley is not to let you on board. Gidley has to do as his captain commands. He does not believe in mutiny.'

'I own that ship,' his voice thundered.

'Only half. And Captain Ben thinks if he sails his half, your half will follow without argument. He said it is odd how ships work that way.'

'You did— You led them all—' He held out a palm, shaking it in the air. 'You are as conniving as Cassandra. I want no part of you.'

She stood. 'Willa's things are already on board the ship, as are mine and Broomer's. I was just waiting to tell you. And...' she picked up Willa, holding her tight '...I am keeping those hideous dresses. And your pillows. I quite like them and they will make her a soft bed on the ship.' She stopped at the door and turned back. 'And the milled lilac soap. You should probably alert your housekeeper that you are running quite low on it.' She sniffed at Willa's hair. 'It makes her smell so precious.'

She waited a moment before speaking again, her words firm. 'Jacob needs you. He will need you especially now. The governess and a footman have taken him on a walk to keep him from seeing us leave. I told them it might happen.'

Then she left and gave Willa a tight hug, hefting her close. They would manage. They would make a wonderful family on Melos. And Warrington could live in London with his dead wife the rest of his life.

She walked downstairs to the hackney waiting across the street and did not turn back.

Warrington did not move. He couldn't. Women were traitorous wretches who did whatever they damn well pleased and could steal a child with-

out blinking a lash. She'd stolen his daughter—
the child—Willa. She'd taken her. Just walked
right out.

Melina was gone. She was leaving the country, and she could get on that ship—that floating
acorn—and sail to the end of the world. He would
give Ben his blessing to take her. He would even
send more pillows.

He opened his mouth. Broomer. She even
took Broomer. He—Broomer—another schem-
ing wretch.

He didn't care if the man was bigger than a
house, he was going to get throttled. And soon.
Warrington rushed from the room.

'Papa…' Jacob's voice, hesitant. He stood directly in his father's path.

Warrington stumbled into Jacob. He reached
out, catching the little boy, stopping his own momentum.

He righted them both, still holding his son.

'Are you leaving again?' Jacob asked, speaking no louder than a whisper. 'I heard you shouting when we came back. And Willa's gone… I
saw the carriage.'

Warrington stepped back against the wall and
his hands loosened. His whole body slackened. He
slid to the floor and looked at his child. 'No. I'm
not. I'm not leaving you. Ever again. You're my
son.' He gathered Jacob into his arms. 'My life.'

He waited, calming himself. 'Now tell me what

you'd like to do today and we'll see how much
we can manage.'

'You're staying with me?'

'Yes. I'm staying. I can't leave my Jacob.'

Jacob relaxed against him. 'I have a bow and
arrow at Whitegate. I could show you how to
shoot it.'

'That sounds like a good plan. I think I might
have one somewhere, too. Perhaps we can have
a competition after you teach me how.'

Jacob's head nodded at Warrington's chest.
War let his arms rest loosely around his son and
stared forward.

'Can we go, Papa? I like Whitegate better than
here.'

'I don't know why I didn't think of it. I'm ready
to return home.'

Chapter Twenty-Five

The town coach rolled to a stop, and Jacob bounced from his father's knees, but Warrington kept a tight grip on the boy's coat. There had simply not been enough room in the carriage for Jacob to sit anywhere else.

Keeping Jacob in his grasp, Warrington stepped on to the docks and saw the *Ascalon*. Someone had already noted his carriage, he could tell. Two men were moving forward, standing, blocking the way on to the ship.

He easily recognised Broomer, and the other, Gidley. They stood side by side, arms crossed.

Striding up to them, he stopped, looked up at Broomer, and said. 'You're discharged without references.' He stared at Gid. 'You, as well.'

'Well, yer got a point,' Gidley said. 'We, fortunately, work for other folks. I hear Mr Broomer has a lady he answers to.'

Broomer's eyes dropped when he spoke to

Warrington and his lips trembled. 'I'm asking your forgiveness. But I had no choice.'

'No choice?' Warrington's words flew from his throat. 'No choice?'

'You'd have done the same thing. A little girl. That sweet woman needing a baby.'

'No,' Warrington snapped. He could not say another word.

'We're here to see my sister.' Jacob's voice broke the stillness.

Broomer took a deep sniff and looked at the boy. 'My pardon, Little Lordship, but we're to say she's not at home.'

Warrington nodded. He turned to the town coach, put two fingers to his lips and whistled.

Three men tumbled out and one of the coach-men jumped from the front. Each held a club. They scrambled up behind Warrington.

'We were at a tavern.' Jacob's voice rose in excitement. 'Papa gave the men sticks, and silver, and he told them they could change the silver for gold if they helped us walk on the ship. We can walk on the ship, can't we, Broomer? I want to see Uncle Ben's ship.' His voice lowered. 'Papa didn't give me gold, but he said if I did everything he asked, I could have a sea biscuit.' He rubbed his stomach. 'I would like that.'

Broomer looked at the men. 'Jack. Mutton. Wilton. Theodoure.' He nodded to them. They grinned back.

'Your sister…' Warrington stared at Broomer '…told us where we might find your friends when I explained how they were needed.'

'You'll have to kill me to get to the lady and that little angel,' Broomer said. 'You can't take 'em.'

'I will not.' He kept his eyes on Broomer and Gidley. 'You have my word, in front of my son, that I will not take her.'

'Papa. I thought you said we—'

'Quiet, Jacob.' He clamped his hand on his son's shoulder. Warrington continued, 'Unless Melina is completely happy to leave.'

The giant of a man ambled back, freeing space for them to come aboard. 'I suppose.'

Warrington stared at the first mate. 'And since you have time left from your guarding duties, Gidley, show my son how a ship works and keep him alive while doing so.' The earl turned to Broomer. 'And if you could take Willa, and keep her with her brother for a moment, I will refrain from telling the men about that particularly warm night in July when—'

Broomer raised a hand to silence him. 'I'll get Willa.' He turned.

'My cabin?' Warrington asked.

'No,' Gid interrupted innocently before Broomer could speak. 'Her cabin.'

Warrington levelled a look at Gidley. If not

for Jacob's ears, this conversation would proceed differently.

Gidley chuckled, his whole body moving, and nodded at Jacob. 'Come along, Little Lordship, let me learn yer the parts of a ship.'

Warrington waited until Broomer and Willa's exodus from the cabin, then he strode inside.

Melina's bottom was propped against the edge of the bunk and her hands clasped the edge. She stared over his head.

He took in the room. 'Devil take it, Melina. Is there a pillow left in my house?' He glimpsed the window. 'And the curtains. How long have you been planning this?'

'Since the letter.'

He saw the basket in the corner. Smoked meat. Vegetables.

He grabbed the side of the door for balance. She planned to go to Melos. 'I suppose Jacob can sleep in Ben's cabin and I can try a hammock,' he said. 'I see there's no room in here for me.'

'You have not been invited.'

He shrugged. 'I'll stay on my half of the ship.' He went to the curtain, pulled it aside and looked out. 'My half should follow Ben's half.' He raised a brow and peered at her. 'Or so I've been told.'

The grunt she gave placed no importance in his words.

'I can see it now,' he said. 'Jacob and Willa on a ship and their tiny little stomachs jolting as we sail to Melos. And the waves. Life-threatening storms. They could perish.' He took a step and planted himself in front of her. 'Or you could stay and marry me, and be the one to guide Willa as she grows into a beauty others will pamper instead of making her do as she should…'

'You do not speak fair.'

'No. If she is to be my daughter, then this time, I will choose a good mother for her. I will not make the same mistake again. Think about it, Melina, because if you say no, I will have to tell my brother Dane that he will be managing the estates and bribe him greatly so I can follow you to make sure you are safe. And two babes will be sailing on a ship, away from nice comfortable beds full of pillows.'

Her eyes flashed dark at him.

He shrugged. 'Think of Jacob and Willa.'

'You will move to Melos?'

'And hope to convince you to marry me. The island will never be home to me. But I can live there and return here to visit.'

'I could not bear to see you leave like I saw my father leave.'

He turned to her. 'Never like your father. I'll expect you to return with me each time. It won't be asking too much, if I am to spend much of my life there.'

He took one stride, pulled her hand to his lips and kissed her palm. 'I can't let you go. I can't.

Since you left my house, I have only had you out of my life for moments, and it has been intolerable agony. I cannot imagine days, weeks or years without you. Let me send Ben for your sisters. They can return here. Your family can share our home.'

She studied his face.

He nodded. 'I have a country estate where I promised to take Jacob. I can add another house if needed. And my lonely, wealthy aunt is batty and cannot find enough people to listen to her stories. Your sisters will be comfortable and we will have enough time to become a true family.'

'What if my parentage is discovered? My father was married to another woman at the time he lived with my mother.'

'Your father's wife knows and I don't wish to cause her any embarrassment. I am quite happy with letting the world know you're a descendent of Aphrodite. Who's to say it isn't true? Certainly not me. I believe it.'

She stood and her eyes softened. 'My mother often claimed she had the spirit of a goddess. So I have heard that nonsense before.'

He took his forefinger and touched her mark, tracing a heart over it. 'Do you think Aphrodite will marry a mere mortal like me?'

She thrust herself into his arms, knocking him back a step, holding him tight.

He held her close, shutting his eyes, and feeling freedom, as if a thousand years of curses had left him.

'I will stay,' she said, 'but I'll give you my answer to the marriage later,' she said. 'I am in no hurry.'

'I'll have to correct that.' He put his cheek against her hair and inhaled the holiday scent of her, and hoped she never lost the trace of all the best parts of the island that clung to her.

Warrington watched Willa and Jacob arguing over her doll while he waited for Melina to return from her walk in the Whitegate gardens. She searched for the perfect spot for her statue. In a few days, Ben should return with the sculpture and with Melina's sisters, and his wife could hardly wait.

Movement beside him caught his eye. 'You do not want the doll, Jacob,' Warrington commanded. 'Give it back to your sister.'

The moment Jacob handed it back, Warrington saw Willa's arm flex. 'Do not hit your brother.'

She looked at Warrington, smiled and said, 'Watface.'

Jacob snickered.

'Jacob.' He glared at his son. 'If you ever teach her anything like that again, you will be forbidden from riding Nero for a fortnight.'

Jacob's body sagged. 'Paapaa…' He dragged out the word.

Willa looked at Warrington. 'Paapaaa...' she copied Jacob's speech and ran to Warrington. He picked her up. Now when he looked into her eyes, he saw sunshine, and when he looked at Jacob, he saw Ben. That was not so pleasing.

'Warrington.' He heard Melina's voice behind him. She never called him by anything but his title, except when they were alone. Then she often whispered to him in her mother's language. Some day he would tell her that his childhood tutor had schooled him quite well in other languages—and his skill with one in particular had persuaded the Foreign Office to ask his assistance with the Greece mission.

'You must be firm with Willa,' Melina continued speaking to him. 'She knows *ratface* isn't a kind word.'

He felt little arms cling more tightly around his neck and a soft cheek snuggled against him.

'Willa,' he said, 'you cannot ride Jacob's horse for a fortnight.'

'Warrington...' Melina put her hands on her hips.

He forced himself not to smile. He was not besotted. He was in love. Totally, truly. And this time, nothing about it felt the same as before. His past wasn't buried. It had vanished. Just like a myth.

'Willa,' he said to her, 'your *mana* and your papa must insist that you only say nice words.'

'Until you are married,' Melina added. 'Then you may speak as you wish to your husband.'

'As you do.' He used his free hand to clasp her waist and pull her close enough to kiss her nose. 'And as I do to you. My Aphrodite. Not a mythological goddess. But better. I recovered the true treasure from Melos.'

* * * * *

A sneaky peek at next month…

HISTORICAL

AWAKEN THE ROMANCE OF THE PAST…

My wish list for next month's titles…

In stores from 1st August 2014:

- ☐ Beguiled by Her Betrayer – Louise Allen
- ☐ The Rake's Ruined Lady – Mary Brendan
- ☐ The Viscount's Frozen Heart – Elizabeth Beacon
- ☐ Mary and the Marquis – Janice Preston
- ☐ Templar Knight, Forbidden Bride – Lynna Banning
- ☐ Salvation in the Rancher's Arms – Kelly Boyce

Available at WHSmith, Tesco, Asda, Eason, Amazon and Apple

Just can't wait?

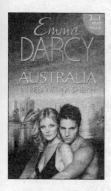

Aa a war blazes across Europe, three couples find a love
that is powerful enough to overcome all the odds.
Travel with the characters on their journey of
passion and drama during World War I.

**Three wonderful books in one from top
historical author Marguerite Kaye.**

**Get your copy today at:
www.millsandboon.co.uk**

Discover more romance at

www.millsandboon.co.uk

- ❤ WIN great prizes in our exclusive competitions

- ❤ BUY new titles before they hit the shops

- ❤ BROWSE new books and REVIEW your favourites

- ❤ SAVE on new books with the Mills & Boon® Bookclub™

- ❤ DISCOVER new authors

PLUS, to chat about your favourite reads, get the latest news and find special offers:

- ❤ Find us on facebook.com/millsandboon

- ❤ Follow us on twitter.com/millsandboonuk

- ❤ Sign up to our newsletter at millsandboon.co.uk